'Don't flatter yourself. I'm not desperate to dance with you like the other women in the ballroom.'

'They want more than dancing from me, I assure you. You noticed my following? It is quite considerable.'

Dulci blushed, as he'd intended.

'What? There's nothing wrong with the words "following" or "considerable".' Jack feigned ignorance of his innuendo.

'Except when *you* say them. I can't say I have noticed your "following", but I've noticed you're still as conceited as I remember you in the orangery.'

Jack laughed at Dulci's pique, the familiar longings starting to stir. He was enjoying this: his hand at her back, the warmth of her body through the thin silk of her gown, his mind taking pleasure in the mental exercise of parrying her comments.

'It's the truth.' Jack swung them into the opening patterns of the waltz. He was starting to wonder if his emotional distance could be challenged tonight. He'd like nothing more than to try his luck at stealing a few kisses…

Author Note

Thanks for your patience over the last few years as Jack and Dulci waited their turn. Jack and Dulci made their first appearance in PICKPOCKET COUNTESS, and they just seemed to beg for their own story. I had many letters asking when it would happen!

Jack and Dulci are wild ones, and a grand adventure in the New World seemed like the right venue for them. When I discovered the beginnings of the Venezuela-British Guiana controversy over a shared but undefined border, I knew Jack and Dulci had found their adventure and I inserted them into history.

Robert Schomburgk actually did a mission in British Guiana in 1835, for mapping purposes, and later went back around 1840 to reaffirm what is now known as the Schomburgk Line. The border dispute continued into the 1890s, until the US stepped in to intervene.

Another interesting point of note in the story: there was indeed gold discovered in the Essequibo River (as Jack suspected), and several other rivers in the region.

You can read more about the history behind Jack and Dulci's adventure in British Guiana at www.bronwynswriting.blogspot.com. Come on by and say hello!

A THOROUGHLY COMPROMISED LADY

Bronwyn Scott

First published in Great Britain 2010
Large Print edition 2010
Harlequin Mills & Boon Limited,
Eton House, 18-24 Paradise Road, Richmond, Surrey TW9 1SR

© Nikki Poppen 2010

ISBN: 978 0 263 21170 2

Harlequin Mills & Boon policy is to use papers that are natural, renewable and recyclable products and made from wood grown in sustainable forests. The logging and manufacturing process conform to the legal environmental regulations of the country of origin.

Printed and bound in Great Britain
by CPI Antony Rowe, Chippenham, Wiltshire

Bronwyn Scott is a communications instructor at Pierce College in the United States, and is the proud mother of three wonderful children (one boy and two girls). When she's not teaching or writing, she enjoys playing the piano, travelling—especially to Florence, Italy—and studying history and foreign languages.

Readers can stay in touch on Bronwyn's website, www.bronwynnscott.com, or at her blog, www.bronwynswriting.blogspot.com—she loves to hear from readers.

Recent novels from Bronwyn Scott:

PICKPOCKET COUNTESS
NOTORIOUS RAKE, INNOCENT LADY
THE VISCOUNT CLAIMS HIS BRIDE
THE EARL'S FORBIDDEN WARD
UNTAMED ROGUE, SCANDALOUS
   MISTRESS

and in Mills & Boon® Historical eBook *Undone!*:

LIBERTINE LORD, PICKPOCKET MISS
PLEASURED BY THE ENGLISH SPY

For Wendi,
thanks for your support of the
Brenda Novak auction to raise funds for
research in the fight against juvenile diabetes.
Your contribution makes all the difference.

For my family and friends
who are all so supportive of my writing,
especially the kiddos, Ro, Catie
and Brony, who let their mom write.
And for my editor, Joanne, too,
who worked extraordinarily hard
to make this story just right!

Chapter One

London—spring 1835

Jack Hanley, the first Viscount Wainsbridge, firmly believed that ballrooms were for business. Chandeliers, potted palms, sparkling champagne—all the standard trappings of festivity aside, ballrooms were a gentleman's office. They were the places a gentleman conducted the most important business transactions of his life: ensuring a place in society and arranging his marriage. Jack had already done the former and had no intentions of doing the latter. Tonight was no exception.

Jack stopped inside the arched entrance of the Fotheringay ballroom, halting a moment to adjust the sleeve of his evening jacket and surreptitiously scan the room. He took mental roll of the attendees. For all intents and purposes, it was an assembly of the usual suspects. That suited him well. This evening, his business was with the newly arrived Venezuelan delegation. He had very specific orders to meet them, and determine if there was any substance to the quietly circulating rumours that Venezuela was spoiling for a fight over undeclared borders with British Guiana.

'Wainsbridge!' An excited female voice broke over the dull din of constant conversation. His hostess bore down upon him with a gaggle of females in tow. Jack swallowed a groan. The horde was descending slightly earlier than anticipated. That was the price of being a newly titled, attractive bachelor with a certain reputation with the ladies. It didn't help that he was still something of a novelty since his work for the Crown seldom brought him to London on a regular basis.

'Lady Fotheringay, how charming you look tonight.' Jack pasted on a benign smile that hid his cynicism. Women in ballrooms had their business too.

'I want you to meet my nieces, Wainsbridge.' The purple ostrich plumes in Lady Fotheringay's hair bobbed dangerously. There were five of them, all named after flowers—nieces, that was, not ostrich plumes, although he wouldn't put it past the silly woman to name them too.

By the time introductions were completed, Jack's court had grown substantially, filled with females clamouring for their hostess to introduce them to the handsome, newly minted viscount with the mysterious antecedents. For the moment he was hemmed in on all sides and not another man in sight. He could only guess where his fellow males had taken themselves off to—cards and the good brandy, no doubt.

Jack was listening with feigned interest to Miss Violet Fotheringay's rather unenlightened dissertation on the year's fashions and contemplating how he might extract himself from his group in order to find the Venezuelan delegation when he heard it: the unmistakable whisky-and-smoke sound of Lady Dulcinea Wycroft's laughter.

Even in a crush such as this, the sound was distinctive in a pleasant, provocative way, something akin to Odysseus's sirens; a sound that would make a smart man fear for his bachelor status. Of course, that assumed the woman in question wanted to marry at all. Dulcinea had shown no inclination in the eight years she'd been out to want to give up her reign as London's supreme Incomparable, although there had been many chances to do so—six proposals Jack knew about and probably a string of others he'd missed in his long and varied absences from town.

Such a resistance to matrimony made her all the more delightful in Jack's opinion. If there was one temptation Jack could not quite resist, it was a witty, cleverly spoken woman who was apparently as staunchly committed to remaining unmarried as he was.

Such a similarity made her a complex creature who was both potential companion and challenge. He loved nothing more than a good challenge and over the years, Dulcinea Wycroft had certainly proven to be that to the good men of the *ton*, none of whom yet had succeeded in walking her down the aisle, although it wasn't for lack of trying.

With careful eyes, so as not to neglect Miss Fotheringay, Jack followed the laughter to its source. Ah, that explained where the men were. His was not the only court. Two pillars down the ballroom, Miss Wycroft reigned at her court of wit and beauty, surrounded by the cream of London's bachelors. This evening, gowned in

striking pomegranate silk, the sheen of her im-
possibly blue-black hair catching the light of
chandeliers, she was a veritable Helen of Troy.

Jack was not immune.

Neither was most of male London.

She was besieged with admirers. If he was the
ton's bachelor of note, she was the female equiv-
alent. Like him, she'd not be conquered easily
and certainly not by that gathering of pups. Jack
stifled a smirk of superiority at the sight of the
men clustered about her. The fools. Didn't they
know they hadn't a chance? They were insignifi-
cant moths to her all-consuming flame. And
really, who could blame them? She was vivacity
personified in a room full of pattern-card women
like Violet Fotheringay, all playing their assigned
roles in life.

Those admirers would fare no better against
her fire than the unlucky moth fared against the
light. She would burn their ambitions as assuredly as she'd burned the would-be suitors that
preceded them. A woman like Dulcinea would
never settle for a typical *ton*nish marriage. Such
a passion for living could not be caged inside a
Mayfair mansion. Jack privately marvelled that
such passion hadn't ruined her already. It was his

experience in general that the brightest flames often consumed themselves. It was perhaps inevitable that Dulci's fire would be her eventual downfall. Jack thought it rather miraculous it hadn't happened already.

He turned his gaze back to Violet, but his thoughts remained firmly elsewhere in the mental vicinity of Dulcinea. As a long-time friend of her brother Brandon, the earl, he'd known Dulci vaguely through the years although he hadn't known her well. He'd been filling various diplomatic posts in the Caribbean and had only just returned to England four years ago. It had been something of a surprise to return and encounter, on his brief appearances in London society, the incarnation of the current Dulci Wycroft. Breathtaking, too—not only in beauty, he discovered, but also in wit.

When he was in town, they ran in similar circles and were inevitably in attendance at the same dinner parties and political functions, not to mention larger events. This past winter, when his schedule had allowed him to rcmain in town, he'd found himself enjoying the exchange of verbal ripostes with her on several occasions.

Jack's thoughts paused and took another path.

During the Christmas holidays, they'd exchanged more than ripostes, spurred on perhaps by the mistletoe and holiday spirits—he meant that literally. He'd kissed her in Lady Weatherby's orangery. Those kisses had unleashed something raw and dangerous between them.

Normally, such an attraction would lead to its natural conclusion where Jack was concerned. But Dulci superseded such logic and placed him in a double bind; the secretive and private nature of his work precluded the opportunity to pursue any kind of relationship—not that he was desirous of anything permanent, which led to the second bind. The relationship he would most likely pursue would hardly meet with Brandon's approval. One did not make a mistress of or have an affair with one's best friend's sister. And Jack wasn't about to marry her over a few wassail-driven kisses no one knew about.

Lord knew *that* particular encounter might have ended better—or worse, depending on how one looked at it—if he hadn't been unexpectedly summoned away from the house party. As it was, he'd been lucky to escape with only one pot being thrown at his head. Dulci had been furious over what she saw as his imposition, although Jack suspected she'd enjoyed the kiss just as much as he had. She wasn't angry with him. She was angry with herself.

The result was that these days their banter had taken on a slight edge. No matter. One look at her tonight and his body was perfectly willing to pick up where they'd left off, pottery shards and all.

So was every other man in the room. By rights, Dulci should have picked one of them by now and settled down to life as a society matron. But Dulci didn't do anything by the rules. She made no secret of her independence, of her enormous interest in the Royal Geographic Society and fencing, and that she enjoyed far more freedom than other unmarried women of good families. Such confidence in her own consequence was an enormous part of her appeal. No gentleman ever assumed for long that Dulci Wycroft *needed* a man to rely on.

She got away with it and much else, Jack knew, because she was very careful not to break the one rule that mattered most. There was no blemish on her name in terms of maidenly modesty. Whatever wild streak Dulci might possess in conjunction with her independence, it did not extend into the realm of sexual exploits.

Jack thought of the orangery and reorganised his thoughts. Well, at least not beyond a few stolen kisses.

Not far down the room, Dulci leaned forwards, showing great signs of interest in the man on her left—and a considerable amount of bosom, in Jack's opinion. The man was a strikingly handsome Spaniard. Jack swore silently. Damn and double damn. He would have to go through her to get to them. With the episode in the orangery still between them, he'd have preferred to keep his business and pleasure separate.

He should have known. It stood to reason she'd be in the centre of the excitement. Dulci knew everyone in society. Those she didn't know, she made a point to meet. The delegation had only been in town a short week and Dulci had already managed to meet the guests of honour, the very people he'd come to investigate. According to the descriptions Jack had been provided with, the man at her side adroitly ogling her bosom was none other than Calisto Ortiz, one of the Venezuelan delegation, nephew to a high-ranking government official with ambitions. No doubt the others were somewhere in the crowd around her. He'd definitely have to get through Dulci to get an introduction. That meant there'd be a scene, at least a small one.

Considering their last words in the orangery, it was to be expected. In truth, it was Dulci's due. He'd behaved badly. One did not steal kisses and then have to dash off in the middle of stealing a bit more.

Jack was suddenly aware that Miss Fotheringay had stopped talking. 'Quite insightful,' Jack said quickly, smiling at the young woman who looked at him expectantly. 'I am positive many young girls share your opinion.' He was sure they did, although he couldn't recall what those opinions might be. It was deuced awkward to be caught out with one's attentions fixed elsewhere. Time to be moving on.

'I have enjoyed this immensely, ladies, but I see some people I need to meet, if you would excuse me?' Jack moved smoothly through his court and discreetly headed towards the group around Dulcinea. He took the long route, careful not to hurt anyone's feelings. It wouldn't do to be immediately seen going from one set to another.

Jack tugged on his waistcoat, girding himself for battle. When he was with her, everything was a competition—a delightful competition, but still a competition—and he had to be ready. 'Steady on, old chap.' Jack muttered under his breath. He had nothing to fear. What fire didn't burn it made stronger. When it came to women like Dulci Wycroft, Jack was tempered Damascus steel.

Jack circumspectly dislodged a young admirer whose only crime was to stand next to Dulcinea. Good lord, the ring of admirers got younger by the year. Lord Baden's son was among the lot tonight. Was the boy really old enough to come up to town now? These men were barely men at all, merely overgrown pups. Or was it simply that he was getting older? At four and thirty, he felt quite the veteran standing amongst Dulci's collection of young bucks. Regardless, they were no match for Dulci's wit. Not one of them had a chance of holding her attention.

'Good evening, everyone.' His eyes briefly swept the group by way of greeting.

The group's collective eye fixed on him, their collective breath held, waiting for the sport to begin. It had become something of a ballroom sport for guests to watch Dulci and he spar. Well, sparring wasn't quite accurate. They didn't fight. They *volleyed* with dares and words carefully wrapped in a socially acceptable package. Jack preferred to classify their exchanges more along the lines of lawn tennis. With practiced charm he drawled, 'Good evening, Lady Dulcinea.'

The match was engaged.

Heads swivelled to Dulci. If she was surprised by his presence, she did not show it. Her greeting was coolly polite, the type one offered to a passing acquaintance although they were far more than that.

'Wainsbridge, I did not expect to see you tonight.' Dulci subjected him to a liquid blue perusal, taking in every inch of his attire.

Jack readied for the forthcoming quip. Amid her sea of dandies with their bright waistcoats and popinjay fashions, his sombre apparel, broken only by the dove-grey brocade of his waistcoat, took on a more austere cast. The king's prized adviser could not strut around looking like a peacock of the most frivolous order. Although what he advised the king on remained a mystery to many.

'Wainsbridge, are these gloomy tones the best you can do? Such a choice would put a damper on even the most festive of occasions.' Dulci quizzed him with a perfectly arched black eyebrow. Heads turned back to him, everyone considering his apparel.

Jack bowed, taking the reprimand with consummate ease. 'I am at your disposal, Lady Dulcinea. What colour would you prefer I wear? The rainbow is yours. Pluck a colour from it and I will see it done. By this time tomorrow, I shall possess apparel done up to your satisfaction.'

The group stared at Dulci, waiting for her pronouncement. Jack thought it highly likely he wouldn't be the only person sporting Dulci's colours by this time tomorrow. Tailors all over the city would be busy in the morning.

Dulci snapped open her fan and speared Jack with a knowing look. As he intended, she understood entirely the dilemma he'd placed before her. She could not dare him to wear a hideous colour without making her court appear ridiculous along with him. Nor could she take the uncreative neutral option since she'd been the one to throw down the gauntlet. She had a certain reputation to uphold just as much as he.

'Azure. I choose azure,' she announced coyly over the top of her painted fan after pretending to give the answer a great deal of thought. And perhaps she had. Jack had to admit blue was the perfect choice for a careful answer. There were so many shades of blue; a gentleman could pick a hue of his own comfort level.

Jack bowed again. 'Azure it shall be, Lady Dulcinea. I duly accept your charge with all these gentlemen as my witnesses. Tomorrow night, at the Danby rout, I shall carry out my commission.'

Jack turned his gaze to the man next to him in the circle as if noticing the Spanish gentleman for the first time. 'Lady Dulcinea, I must beg an introduction. I believe this gentleman and I are not acquainted.' The match was over. Dulci had won the dare, but he'd got what he came for. The rest of the group wouldn't realise that. But Dulci would.

Dulci gave a deceptively sweet smile and made the introductions. 'Wainsbridge, this is Señor Calisto Ortiz, of the Venezuelan diplomatic delegation. I had the good fortune to meet him at a Royal Geographic Society dinner a few days ago. *Señor*, allow me to present Viscount Wainsbridge.'

The Spaniard bowed smoothly and introduced two other gentlemen in turn, a Señor Adalberto Vargas, who was clearly the august leader of the delegation, and Señor Dias, whose mediocre clothing clearly marked him as the hanger-on.

Ortiz was all handsome manners and Jack disliked him immediately. Younger than his Venezuelan counterparts by over a decade, darkly handsome with inky hair, and expensively dressed, Calisto Ortiz radiated a rather obvious appeal of the kind women found charming. He did not endear himself to Jack further when he turned that charm on Dulci.

For tonight, he'd tolerated enough of the man's covert ogling of Dulci's bosom, as deliciously displayed as it was in the tight bodice of her gown. Like recognised like, and Jack recognised Ortiz to be a womaniser of the highest order.

It was time to throw down the gauntlet, in the politest of fashions, of course. A little competition always brought one's true colours to light and he did not expect Ortiz to prove the exception to the rule. Instead he fully expected Ortiz to prickle in response to a few well-placed remarks. It wasn't Jack's job to make friends. His orders were very clear: take the measure of the delegation. There wasn't a single word mentioned about befriending them.

Jack inserted himself into the general conversation during a lull, casually launching his first sally. 'Señor Ortiz, *como le gusta Londres*?'

His fluent command of the language had the desired effect. Ortiz looked momentarily surprised at hearing Spanish. Jack wanted him to be surprised and warned. The Venezuelans might be thousands of miles from home and those who knew the territory, but the English were not without their resources here. The Venezuelans would not be dealing with London-based politicians ignorant of the New World's geography.

Ortiz favoured him with a cold smile. 'I assure you my English is quite fluent.' His terse answer imbued a level of tension into the group. Touchy young man, Jack thought, to be so thoroughly insulted on the acquaintance of six words.

'*Je parle français, aussi,*' Ortiz went on, his steely gaze fixed intently on Jack.

'*Très bien. J'aime parler français,*' Jack smoothly switched into French. He could play this game for a while if Ortiz was so inclined. He might not have the formal degrees of a polyglot scholar, but Jack could bed a woman in six different languages.

Señor Vargas intervened swiftly. 'Señor Ortiz has been educated at the finest of schools. He's the nephew of one of the viceroys posted to our region.'

'Ah,' Jack exclaimed with all the appreciation he could summon. Señor Ortiz's role in the delegation was becoming clearer. 'Are you considered to hold an official diplomatic post, then?'

His enquiry hit the mark. It was petty gratification to see the handsome man's smile fade into a grim line. 'I'm an ombudsman.'

'I see. That's quite an impressive *title*.' Jack's steely tone conveyed the rest of the message to Ortiz. They both knew an ombudsman operated in a limited capacity. The title was honorary at best, a sop to one's ego.

Ortiz's dark eyes flashed dangerously. Jack answered with a cool smile. The man fully understood his allusion and had the good grace to be insulted. But the flare in his eyes suggested he did not have the good grace to be defeated. Ortiz would bear watching. His temper suggested he was a man quick to anger, quick to take impulsive actions that might later be regretted.

Dulci placed a hand on Jack's sleeve. 'It is time for that dance you promised me.'

Jack gave her easy compliance. There was no more to be gained from provoking Ortiz. He'd got what he came for. He'd taken the measure of the delegation and it was quite telling.

Chapter Two

Dulci's announcement was immediately unpopular with everyone except Jack. 'But the next waltz is mine,' a rather dull-witted fellow, the Earl of Carstairs's son, stepped forwards to protest.

The boy was not fast enough. Jack claimed indisputable possession, covering Dulci's gloved hand on his sleeve with his own. 'I'm sure Lady Dulcinea has something saved for you later.'

'I have a country dance free in the fourth set.' Dulci quickly offset the boy's sour face.

'Good choice,' Jack remarked in low tones, leading her towards the dance floor. 'Less conversational opportunities with a country dance. You're probably doing him a favour. I doubt he has the requisite half-hour of conversation saved up to get through a waltz.'

'I'm doing myself a favour.' Dulci placed her hand on Jack's shoulder as they positioned themselves. 'The man's got the brains and build of an ox. He stepped on my feet no less than five times last week at the Balfour ball.'

'Here I thought you were protecting Ortiz when in reality you were angling for a dance with me.'

'Don't flatter yourself. I'm not desperate to dance with you like the other women in the ballroom.'

'They want more than dancing from me, I assure you. You noticed my following? It is quite considerable.'

Dulci blushed as he intended.

'What? There's nothing wrong with the words "following" or "considerable".' Jack feigned ignorance of his innuendo.

'Except when *you* say them. I can't say I have noticed your "following", but I've noticed you're still as conceited as I remember in the orangery.'

Jack laughed at Dulci's pique, the familiar longings starting to stir. He was enjoying this: his hand at her back, the warmth of her body through the thin silk of her gown, his mind taking pleasure in the mental exercise of parrying her comments.

'It's the truth.' Jack swung them into the opening patterns of the waltz. He was starting to wonder if his emotional distance could be challenged tonight. He'd like nothing more than to try his luck at stealing a few kisses.

'That all women are dying of love for you?'

'No need to be envious. It's not as if you don't have the other half of London at your feet.' Jack shot a look at the jilted heir on the sidelines. 'I would have thought women found him rather handsome. He's tall, muscular in a beefy sort of way. Quite the pride of English manhood.'

'It will all run to fat in ten years,' Dulci said matter of factly. 'I prefer a leaner sort of man. Big men don't tend to dance well.'

'Your brother's tall,' Jack argued for the sake of disagreement. With Dulci, anything was fair game for an argument. 'The ladies love dancing with him whenever Nora gives them a chance.'

'Brandon's an exception.'

'Speaking of Brandon, I had a note from your brother a month ago. He and Nora are doing well.' Brandon was the one safe topic of conversation they had between them. 'I gathered they aren't coming up to town because of the new baby.'

'No, they won't be coming up. It's to be expected. They are the most doting of parents.'

A small smile played across Dulci's lips at the mention of her new nephew, giving her features a rare soft look. It occurred to Jack that Dulci's long-standing reign as an Incomparable might indeed be a lonely one. The girlfriends who had débuted with her eight years ago would have long since married and started their own families. He had not thought of it in that way before—a price to be paid for her determination to remain unattached. Much in the same way he paid for the lifestyle he achieved. It had been quite unintentional on his part. Was that true for her as well?

It was also a stark reminder that he didn't know Dulci Wycroft all that well, all the ways she'd changed in the years of his absence. She'd come of age and entered society while he'd been off performing the various commissions that had eventually landed him his viscountcy.

Much of his adult life had been spent away from England doing things for the empire he couldn't share with another. The result was that he knew very little about the woman she'd become. Good God, when he'd left England she'd been sixteen, and he a mere twenty-four. Those intervening years were a blank. He knew only that her beauty, her wit, her innate fire for life and the wild side she strove to keep hidden drew him irrevocably despite his better intentions. Jack didn't dare contemplate too deeply the reasons for his inexplicable attraction. Those reasons were best left unexplored for fear of uncovering longings and truths that couldn't be answered or tolerated. He could not afford to fall in love with anyone, especially not Dulci. He'd have a hard time explaining that to Brandon.

Dulci cocked her head, studying him with her sharp gaze. 'What are you up to tonight, Jack? It must be important if it meant seeking me out. For the record, I was not fooled about your reasons for approaching me. You wanted that introduction.'

Jack executed a tight turn to avoid a collision with the less observant Earl of Hertfordshire. 'Do I have to be up to anything? Perhaps I just wanted to dance with the loveliest girl in the room?'

'Doubtful. The last time you saw me, I broke a pottery bowl over your head.' Dulci's eyes narrowed in speculation. 'You won't tell me what you're really doing here, will you?' she accused.

This was old ground. Old ground, old wound. It went beyond the quarrel in the orangery. He'd had this discussion before with other women. He was not at liberty to discuss his business with her or with anyone else. It was rather ironic that while achieving a title had made him socially acceptable and available, he was not at liberty to act on that availability. A woman was only entitled to part of him. The Crown got the other part without question or consideration.

Such a condition was not acceptable with Dulci. Her unattached status was proof of that. If she tolerated half-measures, she would have settled for a convenient *ton*nish marriage by now. But half-measures were all he could give. What he did for the king was of the utmost secrecy and not necessarily 'appreciated' in finer circles. He knew in the absence of such disclosures on his part that Dulci had her own theories about his actions, none of which showed him in a favourable light.

'You're not going to set up any kind of scheme, are you, such as the time you fleeced Wembley out of his thoroughbred over a game of Commerce?' She gave him a stern look and Jack could not hold back his laughter.

'What a little hypocrite you are, m'dear. Why should you have all the fun? Besides, Wembley deserved it.' Jack leaned close to her ear, inhaling the light scent of lavender, fresh and beguiling like the temptress who wore it. 'I heard you won a racing dare in Richmond last week.'

Dulci looked momentarily alarmed. 'No one is supposed to know. Who told you?' She stopped herself in mid-question and shook her head. 'Never mind, there were only two of us who knew. I know very well who told you.' She made a pretty pout. 'I thought Lord Amberston would know better.'

Jack laughed. 'Don't worry, your reputation is intact. However, it does occur to me that you play awfully close to the fire—does society know their darling Incomparable dabbles in scandal on a regular basis?'

Dulci would not be diverted. 'This is not about me, Jack. I want your word. I don't want you playing cards with Señor Ortiz.'

Jack was all mock solemnity. 'I promise you, this is not about cards.' Such a suggestion was almost laughable if the situation wasn't so serious. She could no more conceive of stopping a war before it started than hc could conceive of having nothing more serious to worry about than a card game. The damnable thing was, he could not tell her otherwise.

'Do you promise?' Dulci was sceptical of his easy acquiescence.

'You have my word, Dulci. In exchange, I want yours that there will be no more moonlight horse racing in Richmond. That's dangerous. You should know better than to risk your neck and your horse's.'

'Now who's the hypocrite?' Dulci flashed a teasing smile that showed off the dimple in her cheek. 'You're hardly the arbiter of moral fashion. I remember a few years ago when you masqueraded as a fop to help Brandon catch the Cat of Manchester. That escapade ran fairly close to outright law breaking. My horse race was merely ill advised.'

Jack managed a smile at the memory. 'That's the best service I've ever rendered your brother. I got him a wife in the bargain and he's been happy ever since.'

Dulci held his gaze, returning his smile. Something warm flickered to life in those blue eyes of hers. Jack moved her close to him as they turned. She did not resist his subtle possession. Jack gave her a private, knowing look. He knew she was remembering the thrill of their exploits to save Nora, the midnight wedding ceremony where Brandon, the earl, had married the notorious Cat. Perhaps she was remembering the dangerous sparks of desire that had risen suddenly and unbidden in the orangery at Christmas.

'Don't, Jack,' Dulci cautioned him softly.

'Don't what, Dulci?' Jack prodded with a whisper, knowing full well her thoughts had gone in the same direction as his, his body enjoying the feel of her far more than it should on a ballroom floor. 'Don't remember you in the orangery? Your hair coming down, your lips wet and red, your face tilted up in the candlelight waiting for my kiss? Your body pressed to mine as close as two bodies can be with their clothes on? How can I forget when I've seen you like that in my mind every night since?' The moment had been unpredictably heady. For a man with his vast experience with women, his reaction had played havoc with his senses whenever he recalled it, which was far too often for his own good.

Nothing had proved its equal, although Jack had certainly tried in the ensuing months. Dulci was a woman who demanded all of a man and that was far too dangerous of a commitment for him to make, for her as well as himself. But he was flirting shamelessly now, seducing her with words, his body and mind firing at the thrill of the challenge she presented.

He saw the pulse in her neck race at his words, belying the protest on her lips. 'Don't remember, Jack. We both know it was a mistake and it will be a mistake again.'

'I don't make mistakes when it comes to seduction, Dulci.'

'No, but afterwards you make plenty. Your *seductus exitus* needs work.'

'That's not a real Latin phrase.'

'*Exitus* is and it doesn't change the fact that yours needs work.'

'Only practice makes perfect.' Jack gave a heavy sigh of over-exaggerated disappointment. 'Alas, I have so few chances to practise.'

'That's not what I hear.'

Jack had no desire to talk about those particular rumours—rumours that involved a certain actress, strawberries and a large grain of the truth. If he could get Dulci away from the crowds, away from the eyes that watched their every move, maybe they could just talk, maybe something more. He *did* want to talk. He wanted to find out what she knew about the Venezuelans. Then again, who was he fooling? He wanted to do more than talk. He wanted to see if the sensations were still there. Perhaps Christmas had been an anomaly. It was a risky proposition at best, especially if he was wrong, but tonight his better judgement was no match for Dulci in pomegranate silk and memories of hot kisses.

'A walk in the garden then, Dulci,' Jack breathed against her ear, inhaling the lavender rinse of her hair. He could feel her body giving in, no matter what arguments her mind made. He could feel it answering to his, fickle compatriots to the codes of decency and honour that demanded they take a different route.

'All right, but just a walk,' Dulci consented.

Jack murmured low at her ear, 'I'm sure there'll be something handy to throw at me if you need it.' His hand tightened at her waist, ushering her towards the French doors that led outside. Ballrooms might be for business, but gardens… well, gardens were for pleasure.

The garden with Jack was a bad idea. *Anything* with Jack was a bad idea as she very well knew from gossip and brief personal experience. He had a reputation for a reason, actually several reasons. Dulci wasn't regretting her consent to walk in the garden, but she was *going* to. She knew it and yet she allowed him to lead her down both the proverbial and literal garden path, because she'd been able to think of nothing else since Christmas and Jack was irresistible, flaws and all.

There were definitely plenty of flaws, which worked only to heighten her own curiosity regarding the man behind the rumours—where did he go when he disappeared from London for months on end? What service had he rendered King William that had catapulted a poor squire's son into the ranks of the peerage with a hereditary title? How true was the tittle-tattle circulating behind ladies' fans that Jack was a lover beyond compare? There was probably a reason curiosity killed the cat, Dulci thought. She'd do better to forget such sordid things and to hope that Jack didn't read minds.

It was proving more difficult than expected to banish such thoughts at the moment. Jack drew her aside, slightly off the garden path, having arrived at his intended destination, a small alcove with a burbling fountain and a stone bench, the moon overhead and the paper lanterns that festively lined the garden paths giving off enough light to wander without fear of tripping.

It was a setting that showed Jack to great advantage. The moonlight cast a silvery hue to his winter-wheat hair, giving it the appearance of a smooth, sleek mane, every hair in place. The subtle detail work of his tailor emphasised the breadth of his shoulders, the trimness of his waist and the length of his legs, a reminder that while turned out in the guise of an immaculate, well-groomed gentleman, there was a raw, rough power beneath the clothes, signs of a man who'd led a life full of varied experiences.

Dulci often wondered if anyone else saw that quality in Jack. The longer she knew him, the more she didn't know him. He was a master of illusion. One only saw what Jack wanted to show and she'd been as easily duped on occasion as the rest.

She no more knew what truly drove Jack than any other member of the *ton*. She'd like to know more. Since the night in the orangery she'd been thinking rather a lot about Jack, her attentions drawn to whatever rumour was circulating about him any given week. She'd heard since Christmas he'd been busy kissing Lady Scofield in her big gardens at Lambeth.

A delicious tremor shot through Dulci. Had he

truly brought her out here, into this garden, to do the same? Would she, *should* she, let him? Those Christmas kisses had dominated too much of her mind. She couldn't deny the truth; she wanted Jack to kiss her and perhaps do more than kiss her. Her body could not forget the heat Jack's hands had invoked, the need for something more that his body had awakened in hers. She wanted to feel that way again, wanted him to wake her again.

She opted for a show of sophistication. She didn't want Jack thinking she was overly eager if he actually had seduction on his mind. Nor did she want to be over-eager if he *didn't*; such a miscalculation would be embarrassing and only serve to stoke his already over-inflated sense of self-importance.

'What now, Jack?' Dulci gave him a practised, coy smile. She moved into the alcove, surveying its furnishings with an assessing look. 'The fountain is probably not an option, but perhaps the bench is a possibility.'

'Did you consider I might not have asked you out here to seduce you? I seem to recall in the ballroom that you were rankly against such a venue.' Jack leaned against a stone column at the alcove's entrance, looking urbane and relaxed, very much at home with the situation. But Dulci could feel his eyes, hot and direct, following her movements. She could not fool him for long. He was experienced enough to know the game was afoot.

'Since when has that ever stopped you, Jack? The greater the challenge, the harder you try.' She trailed a hand in the fountain.

'I have been known to rise to the occasion.' Jack grinned wickedly and stepped towards her. 'I have the firmest of resolves, or so I've been told.'

She recognised that *cicisbeo* smile of his all too well. It was his stock in trade in London ballrooms, the smile that said she was the centre of his attention, that every wish, every desire was about to be fulfilled and more. She'd seen many women believe it. It was easy to believe that smile. She believed in it now against better sense.

Dulci stepped backwards, striving to create more space between them. She had not come to the Fotheringay ball looking for this. Indeed, she had not expected to find Jack here at all. The Season was too young. She'd thought she'd have a few weeks to herself before Jack came to wreak havoc on her senses. She'd thought she'd heard he was out of town. 'You've gathered all the other women to your banner tonight, Jack. You have no need of me as well.'

'But you're the only one I want.' Jack was grinning broadly now. Drat him, he knew he had her on the run.

'No, it's simply your arrogance, Jack. You can't stand not having every woman in the room swooning at your feet.'

Jack laughed, the sharp planes of his aristocratic face melting into boyish playfulness. 'By Jove, Dulci, no one quite cuts me down to size like you do, and goodness knows on occasion I need it.' He looked ten years younger, whatever secret cares he bore dissolving, minimising the darkness and mystery that limned him like a nimbus around the sun since his return to England. It occurred to her to wonder what he'd been like before? Surely he hadn't always been this way? How did a man become like Jack?

'Dulci.' The sound of her name on his lips was an invitation to sin. It was enough and it succeeded where all Jack's calculated foreplay had fallen short. She was in his arms in an instant, letting her body savour the strength of him, the feel of him, the almond scent of his soap, letting her mind forget all the reasons this was going to be a bad idea. His mouth took hers in a long, slow kiss, teasing her with its languorous exploration, one hand at the back of her neck, fingers entwined in her hair. The heat in her started to rise.

'I'm sorry about the orangery, Dulci,' Jack murmured, with sincere penitence. How could she not forgive him? Then something caught her eye over Jack's shoulder and she froze, her mind remembering all the reasons.

Jack nuzzled her neck encouragingly. 'Dulci, this is where you say you're sorry too about throwing that pot and you run your hands through my hair looking for any remnants of that damnable lump you gave me.'

'I don't think so, Jack.' Dulci pushed against his chest and stepped back, the moment lost to reality and disappointment. She'd been so ready to believe. She gave a flick of her head, nodding for Jack to turn around. It was the orangery all over again.

A throat cleared in the nominal darkness. A nervous, blushing page dressed in the royal livery of Hanover stammered his message. 'Excuse me, my lord. I have an urgent message from Clarence House. I was told to find you and tell you to come at once.'

Dulci watched Jack straighten his shoulders almost imperceptibly, the boyish pleasure that had so recently wreathed his face instantly subdued. The transformation happened so swiftly, it was possible to think she'd imagined the other. Jack pressed a few coins into the messenger's hand, no doubt meant to buy his silence regarding where and how the boy had found the viscount and sent him on before turning back to her.

'Dulci, I'm sorry. I have to leave. May I escort you back inside?' He was all duty now. Did this happen with all his women or was it just her bad luck? She hadn't heard, but then again she couldn't imagine anyone wanting to brag Jack had thrown them over for a government summons.

'What could the king want this time of night? Isn't he off to his own clubs and entertainments?' Dulci had recognised the address immediately: the residence of William IV.

'England never sleeps, Dulci.' Jack gave her a kind smile that she found condescending.

'Don't patronise me, Jack,' Dulci snapped.

'I'll call on you tomorrow,' Jack offered. But she would have none of his olive-branch brand of pity.

'I will not be home to you. I am not going to become one of your easy women who let you kiss them whenever you pass through town.' Dulci pushed past him, angrier at herself than at him. Jack would always be Jack, whoever that really was. As much time as she'd spent listening to rumours she'd thought she'd have understood that by now. She would find her own way back inside and, after a decent interval, she'd leave. The night had lost its lustre. But he halted her with a warm chuckle that said he didn't believe her bluff for a moment.

'You can't ignore me, Dulci. Very well, don't receive me. But I will see you tomorrow night. At the Danby rout, if you remember,' Jack called softly. 'I'll be the one in azure. Perhaps we can rename the ball the Blue Danby ball. It can be our private joke.'

She didn't want anything 'private' with Jack. Dulci fisted her hands in her gown where no one could see, her temper rising. It was just like Jack to make a joke when she was mad. Damn it all. She'd already forgot about the wager. She allowed herself the unladylike luxury of stomping her foot in frustration on the garden path. She'd known from the start coming out here with Jack was a bad idea; anything with Jack was a bad idea as she'd proven yet again. At least she'd have plenty to berate herself with on the lonely carriage ride home.

The carriage was crowded for all that there was only one person in it, thanks to the enormity of her thoughts, Dulci groused an hour later. She felt slightly better thinking it was Jack's fault, but that wasn't entirely true. He'd merely opened Pandora's box with his kisses and let loose all nature of strange feelings and emotions into her world. Hopefully common sense hadn't got out with the rest. Maybe it still hung there like a butterfly with one wing caught in the closed box lid, the other wing struggling for release. It certainly wasn't still in the box—tonight had illustrated that. At best, she had only half of it left.

Jack had awakened the curiosities of both mind and body. She was twenty-six and seriously doubted she would ever make a marriage that suited her temperament. But that didn't stop her from wanting to know the mysteries of the marriage bed, the secrets of satisfying the passions of the body.

She was not so naïve as to be unaware that a

certain calibre of gentleman had offered to solve that mystery for her. To date, she'd always been quick to scotch any efforts in the direction. Some risks were simply not worth taking. The kind of gentleman who offered such gratification was not the kind of gentleman who would keep her secrets. Good heavens, Amberston hadn't even kept their horse race secret. One could only guess what someone like him would do with an even bigger secret.

Jack was different. The shocking thought nearly jolted her off the carriage seat. An idea came to Dulci. Why not Jack? Any woman with eight seasons behind her, virgin or not, knew when a man desired her and Jack had wanted her. Perhaps he only wanted her for a night, for the novelty of it.

Whatever his motives, he did want her and that was all that mattered. If his wanting lasted only a night, so much the better. She was looking to satisfy her curiosity, nothing long term. Jack had already proven he could wake her passions and he'd already proven he could be discreet. He kept secrets for the Empire. He could surely keep one short liaison from public consumption and he would never tell Brandon.

Dulci tapped her chin with a gloved finger.

Hmm. Brandon might be a sticking point. She would have to overcome any resistance his friendship with Brandon might pose. Then she laughed out loud in the empty carriage at the ridiculous notions passing through her head. She was actually sitting here planning how to seduce the notorious Viscount Wainsbridge! She needed her head examined. What woman of virtue deliberately gave away her greatest asset? Moreover, in her numerous seasons she'd seen with her own eyes what happened to the young girls who'd fallen prey to various pre-marital temptations. The world wasn't big enough for a fallen woman.

A wicked voice whispered its rebuttal: *only if you get caught. You haven't been caught yet. Jack's perfect—discreet, skilled and in no mood to get caught himself. He might even empathise with you...*

She could laugh all night at the odd ideas floating through her mind, but Dulci could not quell the growing sense that in spite of all the decent reasons not to go through with it, she just might.

Chapter Three

Jack Hanley, the *first* Viscount Wainsbridge for all of five years, always answered the king's summons to Clarence House with alacrity and anxiety no matter what time of day or night it came or whose bed it found him in. Alacrity because one did not keep his monarch waiting, especially when one possessed a title as new as his. Anxiety because he knew the summons was merely a prelude to upheaval. William would not have called him if something had not been afoot that needed his special attentions. No doubt there'd been a development with the Venezuelans, but he was suspicious that it had occurred so quickly. He'd only met them an hour ago.

'I need you to stop a war.' William said abruptly as Jack entered. Jack merely nodded as if such statements were commonplace conversation and shut the door of the Clarence House study behind him. He had suspected as much. The initial rumours had been confirmed, then.

'When, your Majesty?' He took in the room with a sweeping glance, nodding curtly to the third man present, Viscount Gladstone from the Foreign Office.

William IV toyed idly with a paperweight. 'The war hasn't precisely happened yet. But I have it on good authority from Gladstone here that it will if we don't take steps now.'

Ah, it was to be a pre-emptive action then. He was good at that. Jack took the liberty of pouring himself a brandy at the sideboard. He took a seat and expertly flipped up the tails of his evening wear, sliding a careful glance at Gladstone. He had personal reasons for not liking the man. Gladstone made no secret of his contempt for Jack's inferior birth and first-generation title. But professionally, the man possessed an astonishing acumen for foreign intelligence.

'Tell Wainsbridge what you've told me,' William said.

Gladstone cleared his throat. 'Venezuela is contesting its shared borders with British Guiana.

They wish to extend their boundaries. It goes without saying that we are not interested in giving up our claims to that territory.' Gladstone stood up and walked to a long table, gesturing for Jack to follow.

With a long finger, Gladstone traced the boundaries on a map spread before them. 'The border in question is south-east of the Essequibo River.'

Jack nodded. He was one of the few who understood the magnitude of rivers in British Guiana. The marshy topography of British Guiana made coastal rivers the only thoroughfares into the interior. 'This is no small contention. We're dealing with approximately thirty-thousand square miles of property.' In a land of marshes and rivers, such territory was worth squabbling over.

Jack looked up from the map, back to where William sat. This information was not new to him. Indeed, it had been at the root of his presence at the Fotheringay ball. What he didn't know were the motives behind it. 'Do we have any speculations as to why Venezuela is suddenly interested in this section of territory?'

For centuries, ever since Britain had first staked a claim to Guiana in the sixteen hundreds, Spain had not done more than establish a handful of missions along the border. The border had been undefined and peaceful. Of course, it was an independent Venezuela now, not Spain that shared the border. Perhaps after a little over ten years of independence, Venezuela was flexing its muscle in the region.

'That's where you come in, Wainsbridge.' William leaned back in his chair, hands steepled.

'Of course, anything, your Majesty. I am always at your service,' Jack said easily, hiding his apprehension. He'd had to train himself over the last few years to stay alert in William's presence. The man acted more like a retired naval officer—which he was—than royalty—which had been a far-fetched possibility once. It was easy to forget that the tall, white-haired man with a soft chin and friendly eyes commanded a nation. Being with the man felt almost ordinary, like being with a beloved uncle until one remembered that, unlike the uncle who could be refused, one could not refuse the king.

'As you know, you've been asked to determine how real rumours of this border dispute are. I am interested in hearing how your evening went with the Venezuelan delegation.'

'I met them, but just barely.' Jack eyed Gladstone suspiciously. None of this was urgent or beyond what he already knew. Why the emergency summons?

Gladstone flicked a glance at William. 'There's been a further development. One of the gentlemen in the delegation is heavily influenced by a private and powerful consortium of Venezuelan businessmen who are eager to profit from the boundary dispute. We want to identify him as quickly as possible. It is believed the gentleman, whoever he is, may be in possession of a forged map that shows Venezuela's "preferred" boundaries. He may try to pass it off as a legitimate document and use it as evidence to force a new treaty of limits.'

Jack immediately thought of Calisto Ortiz, his smooth manners and his 'ombudsman' attachment to the delegation—official but unofficial. Jack returned to his chair and sat back to give his report.

'I think we can eliminate Adalberto Vargas. He's the senior member, in his early fifties. From his manners tonight, he's from a more traditional school of diplomacy. He's not likely to be swayed by such risky and underhanded tactics like a forged map.

'Neither would it be Hector Dias. He does not have either the suave mannerisms of Ortiz or the intellectual background of Vargas.' Jack surmised Hector Dias was a man who'd no doubt begun his career in mid-level staff positions with various embassies and would likely end his career there as well. The cut and cloth of his clothes at the ball had certainly suggested as much. The man hadn't the wealth at his disposal to match the wardrobes of Ortiz or Vargas.

'So that leaves Calisto Ortiz,' Gladstone put in, a note of triumph in his voice that it had been so easy to detect a likely candidate.

'Yes. He's the flamboyant charmer of the group. He's also there as an ombudsman, so the rules he must follow are much more lax than the other two. His English is excellent, and his con-nections even more so. He's a nephew to one of the regional Venezuelan viceroys with family connections to the governor. He's a likely choice.'

'We'll start putting together a more detailed dossier on him now that we know what to look for,' Gladstone said. 'If he's so well connected, British intelligence surely has information on his family. Perhaps he's organising a plantation movement. Plantations are big business in that part of the world.'

'Not *that* big,' Jack scoffed at the theory. Gladstone scowled at him, the old antagonism between them rising.

'I'd love to hear your ideas,' Gladstone retorted.

Choosing to ignore the slight, Jack returned to the map and stared thoughtfully at the outlined area, an idea forming in his mind. Businessmen weren't interested in the natural beauty of a land. There was something lucrative in the river valley, a valuable resource.

He spoke a single word to the room at large. 'Gold.'

'Gold?' Gladstone replied, incredulous.

'You forget, I've actually been to the region. I was there in 1830 after I helped Schomburgk on his Anegada expedition.' Jack smoothly interjected his credentials into the conversation. His work there had laid the grounds for being awarded the viscountcy. 'The river valleys are too wet and the forests in the interior are too dense for serious farming. Businessmen aren't looking to put up a plantation community in this region. No profit.' Gladstone looked like he'd gladly throttle him.

William broke in to defuse the tension. 'We want to be certain in regards to what they're after. We can use that knowledge to grease negotiations if we must. Until then, Wainsbridge, Ortiz is yours. I want to know what has made the area an urgent point of interest and how far they're willing to go to get it.'

Dismissed, they took their leave of the monarch and made their way through Clarence House to the front door. Jack was glad he had his coach. He did not want to share a hackney with Gladstone. They stepped out into the night air.

Jack's coach waited at the kerb but Gladstone couldn't resist a final jab as Jack stepped up to the door. 'I hear we have a mutual acquaintance in Lady Dulcinea Wycroft.'

'You hear the most amazing things, Gladstone,' Jack returned.

'I see them too, sometimes,' came Gladstone's cryptic reply.

'You've never got over Lady Dulcinea jilting you.' Jack's reply was cool, but inside he was seething. Gladstone must have had men watching the ballroom that night, checking out the Venezuelan delegation on his own even though Jack had been given the job. He would not put it past Gladstone to have forced a meeting tonight simply to drag him away from Dulci.

Anger clouded Gladstone's face. 'Behind those clothes you're nothing but a scrapper, a no-account country squire's son. I can only imagine how many boots you had to lick to rise this far.'

'Whereas I am sure you're quite clear on the boots you've had to lick. No imagining there. Your family's been currying favour since the sixteen hundreds. Dirty business that, two centuries of boot-licking.' Jack stepped into his coach and held the door open for a moment. 'Goodnight, Gladstone.'

He slammed the coach door and sank back against the squabs, less sanguine than he'd let on. This was dicey business with the Venezuelan delegation. Negotiations of this nature were always very covert, hardly ever making the public news, but that didn't make them less dangerous. Usually, they were more so. Without the check and balance of being in the public eye, there were no rules to govern them. Still, it would be business as usual if Dulci wasn't involved. But she was—placed right at the centre of the storm because of her connection to the three men most intrinsically concerned. There was going to be trouble. He could feel it in his bones.

Dulci Wycroft firmly believed trouble found you when you least expected it. She had an antidote for that: she expected trouble.

Always.

She'd learned early that collecting artefacts wasn't exactly an old maid's safe hobby. Not that she thought of herself as an old maid, although she'd reached the august age of twenty-six, trailing a string of six refusals of marriage behind her. Nor was she looking for safe.

If she was, she wouldn't be here, or a lot of the other places she'd been. Her hand flexed and closed around the small gun in her pocket, her sharp eyes alert to any suspicious movements in the dim interior of the dockside warehouse. Warehouses in the dock districts were not foreign venues to her. But this one, set in a rough part of Southwark, was by far the worst.

She'd been glad she'd decided to bring her own unmarked coach instead of relying on public hansom cabs. She'd noticed that the deeper into the area she'd journeyed the presence of cabs had dried up, a sure testimony to the unsavoury nature of the environs, the noise and comparable respectability of Hays Wharf far behind them.

A man moved from the shadows. Dulci tensed and then relaxed. She might not completely trust this man, but she knew him. He was her reason for being here in these rather questionable surroundings.

He strode forwards, well-dressed and olive skinned. *'Señorita, buenos días!'* he effused, lavishly bowing over her hand, too lavishly. Sweat lightly beaded his upper lip and Dulci noted immediately that the lavish gesture was a mask for the man's anxiety. The usual self-confidence the man possessed seemed oddly absent today.

Dulci withdrew her hand as soon as it was politely possible, her tones haughty and clipped. 'Señor Vasquez, let us dispense with the pleasantries. What do you have for me that is so urgent it could not wait out the afternoon?' Señor Vasquez's note had ruled out the chance to catch the Royal Geographic Society's lecture on the West Indies in its entirety, but with luck she might still make the last part.

'I have artefacts from the Americas.' He

gestured towards an opened crate, but Dulci didn't miss the quick dart of his eyes.

'Are you expecting anyone else, *señor*?' Dulci asked keenly, her own eyes conducting a quick investigation of the warehouse too.

'I have many appointments, *señorita*. I merely wish you to see these items privately. They're from Venezuela, your latest area of interest.'

'Really?' Dulci replied coolly, raising her eyebrows a fraction of an inch to indicate only mild appreciation. A display of unabashed delight would only serve to increase Señor Vasquez's price.

Dulci reached into the crate with one hand, parting the straw packing with one gloved hand. The other hand cautiously remained in her pocket, her eyes unwaveringly fixed on Señor Vasquez. Her hand met with stone and she pulled out a carved statue. Vasquez did indeed know her interests well.

'It's a *zemi*.' Dulci fought hard to keep the rising excitement out of her voice, studying the object reverently in the poor light. The idol was devoid of any garments and the stone carving indicated breasts and a rounded belly. 'It's an idol of a native god, or goddess in this case. Unless I am completely mistaken, this is a fertility fetish.' She stared at him in stark contemplation, oblivious to his discomfort at such frank discussion. 'Did this come with a—?'

'A bowl?' Vasquez finished for her. 'But of course, *señorita*.' His eyes flashed with a mocking chagrin. 'I would not give you only part of a set.'

Dulci set down the carving and with both hands delved beneath the straw packing. She felt the shallow dip of a bowl. 'Yes, there it is.' She withdrew a stone bowl and set it in place. 'There, Señor Vasquez, you can see how it all goes together. The idols are flat headed so that a stone bowl can be placed on top of their heads for worship.'

'*Buena, señorita.* Name a price, and it shall be yours.'

He seemed far too eager to get rid of her after the demanding note requiring an immediate meeting.

'I would prefer to see the rest of the contents,' Dulci said, proceeding to empty the crate and offering an exposition on each piece she extracted. 'This is likely to be an amulet, this would be a *metate*, they used it for grinding seeds...' She spoke absently, more to herself than for the edification of Señor Vasquez.

Dulci dusted off her hands and surveyed the artefacts, seven in all. She was cognisant of the fact that Señor Vasquez had checked his watch twice while she'd unloaded the crate. He was clearly expecting someone else, or perhaps hoping to avoid the expected visitor. The collection was certainly splendid, but, while it was exciting to her, she had not forgot the urgency of Vasquez's summons. 'Is this everything?'

'All but this final item.' Vasquez handed her a worn leather book the size of a journal.

She eyed him speculatively. 'Saving the best for last?'

Vasquez placed a hand over his heart. 'I seek only to please you, *señorita*. I know how much you like to read. Look here, there's even a few maps, very detailed.'

Dulci thumbed the pages, noting the drawings of strange plants and places. 'An explorer's journal? Perhaps a missionary's log?' Dulci asked. It was written in English and she immediately thought of Jack. The journal would make a fine gift for him, a remembrance of his own work in that region a few years back. Not that he deserved such a gift after last night, she reminded herself.

'I can only guess, *señorita*. My English is not

good enough for reading,' Vasquez hedged. 'I am a mere importer.'

Dulci was instantly suspicious. There was nothing 'mere' about Vasquez. The Spaniard was rich, his wealth made from the lucre of Spanish interests in South America. 'How did you come by this book?'

Vasquez shrugged gallantly. 'It was in the same crate as the statue. It was on the last ship. I unpacked it and thought of you, that is all.'

Nothing was ever that straightforward. When it was, it was time to start asking the hard questions. 'Are the artefacts stolen?' Dulci cocked her head to one side in an assessing tilt. She'd done business with Vasquez before. He'd proven to be a reliable contact, visiting London twice a year from Spain. Still, something didn't seem quite right.

'Of course not, I am a legitimate importer. Such chicanery would damage my reputation,' Vasquez argued, putting on an offended air at the suggestion.

'If they're not stolen, then why the urgency? We had an appointment tomorrow morning. What difference can a day make?'

'Ah, yes, *señorita*, please forgive me for worrying you. I must leave for home on the morning tide instead of leaving later in the week as I had planned. It is a personal matter. I did not want to leave without meeting with you.' He lowered his voice conspiratorially. 'There are others who were interested in the artefacts. I am to meet with them tonight. But I confess I wanted you to have first pick.'

Dulci nodded, her concern ebbing slightly in the wake of his explanation. The man was a consummate salesman. No doubt he'd arranged all this to increase his price. Urgency was a well-proven ploy for adding spice to a negotiation. 'I'll pay one hundred pounds for the crate and the journal.'

'One hundred pounds? *Madre de dios*, but I could not part with them for such a sum.' He protested neatly. 'Surely you understand, *señorita*, the effort to transport such goods across the Atlantic and bring them to London?'

Dulci's tone was brisk. 'Surely *you* understand, I am in no mood to haggle like a fishwife in the market. I am late for a much-anticipated lecture and you are fully cognisant of the fairness of my price.'

'Because you are my favourite, I will indulge you.' Vasquez relented with an exaggerated shrug. 'A hundred pounds, *señorita*.'

Dulci gave a curt nod. 'Deliver the crate to my town house promptly and you'll receive instructions for payment. If you are quick, you'll have no trouble getting your money before you sail. As always, *señor*, it is a pleasure.'

Vasquez bent over her hand. 'The pleasure is most assuredly mine.'

The pretty *señorita* had barely exited the building before he began rapidly packing up the artefacts. The sooner this crate was out of his hands, the better. He had not told her any lies: the artefacts were not stolen and he did have an urgent personal need to sail tomorrow—he valued his health. Having those artefacts found in his possession would endanger that health greatly.

It had recently come to his notice through his vast networks that someone highly placed in the Venezuelan government wanted them in deadly earnest. The artefacts didn't look particularly dangerous or valuable, just stone and wood carvings, most of them done with a crude skill at best.

It didn't matter. They could have been jewel studded and he'd still have wanted to be rid of them. Originally, he'd thought to make a tidy profit on them, but whoever wanted them had not wanted to purchase them. There'd been no interest in a business transaction. Whatever the reason, these items had not been meant to be seen by others. The possessor of these artefacts, for reasons he could not ascertain, was as good as dead. The artefacts were out of his hands now. He was safe. He'd been careful to erase any mention of them in his ship's manifesto and if his London warehouse was searched, they would find nothing that traced the artefacts back to him.

He didn't worry overmuch about the artefacts being discovered in the eccentric Señorita Wycroft's possession. If the artefacts couldn't be traced to him, they couldn't be traced to her. He supposed it was entirely possible the objects could be found through other avenues, but that would be a random happenstance completely out of his control. In all probability, the artefacts and whatever they hid would fall into obscurity, displayed inside a nice glass curio case in the *señorita*'s town house. His ethical conscience, such as it was, was clear. Señor Vasquez closed the lid on the crate and breathed a much-desired sigh of relief.

Chapter Four

Calisto Ortiz aimed a frustrated kick at an empty packing crate and swore in a fluid torrent of Spanish for all to hear. There was inept and then there was outright incompetence. His men had bungled the job again. How hard was it to retrieve a map no one knew existed? Yet his men had failed to recover it in Venezuela after the map-maker had mistakenly packed it with his other archaeological finds for shipping back to Spain. Here in London, the map had slipped from their grasp a second time. After having tracked it to an importer named Vasquez, Ortiz had thought his work was nearly done. He simply had to run Vasquez to ground and claim the map. But he was too late. The warehouse was deserted, but only freshly so. The crates were empty and bore the markings of Spanish freight. They also looked new, lacking the dirt and gouges that often accompanied crates over time.

Calisto Ortiz barked out new orders to his men. 'Search the docks, maybe the ship hasn't sailed yet. Search the taverns and inns for Vasquez too.'

The men rushed to do his bidding, leaving him alone in the warehouse. Calisto upended a crate and sat down upon it, heaving a sigh. He cared less about finding the ship than he did about finding Vasquez. Vasquez was fast becoming a valuable link in this game for two reasons. The first reason was of a practical nature. If he didn't find Vasquez and hence the map, it would mean the map was loose in London. The search would take on a needle-in-the-haystack quality.

The second reason was more symbolic. Vasquez was moving fast. By all reports the ship had only been in London a short time ahead of his own arrival and now it was potentially gone, the warehouse cleared out. Vasquez knew he had something dangerous and he'd come to London to pass it on to someone, to unburden himself. It meant the map was no longer a well-guarded secret. The mission had now taken on two goals:

retrieve the map *and* silence those who knew about it.

Ortiz ran his hands through his dark hair, breathing deeply to calm his racing mind. He had to take one step at a time, one assumption at a time. Until he found Vasquez, he had no way of knowing if Vasquez understood the value of the map. It could be that Vasquez only knew he had something of dubious worth, but didn't know what it was. Along with the map, there were figurines, *zemis* and *metates*. Then of course, he'd have to hunt down whomever Vasquez had sold the items to.

He had to be prepared for best- and worst-case scenarios, the best being that the map had passed from hand to hand without anyone detecting its importance. The worst was that Vasquez did know the significance of the map and had sold it for a nice profit to someone who'd appreciate the map's value in the discussions that would soon open up between the Venezuelan delegation and the British government in regards to the questionable border Venezuela shared with British Guiana.

Calisto knew he played a dangerous double game, not only with the British but with the Venezuelan government as well—not that the latter would mind if they came out the victor.

Some would claim the map was a forgery, but Calisto preferred to think of the map merely as potentially biased. He wouldn't be the first person in history to sponsor a map-maker to tweak the boundaries a bit here and there. In all reality, the interior of British Guiana was so underexplored, who could say where the borders really were?

It would take years to disprove the boundaries on his map and ownership was nine-tenths of the law, as the saying went. In the meanwhile, Venezuela would be in possession of a very lucrative piece of land containing riches untold and he and his uncle would be wealthy men.

Everything would work out. He was a man who knew how to cover his tracks and follow all necessary leads. His men were hunting down Vasquez right now. There was nothing more he could do at the moment. He flipped open his pocket watch. He had just enough time to change and dine before the Danby rout. With luck, the delectable Lady Dulcinea would be in attendance without her surly polyglot friend.

Luck was in short supply all around. The Danby rout was fully engaged by the time Jack arrived.

He'd meant to come earlier in hopes of stealing a moment with Dulci before she was surrounded. He'd wanted to set the record straight about their most unfortunate interruption the prior evening. It was not how he imagined their reunion. But business had conspired against him. He'd spent the afternoon discreetly following Calisto Ortiz to an empty warehouse in a seedy part of Southwark.

The unplanned adventure had been enlightening, posing several interesting questions, such as why a man of Ortiz's station would be down at the docks. Ortiz's behaviour had been telling as well. There was no doubt that whatever had taken place in the warehouse upset Ortiz greatly. As to what that might have been, Jack could only speculate. Although he'd explored the warehouse after Ortiz's departure, he'd found nothing more than the same empty, Spanish-stamped crates that had upset Ortiz. By the time he'd reported his news to Gladstone and picked up his newly tailored waistcoat of deep periwinkle blue, afternoon had swiftly turned into evening, leaving him hard pressed to find time for a much-needed bath and *toilette* before setting out for the night.

There was no hope of catching Dulci alone, a

fact attested to by the sea of blue surrounding her four men deep. Squaring his shoulders and setting aside the cares of the day, Jack cut through the crowd of admirers to place himself in front of her. He made a courtly leg. 'It appears I've more than fulfilled my commission, Lady Dulcinea.' Jack gestured to the various hues of blue assembled about her. 'I do believe I've saved the economy for a day.'

Dulci laughed and waved her fan, a painted affair that matched the pale blue hues of her gown. 'Tailors' apprentices across the city are in your debt, Wainsbridge.'

'Certainly that's worth a dance.' Jack offered a charming grin and held out his hand.

There was the sound of grumbling. A few voices were raised in complaint: 'He's stealing all the best dances.' 'He danced with her last night.'

Dulci squashed the protests with a smile. Between her gown and that smile, she looked like an angel come to earth as she moved to take his hand. Her beauty never ceased to entrance him. But Jack knew better than to be misled. If Dulci Wycroft was any kind of angel, she was an avenging one. Before he could make his peace with her, she was going to make him pay. Would she start with the wager or the interruption from last night?

'This deep periwinkle is an improvement, Jack.' Ah, it was to be the wager. 'Still, it's a far cry from what you used to wear. I remember in Manchester you had an evening coat with diamond buttons. Brandon said you wore it to his betrothal ball. Whatever happened to all those shirts with yards of lace for cuffs?'

'I burnt them,' Jack answered succinctly. 'I have not played the fop for years now. Such a façade does not suit a king's adviser.'

'It did once. You used to say people were unguarded in their conversation because they assumed a fop had stuffing for brains.' There she went, probing again for the things he could not tell her.

'I'm an adviser, not a spy. A man with stuff for brains is not a man who is ultimately respected. Playing the fop had rather obvious limitations after a while for an adviser.' Jack kept his answers abrupt.

'How long do you suppose we have before we'll be interrupted by a government summons tonight? Do you think we might make it through this dance?' Dulci quipped, with an edge to her voice that warned Jack he was not entirely forgiven.

Damn Gladstone and his interference. But Jack would not make excuses about who he was and what he did. He turned them sharply at the top of the ballroom and decided it was time to change the conversation to something lighter.

'I'm surprised you're angry over the interruption last night, Dulci. You were the one who didn't want to go out to the garden in the first place. Admit it, you like my kisses.' What was he doing? He was flirting with her as if he meant to take this interlude further. *Which of course you do*, his conscious prompted honestly. *Admit it, the experiment last night failed. The kisses at Christmas weren't an isolated incident. You burn for her.*

'They're pleasant enough when there's nothing better to do,' Dulci teased knowingly.

'Is there usually something better to do?' Jack challenged with a grin, liking the way her smile lit her face when she teased him, liking the confident, bold way she flirted. But he had to tread carefully here. Dulci could not be handled like the experienced married women of the *ton*. She was far finer than that and she'd expect far more than they if he led her down that path.

'There was today.'

'No more dangerous wagers in the moonlight, I hope.'

What he really hoped was that she hadn't spent any more time with Calisto Ortiz. He knew, of course, where Ortiz had been later in the afternoon, but that didn't preclude Ortiz having made an earlier call. From what Jack witnessed of the man on two occasions now, he wanted Ortiz as far from Dulci as possible.

'This morning I worked with my fencing instructor.'

Jack's eyebrows rose slightly at this. They rose further after the next pronouncement.

'Then, this afternoon, I picked up some new additions to my collection of artefacts from the new world. Your part of the world, actually. Somewhere near Venezuela, or maybe Guiana.'

'What collection is this?' An alarm rang somewhere deep inside him at her reference, but it would be premature to jump to conclusions.

Dulci's excitement was evident in the sparkle of her eyes as she explained. '*Zemis*, tribal fertility fetishes and other assorted items of interest. They're from the Arawak tribes.'

Alarm was no longer premature. The Arawaks lived on the south-eastern border near the

Essequibo River. His well-trained face must have betrayed him momentarily because Dulci peered at him sharply.

'Have I shocked you?'

Very little shocked Jack after his travels. But that didn't mean he couldn't be terrified. His mind rushed to assimilate the information. This was far worse than his earlier concern over her involvement.

Last night he'd merely been concerned because she'd become a bystander who could be implicated, someone known to all three men: she was a woman in whom Ortiz was showing marked interest; she was the woman Gladstone had once aspired to marry; she was someone he'd paid recent social attentions to and that could put her at risk by association once Ortiz worked out his interest in the Venezuelan delegation. If Ortiz chose to strike out, Dulci would be a likely target.

But now her eccentric hobby had suddenly catapulted her into the forefront of the action. It begged the question whether Brandon had any idea what Dulci did with her time; first fencing and now this gadding about town collecting artefacts that were most likely stolen.

Was this merely coincidence or did Dulci

actually possess the cargo Ortiz had been searching for? The dance was ending, but he could not return her to her court without knowing more. A strong urge to possess and protect her surged. He told himself the feeling was out of a sense of duty. With Brandon absent from town, it was his job to act as a surrogate protector. His more honest side didn't accept that lie for a moment. Something far deeper was at work here and it scared him.

'I had no idea your interests ran in that direction,' Jack said benignly, subtly ushering her towards the verandah.

'I have you to thank for my interest. After your work with Schomburgk, I turned my attentions from the Egyptian excavations to the New World. After all, these artefacts are from living tribes. They're clues to a way of life that is taking place right now, not thousands of years ago. I find that much more fascinating. I see you're surprised. There's a great deal you don't know about me, Jack.' Dulci laughed up at him, but not unkindly.

'Then tell me more,' Jack flirted, the coldness receding a bit. He was back in control now. He had a strategy. He would take her outside and quiz her thoroughly until he had his answers, kiss them out of her if need be. He'd probably kiss her anyway whether he needed to or not. 'Where did you come by these artefacts?'

'A Spanish importer named Vasquez has been supplying me with items over the past two years.'

A new type of alarm coursed through Jack, not all of it having to do with his concern over the current situation. Good lord, didn't the woman know the risks? Didn't she realise how easy it would be to buy stolen goods? The Americas were rife with men of questionable repute who looted tribal grave sites or stole religious icons from the natives in the hopes of selling them back home to unsuspecting purchasers.

Those were the honest men.

The dishonest men simply passed off imitations and forgeries as the real thing.

'I hope you're careful, Dulci,' Jack said. 'There are men who'd take advantage of a woman in that market.'

Dulci's reply was glib and self-assured. 'Oh, I am careful, I always take my gun.'

Jack gripped Dulci's arm, fear returning anew. 'Your *gun*? Where do you go?' He hadn't meant his comment in that way. He'd meant it as a warning about the quality of goods she was dealing with. But now, his concern grew exponentially. Clearly this Vasquez did not call safely at her home with his wares.

'To the wharves, of course, Jack.' Dulci fixed him with an incredulous look. 'Where else does one retrieve goods from ships?'

Oh God, oh God, this was getting worse by the moment. 'And today, Dulci? Did you go to the docks today? Where?'

Dulci's brow furrowed in puzzlement. She pulled her arm away. 'What is this, Jack? You didn't even know I collected until a few moments ago and now you're suddenly full of chivalrous concern for my well-being. I've been doing this far longer than you realise.'

It would do no good to worry Dulci. He'd be unable to tell her anything useful if she asked and that would only serve to anger her. Jack shrugged and dispatched a quick half-truth. 'There's been some concern about activity at the docks lately, that is all. It's been rougher than usual.'

'I went to Southwark and all was fine. Although I will admit that it was a section that was more run down than the usual areas I frequent. The artefacts are splendid. Their arrival is quite timely with the Venezuelan delegation in town. I am looking forward to showing them to Señor Ortiz. He may know something more about them than what I can find in the libraries. I want to write an article for the Royal Geographic Society about them.'

No! All of Jack's instincts rebelled at the notion of Dulci showing Ortiz. But he could not overtly steer her away from the man without raising suspicions or looking like a jealous suitor. Neither was an appealing prospect. Well, he'd just have to get there first.

'I'd like to see your collection. I can serve in Ortiz's place. Perhaps I'll recognise some of the items and be able to shed some further light on them. I have an inspiration—let's take a night off from all this social whirl. I'll call tomorrow evening after dinner. We can fence and I'll tell you if your instructor is any good. Afterwards, we can go over the collection.'

It was an audacious request. A gentleman never called on a lady at such a time and Jack was inviting himself. If it had been anyone else, his intentions would be clear. But Dulci was also a family friend. He was trading on that connection quite liberally with the request.

'Do you think you can best me, Jack?' Dulci's eyes twinkled with challenge at the mention of fencing. 'You might be in for another surprise.'

Chapter Five

The enormous chandelier lit up the Stockport House ballroom. Dulci cut the air with an experimental slice of her rapier, upsetting the lazy waltz of the dust motes in the streams of light. Satisfied with the balance of her weapon, she slid a button over the point and tossed another button to Jack. 'Too bad we can't put a button on the sharp edge of your wit. Everyone was talking last night about how you fairly skewered Señor Ortiz the night before with your linguistic prowess.'

Jack slid the button over the rapier point. 'Are you defending him, Dulci?'

'Only because you were acting like a dog in the manger.' Dulci took another practice slash.

'I disagree.' Jack executed a lunge against an unseen opponent. 'I was clever and he'd been ogling your bosom far too long to be appropriate.'

Dulci made an arcing slash. 'Is there an appropriate amount of time for that? Perhaps some kind of hidden gentleman's rule?'

'About bosom ogling?' Jack lunged, stretching his leg muscles, thinking for a moment before responding. 'Yes, no more than two seconds and then one's eyes must revert back to the lady's face and not stray again. That way, she'll wonder if you ever looked in the first place. Of course, if one's partner is especially well endowed in that region and one is very skilled, one can sneak a few more glances by adopting a contemplative look during conversation and drop one's eyes without a move of the head. But I wouldn't recommend it for everyone, it takes a lot of practice to perfect.'

'That's perfectly appalling,' Dulci scoffed. 'You don't have a rule, you have a whole treatise!'

'Makes one wonder what other hidden rules govern the lives of gentlemen, doesn't it?' A wicked gleam lit Jack's eyes. He raised his rapier in a fencer's salute. '*En garde*, my dear.'

En garde indeed! How was she supposed to

concentrate after that? They fell into first position. Jack thrust forwards and Dulci parried with expert ease out of reflex, struggling to drag her thoughts back from the conversation.

Jack made a daring lunge and caught her rapier arm out of position. Dulci tried to recover, but was not fast enough to deflect the strike.

'*Touché*. Round one to me.' He winked. 'You weren't concentrating. Perhaps it was my exquisite physique that distracted you.'

Dulci flashed Jack a withering look and determinedly took up her position. 'I'm just not used to seeing you in such light colours.' In truth Dulci did find it something of a novelty to see Jack in a plain white shirt and tan breeches. Such clothing didn't hide anything and her imagination was embellishing heavily, firing her already active imagination to indecent levels. She'd end up skewered by her own blade if she wasn't careful.

He looked almost normal, standing in her ballroom wearing regular clothing. Except for the fact that there was nothing ordinary about Jack regardless of what he wore. It didn't matter if he was the diamond-buttoned fop or the sombre gentleman, Jack drew people to him by the sheer force of his personality, a unique blend of the light and sharp witted, underneath which lurked a dangerous intelligence that men respected and women yearned to possess.

She was no different in that regard. Dulci wished she could unlock the secrets of his mind. But Jack was a guarded man, a puzzle she had yet to solve, which probably explained why he was standing in her ballroom fencing with her, when she was supposed to be mad at him.

'Are you going to engage any time soon?' Jack drawled, scolding her for wool gathering.

'I was wondering why is it that you're here when I'm supposed to be upset with you.' Dulci took the offensive and pressed him hard with a series of attacks.

'Do you have an answer?' Jack asked with a sharp riposte that bought him back some ground.

'None that I like.' Dulci flicked her wrist and delivered a complicated stroke that nearly disarmed him. She grimaced in disappointment. That move always worked on other opponents. Jack must have wrists of steel to successfully deflect it.

Jack groaned. 'That's hardly a resounding endorsement.'

A smile twitched at her mouth. Dulci felt a laugh coming on that would surely disable her. 'Don't make me laugh, Jack. You're not fighting fair.'

Jack grinned deviously and Dulci knew she had to hurry if she meant to win before she burst into laughter and dropped her guard. Dulci feinted, parried two more quick strokes, then suddenly changed hands. Her left wasn't her strongest arm, but she was counting on the surprise giving her a few seconds' advantage.

This time her tactic worked. Dulci claimed the round four strokes later.

'Nicely done,' Jack commented, graciously ceding the round. 'I underestimated you. I didn't know you'd developed your left arm.'

Dulci ran a towel along the length of blade, wiping it clean out of habit rather than need. 'Turnabout's fair play. I underestimated you in the first round. No one has successfully deflected the move I used towards the end.' Dulci paused, the easy conversation catching her off balance. It was a moment between equals. Eyes met and held. Jack was on the move, crossing the small distance between them.

'You could do better with it. Let me show you a stronger way to deliver that blow.' Without waiting for permission, Jack slid behind her, his hand covering hers on the hilt of her rapier, his other arm about her waist, drawing her against him as he directed her into position.

The nearness of their bodies swamped Dulci with an acute sense of intimacy. She was so close to Jack she could actually smell him right down to identifying the brand of gentleman's soap he'd used for his *toilette*: an almond scent sold at an exclusive store on Bond Street.

She could identify other things, too: the fact he was five inches taller than she; that she could use the hollow of his shoulder to rest her head and in turn he could use the top of her head to rest his chin; the surprising strength of his arm. Beneath his clothing, Jack possessed a remarkably fit body, built to a fencer's perfection: lean and trim, deceptively muscular, with narrow hips and long legs. An ideal build for stealth and speed, two useful tools an épéeist relied on regularly.

Dulci's face heated at the direction of her thoughts. She was thankful Jack was behind her. She didn't want Jack thinking she could be had too easily like his strawberry actress. Besides, this was all meant to be a purely academic exercise between fellow fencers. But with Jack one could never tell. Jack had the ability to turn the most mundane gestures into a seductive prelude to all sorts of pleasurable sins. After all, they'd only gone out to the garden for a harmless walk.

Jack's hips shifted against her back, his voice soft at her ear in a most non-academic tone. On purpose? Dulci wondered. 'Let's take a step forwards and try it now with the steady wrist, no flicking this time.'

They moved together, stepping and striking. 'There, do you feel how much stronger the blade's position is without the flick at the end? Good. Whoever taught you that was more interested in showmanship than real prowess.

'Now, try it against me.' Jack left her and picked up his own foil. She felt strangely abandoned without the warmth of Jack, the feel of Jack, behind her. Dulci was half-tempted to ask him to show her the move again. The only thing stopping her was her pride. Such a trick was a ploy other women would use. She would not stoop, hard as it was.

Dulci gamely readied herself and engaged. This time the move worked and Jack found himself disarmed in short order.

'Very good,' Jack applauded, his admiration

obvious, as was his approval. Overt approval was not something she was used to. Men might admire her, and she knew very well that many did. But admiration was not the same as approval. It had taken her a long time to understand the nuances that separated the two.

Men who considered themselves modern and above the traditions of their station might enjoy privately fencing with her, might take pleasure in discussing her collection of histories and artefacts, might even applaud her personal studies from a distance. All of that was well and good in their minds until it came to marriage. A man could admire such traits from afar, but no man wanted to be shackled permanently to a woman who possessed those traits. It had taken six marriage proposals for her to fully understand.

But Jack was different. She supposed it was because he'd openly declared himself not the marrying kind and she could trust him to stand by that declaration unlike Gladstone, her sixth miserable proposal. Gladstone had declared no more than friendship and respect for her and then surprised her with a marriage offer accompanied by a list of demands regarding the things she'd need to give up as his viscountess.

In those terms at least there was no risk of such a misunderstanding with Jack. She understood Jack perfectly. Rumour could be trusted in this regard: he offered a moment of physical pleasure, no promises attached. A relationship would last only as long as Jack's work didn't encroach. In many ways, a relationship with Jack was over before it started. A woman who gave herself to Jack would have to be happy with whatever she could salvage. In the long term, Dulci doubted she could do such a thing. But it hardly mattered. She wanted only the experience he offered and then they could go their separate ways.

The thought haunted her throughout their work out. Dulci was glad for the excuse of exercise. She could pretend the flush on her cheeks was from their exertions.

They worked a while longer on footwork and various techniques until both were well exercised from their efforts. Dulci stopped and wiped her face with a towel. 'I'm finished, Jack. How about you? I'll have a tea tray sent to my collections room. We can eat a little supper and I'll show you the new batch of artefacts. I've just begun cataloging them. You can see for yourself that I've not been hoodwinked into buying fakes.'

* * *

The collection room far exceeded any of Jack's preconceived expectations. Two adjoining drawing rooms had been devoted to Dulci's work, the dividing doors between them pulled back to maximise the space; tall windows overlooking the back garden let in copious amounts of light during the day. Where the light was best, a long work table sat against a wall, strewn with stones, statues and wood carvings. Bookcases were laden with atlases and treatises from the Royal Geographic Society. Free-standing curio cabinets with glass shelves stood about the room, compelling the visitor to wander, stopping to look at each treasure.

And they were indeed treasures, Jack noted, studying each case in turn. It was impossible to tell how honestly anyone had come by the items, but they were authentic. He could rest easy on that account. Dulci had not been misled into purchasing frauds. He stopped to eye a splendid lapis-lazuli-and-gold Egyptian collar. 'These are very fine items, Dulci.'

He studied a cabinet containing a set of bronze elephants with jewelled eyes. 'From India?'

Dulci moved to stand beside him. 'From a maharajah. An old friend brought them back for me a few years ago.'

'Is that wistfulness I hear?' Jack asked, tossing her a sideways glance. 'Would you like to go to India some day?'

'I'd like to go anywhere.' Dulci ran an idle hand over a mask, tracing the contours. 'India, Egypt, the Americas. There's a big world out there—' Dulci waved a hand '—and I've seen so very little of it.'

A footman entered with the trays and Dulci crossed the room to direct the setting out of the tea and supper on a vacant table. Jack studied her as she gave instructions, her dark hair hanging in a thick braid down her back, the shapely curve of her hips in the tight fencing trousers she wore.

A stab of jealousy went through him. He was an only child and had never acquired an appreciation for sharing. Had Gladstone seen her dressed thusly? Probably not, Jack reasoned. No man could see Dulci turned out in tight trousers and white shirt and blithely let her go. He could feel himself rising appreciatively at the provocative sight of her backside. On the other hand, maybe Gladstone, traditional bastard that he was, had seen Dulci like this and promptly run the other way. Gladstone wouldn't know what to do with a woman like Dulci.

Jack knew. Whether or not that was a credit to him, however, was in dubious question. Dulci was a woman full of passion, a woman ready to burst with it. He recognised it in her smiles, in her blue eyes so full of life. It was there in her dares, those stupid dares that would bring her down sooner or later. She would not be careful for ever. One risk would be to go too far with the wrong sort of gentleman who would covet her *joie de vivre*. He would spare her that humiliation, that fall from grace if he could. But Dulci would not tolerate being reined in.

She'd done an admirable job of fooling London society so far. He could hardly reconcile the perfectly coiffed Incomparable who took to the dance floor every night of the London Season with the energetic virago who'd bested him at fencing and took a serious interest in anthropology. He supposed it was something of a revelation to learn he wasn't the only one who wore a mask. In that, he and Dulci were quite alike.

The one thing that had become abundantly clear to him in the past few months since Christmas and intensely so in the past few days, was that he wanted her. Kissing her in the garden had only served to re-ignite his previous desire. He wanted all that energy, all that beauty, all that wit, in his bed. He knew too that it would have to be her choice, her understanding of what such an arrangement would mean and what it would not, both for her as well as for him.

There were so many reasons not to pursue this mad passion any further; she was untouched and he had nothing to offer—nothing he *would* or *could* offer. This decision would cost her far more than it would cost him. It would not impede his chances to marry—not that he had any plans in that direction—but it would impede hers should she ever change her mind and accept some erstwhile suitor in the future. But the body defied logic. Such reasons did nothing to staunch his desire.

The supper things were settled at last to Dulci's satisfaction and Jack took a seat on the sofa across from her, picking up the thread of their interrupted conversation. 'If you want to travel, why don't you?' Jack reached for a plate of cold meats and bread.

Dulci laughed. 'I haven't the same freedoms as a man, Jack. I can't pack my maid off to Egypt with me as if it were a trip to Bath.' Dulci bit into her meal with a ferocity that echoed her disapproval of such strictures.

'Of course not. Surely something can be arranged. There are guidebooks and tours these days. You'd hardly be alone.'

Dulci shook her head and made a face. 'I don't want to travel with a tour. It would be incredibly boring, visiting all the same places everyone else visits. I want to explore. You've seen land no Englishman has ever seen. It's simply not fair. You got to because you're a man.' Dulci sighed and sank back against her chair. 'You don't know how lucky you are, Jack. Your life is portable, your body is portable. I wager you could walk out this door and be on a ship to anywhere by the tide, or a mail coach within minutes of leaving my house.'

Dulci's eyes burned with a need so intense Jack felt it sear him deep inside. Shame on society for having no idea or tolerance for such a fire. Inside the walls of her brother's house, she could wear trousers and fence, write her articles, collect her artefacts. But not beyond. Outside Brandon's home, she was trapped by society's rules and by her sex.

'Is that why you haven't married?' Jack took an

educated guess. Dulci could no more bear half a life for herself than she could half-measures from anyone else.

'Whatever does that have to do with anything?' Dulci's answer was sharp and defensive. He didn't blame her. His comment sounded entirely *non sequitur*, only it wasn't. He could see the connection. Marriage would take her out of Brandon's house, out of the only place she had any freedom. Jack loved women, but he was heartily glad he'd not been born one. He wanted to say something that would comfort her, but he could not give her empty words. She would know they were just that.

'For your information, I haven't married because I haven't met the right man.' Dulci took a defiant bite. Jack fought a smile. It wasn't anyone who could convey all manner of message by simply eating.

Jack wasn't ready to let the conversation go. It was proving to be far too interesting. 'The right man would be...' Jack let his words fall off.

'Out there somewhere.' Dulci fluttered a hand. Not the answer he was looking for. He'd been hoping for a list of itemised qualities. 'I am in no hurry. I have no reason to marry.' She fixed him with a pointed stare. 'Unlike yourself. What are you now, Jack? Mid-thirties? You need an heir for that new title of yours.'

'Same reasons as yours, I suspect.' The conversation was suddenly not as interesting as it had been. Thoughts of an heir and how they were begot had aroused him. He set down his plate and rose. 'Come and show me the Venezuelan items. It is why you brought me up here, isn't it?' he charmed shamelessly. 'Or is this a new rendition of showing off the etchings?'

Dulci led him to the long work table beneath the windows. The items were laid out by groupings, some already tagged with notes lying beside them. 'These are cooking implements from what I can tell—a *metate*, a pestle.' Dulci reached for a book nearby on the table and turned to a marked page. 'The items match the drawings here and the brief description.' She showed Jack the page. 'I'd like to know more, though. These items suggest a certain diet and they rule out the presence of other foods. One can grind grains and seeds with these, but I have yet to find any tools that would be good for meat dishes. It tells me these people don't eat meat at all or at least very little.' She stopped herself. 'I didn't mean to go on. Am I boring you?'

'Hardly.' He could listen to Dulci talk all day, although given the choice there were other things he'd rather do with her. He'd wanted to see the artefacts but this evening appointment was proving ill founded. Fencing had been quite a stimulating exercise, her body pressed to his as he showed her the appropriate move and she'd not been immune.

Jack was impressed with her reasoning and said so. Dulci shrugged. 'I've picked up many tips from the lectures at the Royal Geographic Society. When they say something like that it seems so obvious, yet I wouldn't have thought of it on my own. It's quite a reminder about how locked into our worlds we get, the blinders we wear without knowing it.'

'Still, your applications of the knowledge are very insightful,' Jack complimented.

'I am hoping Señor Ortiz can fill in some blanks for me, however. The British library was severely deficient in any relevant texts, another reason why I want to do an article,' Dulci said with more enthusiasm than Jack liked. It was the second time she'd mentioned wanting to use the Spaniard as a resource.

Jack had to prevent such a discussion from happening. It didn't matter if this was the same cargo Ortiz was looking for, suspicion on Ortiz's part would be enough. Jack did not want to think what lengths Ortiz might go to in order to retrieve the cargo. But now wasn't the time to dissuade Dulci. He had to choose his moment. Jack picked up a heavy mortar to examine. He ran his hands over the smooth rock surface, an idea taking root. If this was the missing cargo, what would Ortiz be looking for? An artefact with a hidden cavity? If he could find the map first, he could use it to lead Ortiz away from Dulci.

'The tribes Schomburgk and I ran into on the Anegada mission were infamous for their booby-traps. There were all kinds of secret levers and counterweights to spring trap doors and such. Do you think the Arawak have secret hiding places? Have you read of any similar traditions?' Jack kept a certain amount of levity in his tone. He didn't want to appear too eager.

Dulci knitted her brow, making an honest effort at recalling. 'You mean like a false bottom? I haven't heard of anything like that. It would be exciting though, wouldn't it, to find a hidden treasure.' She scanned the assortment of items on the table. 'I am afraid most of these items are too small, and I'd doubt stone is very easy to carve out a hidey-hole in.'

'I suppose so.' Jack assented. Many of the items *did* look too crudely carved from hard stone to hide a secret compartment with much skill. But his eyes silently lit on a wooden statue at the far end of the table and a collection of boxes with carved lids. He'd like to study those further without drawing Dulci's attentions. Maps could be folded. They didn't have to be rolled. Folded, they would take up far less room. A paper map could be folded down quite small.

'A single item contains an entire belief system if one knows how to look at it. This one tells me about their religious preferences. Nature is their god,' Dulci was saying. 'I think this item is almost beautiful.' It was the soft, reverent quality of Dulci's voice that drew his eyes to her and the item she held in the palm of her hand, a fertility fetish. 'It's been carved out of turquoise and someone spent hours polishing it. Perhaps it belonged to a tribal queen.'

The fetish *was* beautiful and highly corporeal with its full breasts and round belly or maybe the moment owed its sensual overtones to Dulci's voice. Jack felt his member stir in response. It had been stirring for the past three days since the first night in the ballroom, if the truth be told. Did Dulci have any idea how she was affecting him? The evening, the delightful company, the temptation of Dulci's fire were overpowering. Perhaps they could play a little without too much harm, Jack's inner devil suggested.

He took the fetish from her. 'Maybe it was a gift from her lover.'

This time there could be no mistaking his statement as an academic assessment. Jack's words were charged with explicit seduction. Something potent and hungry sprang to life between them. Jack let her see his rising need in the slow gaze that caressed her face, in his fingers' deliberate stroking of the little fetish—a move calculated to look absently done. He dropped his gaze down her body. It had the desired result. Dulci bit her lip, stifling a little gasp at his boldness.

'Stop it, Jack,' she scolded, a nervous, excited tremor in her voice. 'That was more than two seconds.'

'I am making my intentions known.' Jack took her hand. 'Don't pretend you didn't see this coming.'

'No, I won't pretend it.' Dulci trembled as he ran

his knuckles gently the length of her arm. 'I've wanted it. It's time to finish what we started in the orangery.' Her voice was nothing more than a breathy whisper, her desire getting the better of her.

'And the garden, don't forget.' Jack reached for her, pulling her hard against him for a slow kiss. She was an innocent wanton. 'Do you know what we started?' he whispered, testing her.

'I have no idea, not really.' She parted her lips, wet and wanting. 'But I want to know, Jack. I want to know everything and I want you to show me.' Those blue eyes of hers smouldered with want; every man's fantasy, his fantasy—Dulci in his arms, giving him permission to unleash her passion, to show her what her body was made for. It was a potent, frustrating elixir that worked all kinds of magic, undoing his tenuous grip on the realities beyond this room, this night.

'Do you know what you're doing, Dulci?' he asked one last time. He wanted to be patient, but it was difficult to be patient when one was rock-hard and had been for some time.

'I know, Jack. This is what I want.'

Jack nodded and stepped away from her.

'What are you doing? Where are you going?'

'I'm locking the door. No more interruptions, not for this.'

* * *

Dulci waited for him at the sofa, watching him as he locked the door. He was playing for time for her sake, giving her a last moment to make her decision. The die was nearly cast.

It wasn't a question of wanting him.

She did.

It was a question of wanting him enough to live with the aftermath. Not the aftermath of lost virginity—virginity was highly overrated in her opinion, its importance a myth perpetuated by men who didn't want women to have the same freedoms they enjoyed. It would be a relief to surrender hers and have done with it. That was not the aftermath that concerned her. She had grappled with the social implications of virginity since the night in the carriage.

What worried her most in the few moments she had left was whether or not she could let Jack leave as he most assuredly would; whether or not she could stand knowing that something which would mean so much to her would mean so little to him, certainly not enough to stay. It was the way she wanted it, but she was not naïve enough to believe the event would carry no emotional weight for her.

Jack turned from the door and faced her. This was her last chance. She could call a halt or continue with an encounter that would satisfy her curiosity once and for all and hope that it would be enough.

Chapter Six

She drew a deep breath and squared her shoulders in determination, her decision made. Jack could see the resolution in her eyes. He crossed the room towards her, watching as she reached a hand to loosen her hair, shaking it into a long ebony cascade, and Jack's need ratcheted up another impossible notch. Dulci might be untouched, but she was bold, an undeniably heady combination.

Something flickered in the blue flames of her eyes. Faith, perhaps? Faith that she'd made the right decision, faith in him that he wouldn't fail her? She wrapped her arms about his neck and he pressed her against him, covering her mouth with his in a full-bodied kiss.

The dance had begun. He would start slowly, letting their bodies know one another and then…well, then he would take them both to pleasure. He sensed her impatience, her curiosity. 'Patience, Dulci. I'll get us there, but not too soon. The journey's half the fun. You'll see.'

His hands teased her breasts through the fabric of her shirt, a hand slipped down to cup her through the trousers at the juncture of her thighs, making the presence of clothing seem as erotic as being without. Jack made short work of her shirt fastenings and she changed her mind. His hands worked magic on her bare skin.

'I thought massages were for backs,' Dulci observed languidly, her body boneless beneath the soft caress of his thumbs high on her rib cage, tantalisingly close to her breasts.

'Only for those of a limited imagination, my dear.' Jack lowered his head and kissed her belly. A hot shiver shot through her and Jack gave her an iniquitous smile. 'That would be like saying kisses were only for the mouth, don't you think, Dulci?'

'You're a wicked tormentor, Jack.'

Jack merely chuckled and did away with her trousers, his hands sliding up the bare skin of her legs. 'I love your legs, Dulci,' he murmured, stopping to kiss the inside of her knees and stopping again to kiss the inside of her thighs. 'They're so lithe and so very long, supple enough to wrap around me, you can hold me tight when I am deep inside you.'

His hot eyes shot up to her face, full of want and anticipation, reminders that the pleasure the two of them invoked now was a prelude to the mysterious pleasure yet to come.

Then it was his turn. He moved apart from her and undressed swiftly, letting her look upon him. 'Would you like to touch me, Dulci?'

She nodded, letting him take her hand, guiding it between his legs, to where he wanted her hand the most: on him, at the core of his manhood. He held her there, showing her how to stroke him fully, how to tease the tender tip of him. Dulci was in awe. These were glorious secrets.

He stopped her hand. 'You'd be the death of me if I let you, Dulci. But there's more to come. Let me show you.' He gently pushed her back against the sofa cushions.

He drew a deep breath and lay over her, covering her with his length. She could feel his strength in his reserve; the effort he took not to burden her with his full weight, the power of his erection where it lay between them prodding at her entrance. Jack was kissing her again, taking away any ability to think, reminding her now was not the time for reflection but for action.

She shifted her hips in intuitive welcome and Jack took her in a quick, thorough thrust, tearing away the thin proof of her virginity. She gasped. Jack stilled inside her. She stretched around him and then they plunged together, meeting each other in the ancient mating waltz, finding the exquisite rhythm that pushed them towards brilliant fulfilment. Her legs locked about Jack, holding him deep, her body feeling each intimate tremor as he neared his completion, shattering inside her while she shrieked her own satisfaction, oblivious to the fact that though locked doors can keep people out, they can't always keep sounds in.

It was a while before she wanted to talk again. In the aftermath of their love-making, all she wanted to do was lay on the sofa with Jack, somnolent and satisfied. Somewhere in the depths of the house a clock struck the late hour. The evening had fled. It was now technically morning. It seemed surreal that balls were still going on all over town. That world seemed irrelevant and far away compared to the world she and Jack had created here.

But this could not last and she knew it. Still she could not willingly rouse herself. Not even reality could compete with being tucked against Jack's naked warmth, his sex stirring already against her buttocks, his voice teasing in her ear. 'What shall we do for an encore, my dear?'

'I have an idea,' Dulci whispered, moving to sit astride his thighs, fully ready to give herself over to a night of decadence.

In the early hours of the morning, another idea occurred to her, surfacing from the warm depths of replete desire. Maybe this was why she hadn't found the right man. Who could possibly give her the pleasure she'd found with Jack? Sexual pleasure, certainly, but there was another level of pleasure, too; their sharp repartee in the ballrooms, the other exchanges, too, like when they'd been fencing, when their mutual guard was down. All of that would disappear when she married. No man let his wife keep any male friends she might have acquired previous to him.

Probably for this very reason, Dulci thought, snuggling a bit closer to a dozing Jack; fear that his new bride had a lover prior to him, which in turn created an awkward, competitive triangle. No man wanted to worry about living up to past comparisons, especially if that comparison involved Jack.

Unless that husband was Jack, came the unbidden, forbidden thought. The thought was shocking, a violation of what she'd promised herself with regard to Jack: expect nothing beyond the moment, *want* nothing beyond the moment. He would not stay and this had been about curiosity only.

She must have tensed. Jack murmured in his sleep, his hand warm where it lay splayed across the flat of her stomach.

Jack was self-proclaimed non-husband material and Dulci couldn't disagree. Jack as a husband only *seemed* like a good idea in the aftermath of their passion. It was probably natural to entertain such thoughts. But it wouldn't always be like this. She knew empirically that outside the passion, outside the body he shared to its fullest in bed, there were times when he'd be gone and things he could not share when he returned. She would only ever have part of him. The trail of women he left behind him was testimony enough in that regard.

Needing to distract her mind from such errant and dangerous thoughts as marrying Jack, Dulci rose from their makeshift bed on the floor, the sofa having been outgrown by their antics hours ago. She draped a burgundy throw about her shoulders and went to the work table. Jack groaned his disappointment behind her.

'I'm looking for something I want to show you.' The throw slipped down one bare shoulder as she shuffled through the objects on the table.

'I like the view from here,' Jack murmured appreciatively.

'You're insatiable,' Dulci scolded, but she didn't mind. His comment warmed her on the inside. There was a certain pleasure in knowing she was an equal match for her lover's enthusiasm.

Lover.

It was the most apt term for describing Jack. He was her lover. Nothing more and certainly nothing less, if she were entirely sanguine about it. After last night, they now existed in an erotic limbo between merely slaking physical needs with the other and something more philosophical, more committed. What would it be like to meet in society after this?

Above the work table, the long windows captured the moonlight. Evening had become night.

'Aha! I found it,' Dulci crowed triumphantly, making her way back to him.

Jack levered himself up on one arm. 'What treasure is this, Dulci?'

She sat down beside him on the floor and slid in close. 'It's a journal. Vasquez brought it in the last shipment.' Dulci flipped open the worn leather book. 'The drawings are very detailed. I thought you might recognise some of the things from your trip.'

'Is this a gift?' Jack teased.

'Sort of. I haven't read it yet,' Dulci began. 'It has occurred to me that it might be a good source of information regarding my artefacts. Perhaps I could pass it on to you when I'm finished?'

Jack reached for a strand of her hair and twisted it about his finger. 'It's a lovely gift, Dulci. You may use it as long as you wish. It's like giving someone a book from the lending library as a present, though, if you think about it,' he joked but she could tell he wasn't offended.

Dulci snuggled down against him. She could feel his eyes moving over her shoulder, taking in the pages illuminated by the fading light. Dulci reached for a nearby oil lamp and dragged it to a low table closer to them. She turned up the wick. 'Now you can see better. There's all manner of information in here, birds, plants, even maps, Jack.'

Dulci flipped through the book. Jack offered a comment here and there, but it was becoming exceedingly obvious he was more interested in the warm woman curved against him and the flame-lighted intimacy of their situation. Then something on the pages caught his eye and the hand absently stroking her hip stalled in its lazy motions. 'Wait, Dulci. Go back a page.'

'What is it? Did you recognise a place?'

'The page is creased awkwardly by the book spine.'

Dulci ran her hands along the place where the spine met the page. 'You're right, Jack. The page unfolds into a larger page.' Dulci unfolded the sheet and another carefully folded sheet fluttered out.

Excitement seized Dulci. She scrambled to her feet, eager to lay the new paper out on the table, Jack following close behind.

Dulci lit another lamp at her work table, illuminating the place names and the land contours.

Dulci traced the lines of rivers, pronouncing their names, 'Orinoco, Cassiquiare, the Amakura, the Essequibo.' She paused. 'This is a map of British Guiana. These are the rivers that form the boundaries with Venezuela. The Arawak live along here.'

Excitement thrummed through her. This would help her research immensely. She turned to look at Jack. 'Do you know what this means?'

Chapter Seven

Oh God, did he know. It meant the rumours were right. There was a forged map. More than that, it meant Dulci was in great peril. He could no longer pretend her cargo wasn't the cargo Calisto Ortiz was looking for. The map made it a certainty. Still, there was one more test the map had to pass.

Jack held his breath, his suspicions high despite the plea that ran through his mind like a litany: *Please don't let it be the map.* But he was almost certain it was.

In the dim light, the map looked remarkably accurate based on his knowledge of the region. Jack leaned forwards and scrutinised a faintly darker line along the Essequibo that shouldn't be there. Based on currently recognised boundaries between the two territories, this map was a fraud.

Jack tamped down his fears. His imagination was running away with him. There was nothing to fear yet. No one knew Dulci had it yet. No one even remotely suspected she had it and no one would as long as she didn't tell Señor Ortiz she had recently purchased artefacts or that she did business with a Señor Vasquez.

'What is it, Jack?' Dulci queried at his silence.

'Nothing,' he lied swiftly, placing a light trail of kisses on her shoulder where the blanket had slipped again. With one hand he pushed back the heavy weight of her hair, exposing her neck, his kisses moving upwards. 'I was just thinking how much I'd rather explore you than a sheet of paper.'

Dulci turned in his arms, ready and eager in the wake of her excitement over the map. Jack hated himself. Never, ever mix business with pleasure. That was one rule he never broke. He ought to make his excuses to Dulci and track down Gladstone right away. But for the sake of business, he couldn't risk Dulci, in her excitement, telling Calisto Ortiz about her discovery during casual conversation on the dance floor. There were things he couldn't risk for the sake of pleasure either, such as Dulci's wrath at another interruption. In the wake of the débâcle in the garden, she would not understand another abrupt departure. Especially now their relationship had somewhat changed.

Dulci reached between his legs, duplicating her earlier actions with a smile on her face. Jack groaned in expectation. He had to have time to think: what to do about the map, about Dulci. For now, the rules could go to hell.

Calisto Ortiz lifted his tumbler in a silent toast. He reclined against the leather comfort of his chair in his expensive suite of rooms. He took a sip of the excellent liquor, savouring its mellow tastes. Tonight, he was well satisfied and in good humour with the world. Vasquez had been found, questioned and dispatched. And he, Calisto Ortiz, had the answers he wanted. In a vain attempt to save himself, Vasquez had told his captors who had bought the journal. Ironically, such an admission sealed the importer's fate.

Dulcinea Wycroft.

Calisto swirled the liquid in his glass. It was about as pleasant as surprises got. He'd not perceived the beautiful woman's interests went that deeply. Retrieving the map would be delightful and, with luck, there'd be no more need for another murder. Lady Dulcinea would have no idea what she possessed. Women had no head for politics and maps. All he had to do was gain access to her home and ask her to show off her collection. That should not be difficult. Surely she hosted an 'at home' like other women he'd met here in London and surely, like other women in London, she found him charming enough for an invitation to call. It would be the work of a few seconds to pocket the journal during a well-placed kiss. A little flirtation and his plan would be back on track. Ah, yes, after a rough time, there would be some luck at last.

Two nights later at the Mayfield ball, the easy attitude Ortiz possessed was being severely tried. Dulcinea Wycroft had disappeared from society, making it rather difficult to pursue his plan to seduce the journal from her. He was not a patient man. He nodded politely to a passing group that stopped to exchange pleasantries, hiding his growing impatience. Where in the world was Dulcinea Wycroft?

Where the hell was Wainsbridge? Gladstone checked his watch for the third time on the perimeter of the Mayfield ballroom. He dared not check it again. It was unseemly for a gentleman to glance at his watch too often at a ball. Such a preoccupation with time suggested he was only waiting until he could politely move on to the evening's other entertainments, hardly an endearing endorsement of one's hostess and Gladstone was careful not to upset hostesses.

Gladstone was getting impatient. He had news to share. He'd rather have shared his news in a more business-like setting, but time was short. He had not seen Wainsbridge in two days. It didn't help matters that Dulci had been absent from the usual circuit of entertainments too. Their mutual absence raised all nature of jealous conjecture in Gladstone's mind.

Four years ago, he'd made the delectable Lady Dulcinea an honourable proposal of marriage, knowing himself to be an entirely acceptable match for her. She'd refused him, left London quite suddenly in the dead of winter and turned up at her brother's home where Wainsbridge had also coincidently taken up residence a few weeks prior.

It all looked very suspicious to Gladstone, who could not fathom why Dulci Wycroft would turn him down unless there was another. That the other was a man whose only title had been *earned* through actual *work* and not inherited from the efforts of earlier generations, rubbed salt in Gladstone's wounded ego.

Gladstone glanced about the ballroom, which seemed reserved in its atmosphere tonight without the presence of London's most sharp-witted bachelor and the Season's reigning beauty. Others appeared to sense the difference too. A few columns over, Señor Ortiz, whom Wainsbridge was supposed to be watching, appeared bored with the conversation about him. Every so often, Gladstone noticed the man's eyes drift over to the doorway then, disappointed, drift back to the group surrounding him, many of them women interested in testing the hypothesis of Spanish virility against the real thing.

Volume at the entrance rose suddenly. Gladstone resisted the temptation to look that direction. He kept his eyes fixed on Señor Ortiz, gauging the man's reaction to determine who had walked in. Ortiz's eyes lit up. Gladstone turned slowly to confirm his guesses. Already surrounded by admirers, Wainsbridge and Dulci Wycroft sailed into the ballroom, together, utterly beautiful. There was no handsomer couple in

London. It was as if a great spark had been lit. The dancers whirled faster, the music's tempo was livelier, the laughter of the guests less brittle. Was it his imagination or did Lady Mayfield, the hostess, breathe a little easier?

Gladstone moved towards them, anxious to speak with Wainsbridge.

Dulci saw him coming with a sinking heart, her euphoria over the past two days disappearing with each approaching footstep. It didn't help that she knew it would be like this. Knowing didn't make it any better. She had hoped…oh, how she'd hoped. Gladstone shouldered his way through the crowd with none of Jack's consummate ease, stepping on feet, proverbial and otherwise. A subtle unease crept slowly through her at the determined set of Gladstone's very square jaw and intent grey eyes. Reflexively, she tightened her light grip on Jack's arm.

'I don't think he's here for you, m'dear,' Jack murmured, detecting Gladstone's less-than-discreet progress towards them. 'Tonight, it's me he wants.'

His words were an effective killjoy. Dulci knew what he meant. Back to work. Their sweet interlude was over, and if not over, then definitely on hiatus. When Jack 'worked' he disappeared for stretches at a time. He might surface after a few days or it may be months before he rejoined society. No one knew where he went or what he did until afterwards and then only in vague snatches. Whatever he did, he had done it well enough to earn the accolade of viscount. His services were viewed as valuable to his monarch and to his country.

'Lady Dulcinea, you're looking ravishing tonight.' Gladstone bowed over her hand, his eyes lingering on her face in his usual annoying manner, searching for any sign of affection.

'Gladstone,' Dulci answered with stiff politeness. She dare not give him even the slightest of polite encouragements. After four years, he'd proven to be the most tenacious of all her would-be suitors. Her quiet rejection had not resulted in the desired effect. If anything, the rejection had made him more persistent.

'Wainsbridge, I'm hoping I might have a private word with you.'

'And I am hoping Lady Dulcinea will favour me with a dance.' Jack's eyes twinkled with mischief. 'What do you think our odds are of both of us getting our wishes?' Those around them laughed. Gladstone narrowed his lips into a grim line, unamused at Jack's light humour.

Dulci did her duty, masking her immense disappointment. 'Wainsbridge, go on with Gladstone. I am sure Lord Gilmore can admirably dance attendance on me until your return.' She smiled at young Gilmore, who seemed overwhelmed by the honour she was bestowing on him.

'Very well, it's all been arranged, Gladstone.' Jack shot Gladstone an ungrateful glare. 'I believe there's a library just down the hall that will suit our purposes. If you'll follow me?'

Dulci fought the urge to follow Jack with her eyes, but that was the behaviour of a besotted fool in love. She dare not give the gossips any grist for their mills. People accepted that she and Wainsbridge might occasionally be seen together because of his friendship with her brother and long association with the Wycroft family. Their clever wagers and sharp humour ensured people believed them tenuous friends at best, two persons who would not have sought the other out if it hadn't been for Brandon Wycroft, which had been somewhat true until that evening in the orangery. Dulci had no desire to change society's perception. She did not want anyone speculating about the true nature of her association with Jack, especially not now that she had something truly scandalous to hide. How could anyone understand it, this need that drove her towards him? She hardly understood it herself.

So she danced with Gilmore, and then with Carstairs's son, being sure to avoid his feet whenever possible; when she couldn't, she assured him he hadn't hurt her toes in the least. She managed to laugh, to lightly flirt, to drink the punch they all brought her, and to avoid looking at the ballroom door in the hopes that Jack would come sailing back through when she knew very well that he wouldn't.

Shortly before midnight, Dulci contrived a moment alone and escaped the hot ballroom for the cooler locale of the verandah. The verandah was nearly deserted; most couples were inside dancing the supper waltz and making preparations to go into the late-night meal. Tonight was far different than the setting she'd found herself in the previous night. And far less enjoyable. The last few days had been a whirlwind of experiences and it felt good to get away by herself for a moment. She was still reeling from what had transpired with Jack. It was amazing society couldn't tell the difference. She *felt* different. But apparently all the changes were internal. There was no external proof of her escapade.

Dulci found an empty chair and sank into it, grateful for the respite. Pretending lightness and happiness when one felt neither was deuced hard work.

She closed her eyes and slowly plied her fan. She drew a deep, cleansing breath and expelled it. That was better. She had known it would come to this with Jack, this disappearing without any warning. She'd known it could come at any time, two weeks from now, or the moment they stepped back into Society, as indeed it had. Knowing didn't make it easier to accept. Neither did knowing he'd made her no promises. She couldn't be angry with him for breaking what had never been.

'I do not think he's coming back tonight.'

Dulci's eyes flew open at the sound of the accented voice, soft and close. 'Señor Ortiz!'

'I have startled you, Señorita Wycroft. That was not my intention.' He pulled up a small chair and settled himself on it. 'A lovely woman should never be disappointed by a man. I think you would find many of us would fix our attentions on you more firmly than the viscount's divided ones.' He reached for her gloved hand lying in her lap, and traced a pattern on the back of her hand.

Calisto Ortiz was handsome and intuitive, a deadly combination when it came to a woman's virtue. Dulci recognised it immediately. Jack carried the very same qualities. But with Ortiz, she found herself to be immune.

'One can only be disappointed if there are expectations to be met in the first place.' Dulci smiled coldly, retracting her hand, making sure her message was clear. 'I have no expectations of Wainsbridge. Ergo, I cannot be disappointed by his abbreviated attentions.'

Ortiz was not deterred. He merely gave a Latin shrug and sighed. He sat back in his chair and ran a hand through his dark hair. 'Ah, so that's how it is with Wainsbridge. He is a man who keeps his work as his mistress. What called him away tonight? Was it business with a ship? A new cargo? Investments? Perhaps a new property to consider?' There was an insult in the enquiry— the idea that a real gentleman had no work.

Dulci shrewdly assessed the Spaniard, careful not to give away too much with any admissions. He was flirting for a purpose and he had boldly guessed far too much about her and Jack. What did he want? Revenge for the insult Jack paid him a few nights ago? She would not know if she turned him away. Dulci rose and smoothed her skirts. 'The Mayfield gardens are decent, Señor, and their roses are considered quite fine. I could show you, if you wished. Do you grow many roses in Venezuela?'

'I would love a look. I am an avid botanist myself when I am home. I have an extensive greenhouse.' Ortiz offered his arm. 'Is Wainsbridge a botanist?'

Dulci laughed, a real laugh this time, nothing like the laughter she'd conjured up to please her dance partners. The very idea of Jack puttering with rose clippings in a hothouse bordered on hilarious. Jack could not be caged by walls. His greenhouse was the whole wide world.

Chapter Eight

The library was dark and empty, a stark contrast to the vibrant ballroom. A small lamp burned on the fireplace mantel, offering the only light. Jack shut the door and clicked the lock into place. 'What do you need that could not possibly wait?' He began.

'I would watch your tone with me if I were you,' Gladstone grumbled, making his way to the sofa. 'You're supposed to be tailing Ortiz. You've abandoned your post. I shudder to think what you've been doing instead.' But it was evident Gladstone had a pretty good idea. He spat in disapproval, anger and envy etched into every word.

Jack did not care for the man's insinuation, no matter how true in fact, but not true in emotion. What he'd done was certainly not as despicable as Gladstone implied. There was no shame in what had transpired between he and Dulci. There was no dishonour in honest sex between a man and a woman.

Even in the dark, Jack could find Gladstone's lapels. He gripped them, hauling Gladstone to the wall. 'You will not impugn Lady Dulcinea's honour with such disgraceful aspersions.'

'You forget yourself, sir,' Gladstone growled, struggling in Jack's grasp.

'I do not forget a woman's honour, which is more than I can say for you.' Jack let go and stepped back. He'd like to pummel the man with his fists for the crass thoughts. 'Do you have real news, or is this one of your jealous ploys?'

If there was nothing to report, Jack *would* pummel the man, all thoughts of propriety and decorum be damned. He'd been disappointed to be pulled away from Dulci so soon. He'd known it would happen but he'd hoped for a dance or two before Gladstone caught up with him.

They'd had two private days together, two days of protection for Dulci while he thought it all out, although she didn't know that. He couldn't risk not connecting with the outside world any longer. He needed to learn what might have occurred during his absence.

Lacking information left him less capable of protecting her.

Gladstone shrugged, straightening his jacket. 'As it happens, I do have news. While you were "otherwise engaged"—' he gave Jack a hard look '—a Spaniard was fished out of the Thames with his throat cut, a nasty piece of work.' Gladstone ran a hand over his mouth as if remembering the ghastly corpse.

'Normally, I'd not pay attention to such a crime, unfortunate as it is. Bodies wash up all the time from suicides to murders. But this man had been beaten long before his throat was cut and whoever did the job left a piece of identification on him. Either the murderer was not cautious or simply didn't care. I think it was the latter, suggesting that the man didn't live in England but was only visiting. The man was too far from home for anyone to come looking for him—'

'Well?' Jack interrupted impatiently. Gladstone was a tyrant when it came to detail and it showed in the man's storytelling. 'Who is the man?'

'Señor Domenico Vasquez, who, we've discovered, rents warehouse space in Southwark.' Gladstone paused to let the information settle.

'The warehouse I trailed Ortiz to.' Jack's

insides roiled. He fought to keep his outer façade collected. 'I doubt there are two Spanish importers renting space in Southwark.' Jack spoke solemnly. 'It appears we have a match. Calisto Ortiz is a murderer.'

'We have a *likely* suspect. I doubt he did the actual killing in any case,' corrected Gladstone.

Anger over Gladstone's excessive caution fired Jack's temper. 'Make no mistake, Gladstone, this was not an accidental death. If he was beaten first, it was not a quick crime, done in the heat of the moment by a surprised cut-purse who didn't mean for things to go so far.'

Gladstone looked slightly offended. 'No doubt you're in a position to know such things with all your vast experience.' His tone was not friendly and Jack knew he'd inserted a veiled jab at what he viewed as Jack's inferior birth.

'Vasquez's death confirms much, Gladstone,' Jack said sharply, choosing to let the insult slide. 'Vasquez was in possession of something dangerous, something Ortiz did not want disclosed. We cannot ignore this.'

Gladstone scoffed. 'I must caution you, Wainsbridge, not to be so hot headed. We don't have any proof that Ortiz committed the murder, only that Vasquez is dead and Ortiz visited the warehouse.'

'Connect the damned dots,' Jack growled in disbelief. 'The Venezuelan delegation comes to town followed by rumours of a potential land swindle and the importer is killed on whose ship the cargo in question was suspected of vanishing. The connection seems obvious to me.'

'Señor Ortiz is a Spanish nobleman, he deserves the courtesies one gentleman extends to another,' Gladstone said severely. 'We must tread carefully here in order to avoid creating an international incident. Of course, I don't expect you to know anything about such a code.'

'It sounds quite similar to honour among thieves,' Jack ground out. 'At the very least, we should have Ortiz questioned.'

'Definitely not, it would expose our hand. Then the delegation would know we suspected unfair dealings on the land negotiations.'

'They'll know eventually when we confront them.' Jack thought of the map, but now was not the time to tell Gladstone. He would wait until everyone met together tomorrow to share the map. 'Besides, there's a chance that knowledge could be leverage with Ortiz. The others in the delegation may not know he's attempting to pass off a forgery as the real thing.'

Gladstone's voice was solid. 'Wainsbridge, we do not take chances. That is an uncalculated risk at the moment.'

Very well. If Gladstone would not take action, Jack would take his own measures. 'Then our conversation is over, Gladstone. Thank you for your news.' Jack gave him a short nod and left the room, his strides long as he hurried his return to the ballroom and Dulci. Gladstone was an over-cautious fool. All evidence pointed to Ortiz's guilt and Gladstone was more interested in extending gentleman's courtesies. Such courtesies made no sense when they put a murderer on the dance floor, able to strike again if he should uncover another link in the chain leading to the map.

Jack re-entered the ballroom, scanning the floor for Dulci. He spotted Lord Gilmore leaning against a post alone and made his way to the young man's side. 'Have you lost her already, Gilmore?' he said with an insouciance he didn't feel.

Gilmore looked shocked at the insinuation. 'She needed a moment to herself, Wainsbridge. She went out on to the verandah.'

Jack moved off, eager to reach the verandah. He was glad to see it fairly empty; spotting Dulci would be easy. Then he looked beyond the railing out into the garden. Good lord, Dulci was out there. *With him.*

Suppositions raced through his mind. How much had Vasquez disclosed before he died? Had Vasquez given Ortiz a name? Did Ortiz know already that Dulci possessed the map? Jack prayed he did not. Damnation, ballrooms had become dangerous places.

They'd also become confining. Jack chafed at the limitations his circumstance placed on him. The primal man in him wanted to rush out into the garden and drag Dulci away from Ortiz. But he could not do so without staking a public claim to Dulci, a claim he had no right to entertain. Dulci would not forgive him. And he had no wish to end up like Gladstone: a jilted, grieving suitor. It came as something of a shock to realise just how much the two days he'd spent with Dulci had affected him.

It had started purely as a protective gambit to keep her out of the public eye. The diplomatic front would not go unmanned in his short absence. Gladstone was out there, after all. But reality had become distorted in Dulci's arms, time a fluid, infinite entity, the concerns he lived with daily suspended and surreal in the wake of passion invoked by their love-making. There'd even been times he'd forgot about work entirely, an absolute first for him.

A few couples strolled passed him on the verandah. Jack nodded, but did not encourage prolonged conversation. If the best he could do was play guardian from the steps, then he'd do it with diligence.

A diligence that stung, Jack reflected. It was deuced hard to play the neutral watchdog. They were too far away for him to hear what they said, but he could see them. He could see Ortiz bend close to whisper something to Dulci. He could see Dulci give her head a coy toss.

She stole his breath with the simplest of moves. How had she got under his skin so completely, so entirely? Really, the effect she was having on him was quite unprecedented in his experience with women.

Now that he'd come up for air, had had time to think more objectively about what had transpired between them, he had to wonder—what in sweet heaven was he doing with her? Brandon would skewer him if he knew what his best friend was doing with his sister. But whatever Brandon would do to him for dallying with his sister, it would be far less than what Brandon would do if Jack ever tried to marry her and pull her into the murky instability of his life. Brandon wanted more for his sister than being dragged from peril to peril in the New World, title or not.

Of course Jack *couldn't* marry her. He wasn't a marrying man. His work for the king made any kind of real marriage impossible. Jack couldn't imagine not being able to tell his wife where he went or what he did. The only option was to take a wife who wouldn't care. Since he couldn't fathom *that* cold arrangement, he was left with the last option: not marrying at all.

And if he couldn't marry her, he shouldn't have done it at all. Certainly, Dulci had been adamant in her desires, but he was the one with all the experience. He knew the rules when it came to ladies and maidenheads. Surely he could have stopped their foray into passion's realm if he'd wanted to. There was the rub.

As good as it had been, he was plagued by a twinge of guilt. The bottom line was not pretty: he had seduced his friend's sister. No, not *seduced*. Dulci would never stand for that. Rather, he'd taken his friend's sister's virginity. Never mind that she'd wanted to give it. He was supposed to know better for both of them…and yet he hadn't.

This was just a unique case of unmitigated lust. Dulci had not professed undying love for him and that was for the best. For the time being they were well suited. When the time came to move on, go their separate ways—and it would, he was certain—they'd have no regrets.

That's what he told himself anyway. In reality it was a bit more difficult to imagine. But it was the best he could do in terms of justifying his actions to his conscience—he *did* have one, even if it was slightly rusty from occasional use. This was lust on both their parts. They'd both satisfied whatever curiosity had spurred them. He wasn't dealing with a lovesick girl. He was dealing with Dulci, who was level headed and knew what she wanted.

It *was* better this way. But for now, it was deuced difficult to stand on the verandah and do nothing but watch the object of his erections…er, affections, out in the garden with a very danger-ous man. His only consolation was that if he could see them, they could see him. Jack made himself as obvious as possible, standing at the railing, broad shouldered, his arms folded across his chest, his legs shoulder width apart in a commanding stance. Now, if they would only look.

Dulci looked past Calisto Ortiz's shoulder and smiled, hard pressed to contain a rather sudden burst of elation, unexplainable as it was, at the sight of Jack on the verandah. 'You're wrong, you know. He did come back. It is too bad we did not wager.'

Ortiz chuckled. 'Perhaps you would not have won, *mi querida*. Would you have wagered on his return?' The back of his hand lightly skimmed her arm in a gentle motion Dulci found overly familiar. 'Does this mean I must return you to your escort?'

'Yes, I must not keep Wainsbridge waiting.' Dulci pulled her arm away, grateful Ortiz had too much pride to wait to be asked to return her. A gentleman knew what a lady wanted before she requested it.

Nearing the verandah steps, Dulci saw Jack move towards them. For a man who shunned commitments of the interpersonal type, he was behaving quite proprietarily. Ortiz saw it too.

'May I ask a boon before our erstwhile viscount

reaches us? May I call on you? I have heard of your Venezuelan collection and I would be honoured to offer my humble assistance. It is rare to meet a woman of your intellectual refinements. I find it refreshing.' His voice was low, concupiscent in its tone.

Dulci glanced up at the Spaniard, genuinely moved by his comment, if not by the innuendo. How long had she waited for a man other than Jack to appreciate something more than her pretty face? Perhaps she'd been too quick to dismiss Ortiz, overly influenced by Jack's obvious dislike of the man. 'You are too—'

'Late.' Jack's interruption cut across the quiet moment, brutal and blatant, his face wearing a hard look Dulci had never seen. He wasn't looking at her but at Calisto Ortiz, with a deadly intent that went far beyond ballroom jealousy.

'Pardon me, *señor*?' Ortiz challenged.

'I said you were too late,' Jack repeated, his hands flexing at his side.

Dulci felt decidedly excluded. There was something feral and male at work in the garden, something dangerous. She'd not seen Jack like this, the urbane king's man transformed into a warrior, possessed of a primal fierceness.

Out of an instinctive need for self-preservation, she stepped back from them both. Jack would have some explaining to do when she got hold of him.

Ortiz's eyes narrowed. He was assessing, Dulci thought, wondering if he could best Jack in some way and whether or not such a display was worth it. Would it enhance his standing with her even while it created a scandal?

Gentlemen engaged in fisticuffs would not go unnoticed. Jack's green gaze never wavered. At last, Ortiz relented, losing whatever internal debate he'd carried on with himself.

Dulci let out the breath she'd been holding. The imminent danger had passed.

'If you'll excuse us, *señor*?' Jack reached for her, his hand at her back, forceful and strong as if he expected resistance. 'Lady Dulcinea and I have another engagement to attend.'

Curiosity was a powerful motivator, Dulci noted on the way to the carriage. On any other occasion, she'd have cut up at Jack immediately for manipulating her in such a manner. He'd spoken for her, decided who she would receive and then all but marched her out of the Mayfield ballroom without a word.

A potent silence reigned between them at the kerb while they waited for the carriage. Beside her, Jack stood tall and terse, his eyes habitually scanning their environs. At his side, his hand tapped anxiously against his trouser leg in an impatient gesture. His other hand didn't leave the small of her back.

The carriage arrived and Jack hurriedly ushered her into it, throwing a disgruntled look at the coachman as if to say, 'It's about time.' He didn't relax until they were underway.

'Don't get too comfortable,' Dulci remarked the moment she saw his shoulders ease and settle into the squabs of her excellent seats. 'I'll take your explanation now for your rather boorish behaviour with Señor Ortiz.'

Jack's features still wore the hardness she'd glimpsed in the garden. 'Your importer, Señor Vasquez, is dead. The Thames washed him up yesterday.'

Dulci furrowed her brow, perplexed. Certainly this was a tragedy, but Jack hadn't known the man. It didn't explain Jack's reaction in the garden. 'Dead? How? Was there an accident with his ship?'

Jack's voice was tight. 'No. His throat was cut. It was most definitely an act of murder.'

Dulci fell back against the squabs, her face paling at the thought. 'Why?'

Jack leaned forwards and took her hands in his. 'Someone was after his cargo.'

'Yes, of course,' Dulci said absently. Her mind raced through the conversation she'd had with the man just a few days ago. He'd been nervous, anxious to conclude their business. A horrible thought occurred to her. 'Jack, I have the cargo,' Dulci said slowly, understanding dawning at least in part. 'Whoever killed Vasquez will come looking for me.'

Jack squeezed her fingers and she took comfort from his strength. 'Only if Vasquez gave them a name, my dear.'

It was weak assurance at best. She noticed he said nothing along the lines of 'no need to panic unnecessarily'. Because, of course, there was every need. Dulci knew without being told that there was no way to know what Vasquez had said or didn't say in his last moments. 'In such circumstances, I think we must assume the worst,' Dulci said quietly. 'Tell me everything. Who is behind this and what are they looking for?' She'd meant every word, but she hadn't understood what the worst was.

Jack knew he had no choice but to tell her the truth. 'There's a map with forged boundaries that the Venezuelan government may use to force our hand in the upcoming negotiations over the borders between British Guiana and Venezuela. The map has slipped the possession of its intended owner. It ended up in Vasquez's cargo.'

'Our map,' Dulci stated matter of factly, the pieces of the puzzle becoming clearer. She could see the moment of discovery in her mind, the two of them wrapped in blankets, the firelight, the journal between them, Jack flipping back a page and running his long fingers along the awkward seam of the page. It was hard to conceive of such a simple, intimate moment, playing a critical role in political negotiations.

'Yes, our map.' Jack's face was impassive in the dim interior of carriage. His visage gave away no clue that he shared her images of the map. He was, most unfortunately, all business. Something inside her died and suspicion began to bloom in its place.

Señor Vasquez had been killed for the map. Someone must want the boundaries redrawn badly, badly enough to commit murder. 'What do the lands have that's worth killing for?' Dulci asked.

'I believe there's gold in the contested river valley.' Jack's answer was succinct, direct.

'Do you have any suspects?' Dulci tried to match Jack's business-like tone while her insides churned in anticipation of more bad news.

'Calisto Ortiz.'

Dulci froze, overcome with a morbid chill. The man who'd caressed her arm in the garden, who'd taken dinner with her at the RGS, who'd flirted with her and with whom she'd flirted back, was a murderer. 'How certain are you?'

'More certain than Gladstone. He wants to extend a gentlemanly prerogative to Ortiz and not race to conclusions. I do not suffer from any such compunction.'

'How could I not know?' Dulci was stunned.

Jack shook his head. 'Why should you have suspected anything? You had no reason to think otherwise.'

'He wanted to come see my collection.'

Deceit. A superficial ardour. A kaleidoscope of emotions and motives swirled into hard forms. Nothing was as it seemed. Ortiz had not been interested in pursuing her, but her map. They could not doubt that Vasquez had given him her name. It was the reason Ortiz had sought her out tonight in the garden. If she'd harboured feelings for Ortiz, she might have been hurt by his deception. As it was, she was appalled.

There was a special type of fear evoked from the knowledge of having fraternised with an enemy in such close quarters. That fear was heightened by knowing that the enemy was at large and all secrets were stripped away. There was no longer the protection of shallow façades. She knew now what Ortiz was behind his good looks and easy manners. He knew the same of her. She imagined in his mind she was no longer a pretty belle with whom he could pass his time while away from home. She'd been transmuted from an entertaining interlude abroad to quarry, someone to be hunted and run to ground. If it hadn't been for Jack's interruption this evening, Ortiz would have been easily successful.

Ah, yes, if it hadn't been for Jack… The silence between them in the carriage burgeoned. Dulci took no steps to break it. Earlier suspicions bloomed full in the wake of Jack's disclosures. Jack had been stalking Ortiz from the start.

Façades. Pretences to passion. The kaleidoscope of emotions and motives swirled again, configuring new shapes. Ortiz wasn't the only guilty party here. The difference was that Jack's betrayal hurt. She'd been foolish, believing in Jack's passion, in Jack's promises. Oh, not real promises made with words, but in the promises his body made hers. She'd given herself over to the ridiculous belief that this time it would be different, that she'd be different than the other women he'd been with. And maybe she was. This time she wasn't outside his work like the women he entertained periodically when he was in town. She *was* his work.

The fencing, the desire to see her collection, all an attempt to gauge if she held Vasquez's mysterious, coveted cargo. Then there was the map. He'd known the minute he saw it he'd found the prize, in the middle of an intimate, cherished moment. The following two days—what was she to make of them now? All lies? Perhaps they were nothing more than a delay, waiting to see how events would develop. What promises could she believe? Some of them? None of them?

In all fairness, she'd pushed for the first time, that glorious act of love-making in her work room; she'd wanted that even with the understanding there would be nothing more: no promises, no exhortations of sudden and newly discovered love upon consummation. She'd approached that first time with a judicious eye to reality. But then, there had been more. He'd taken her in his arms and loved her into oblivion, far beyond their initial intentions.

In the two days that followed, she'd started allowing herself to believe things had shifted, that this time, beyond all explanation, it was different for him. She had not realised until now how dangerous that little fantasy had been, how much she'd inadvertently built it up in her mind so that now what he saw as just sex was something she viewed as the worst of betrayals.

'Dulci, say something.' Jack broke into the prolonged silence. 'I understand what a shock this must be.'

The kaleidoscope in her mind stilled, cold objectivity coming to her. She'd heard the rumours about him before, how he seemed utterly devoted and yet possessed the cold-blooded ability to walk away when it suited him without a backwards glance. She'd even been counting on such truths to some extent. She'd wanted no protestations of honour and duty afterwards, no forced proposals more for her brother's sake than hers. Now that she had precisely what she'd counted on, any disappointment she felt was her own fault.

Dulci studied Jack with hard eyes and said simply, 'You're wrong. It's really not shocking at all. It is what I should have expected.'

The carriage pulled into the round drive outside Stockport House. Jack insisted on handing her down, making a great show of searching the area before he let her out of the carriage.

Dulci wished she could sniff at his protective behaviour, but she knew such a gesture was foolish. Whatever she blamed Jack for, she needed him for protection. The one night she wanted to send Jack packing back to his bachelor rooms was the one night she could not risk being alone.

The world she took for granted had become dangerous. How would Ortiz come? This was the most pressing question. His arrival was inevitable. Would he come as a polite gentleman and hope to discreetly lift the map from the collection room? Would he come violently as a thief in the night? Would he stop at that? The other question was how far would he go? Would he assume she was ignorant of what she possessed and leave her alone? Would he assume she understood the value of what she had and seek to subdue her the same way he'd subdued Vasquez?

Dulci walked stiffly to her front door, marshalling her thoughts and her courage. Her motto would serve her well. The antidote for trouble was to expect it and she was expecting quite a lot.

To her dismay, her hand shook slightly with her door key. Jack took the key from her hand and fitted it to the lock.

'I'll have a room readied for you at the top of the stairs,' Dulci said curtly.

If Jack was disappointed in his sleeping arrangements, he didn't argue. 'As you wish, Dulci.'

She wanted him to argue, to put up some kind of protest so she could take it as proof that not all of their passion was a lie, as proof that he understood she was angry with him for deceiving her. But if love-making was on Jack's mind at all, he kept it very well hidden and that infuriated her no end.

Chapter Nine

Calisto Ortiz bent graciously over Lady Mayfield's hand and departed the ball, looking to all he passed like a man headed to the clubs or gambling hells to spend the later hours of the night. He offered no sign of the turmoil seething beneath his well-cultivated surface.

Foiled by Wainsbridge again! It was personally intolerable.

He'd been on the brink, the *very edge* of success! The lovely Lady Dulcinea had been warming to his flirtation, excited by the prospect of sharing her collection with him. Once he'd extracted the invitation, it would have been a simple matter to retrieve the journal and, with it, the map without anyone being the wiser. But Wainsbridge had chosen the choicest of moments to reinstate his curious claim. It did make him wonder precisely what manner of relationship the viscount had with Lady Dulcinea. The man's behaviour spoke of a commitment far deeper than that of a dance partner. Unless there was another reason for Wainsbridge's possessiveness?

It would be in his interest to uncover who the viscount was and the exact nature of the man's attentions. Perhaps Wainsbridge's interests, like his own, were rooted in something more than the attractions of Lady Dulcinea's pretty face.

Calisto Ortiz stepped out into the night and hailed a hackney, giving directions to a tavern on the Southwark docks. If the viscount was indeed more than an ardent dance partner, he would not have the liberty of waiting to act in a more genteel fashion. Wainsbridge would know what he was after. It was imperative that he act tonight. He knew men on the docks who would gladly perpetrate a break-in. He could not commit such a crime himself, but he could send others to act on his behalf.

The crash of shattering glass woke Dulci shortly after four in the morning, according to the little clock beside her bed. Protection and defence drove her instincts. She pushed feet into slippers, arms into the dressing gown hastily discarded at the end of her bed, her hand snatching up the heavy silver candlestick from a long narrow table as she flew down the hall. There was no time to go for her revolver in the library in her desk drawer. Who would have thought she'd need a gun in her own house?

'Jack!' she called loudly, running past his room, but his door was wide open and he was gone.

Dulci flew down the staircase, her feet certain of their destination: the collection room. The fight was already engaged. Later, when she remembered that night, she'd be glad Jack had got there first. What would she have done against two masked intruders with nothing more than a candlestick?

Dulci gasped at the sight of her beloved room in a shambles. The long windows she adored for their work-light were nothing more than jagged shards of glass, the remnants of the panes laying in a shower of sharp, sparkling rubble on the floor. A few curio cases, which had had the misfortune of being in the battle zone, were turned on their sides, their panels broken. In the middle of it was Jack, shirtless and brandishing a knife she hadn't known he carried. He feinted and dodged, using a curio case as a shield against one of the attackers. Dulci cringed. If only she had her rapier or her gun! But by the time she retrieved either the fight would be over.

Under other circumstances, she might have been riveted by Jack's bare-chested skill, all lean grace in the moonlight streaming through her ruined windows. But the other attacker drew her attention, slinking around to the side of the long work table while Jack was engaged.

Dulci sprang into action, racing towards him. These men would not take a thing from her! Her slippers crunched glass beneath their soles. She brandished her candlestick, swinging it like a medieval mace, screaming a banshee yell. The intruder looked her way in time to see the candlestick seconds before it connected with the side of his face. He staggered backwards into the table and collapsed with a cry.

The cry brought the other attacker. Darting away from Jack, the masked man lunged for Dulci. In reflex, she put up the candlestick to ward off a blow. The blow glanced off the silver of a blade, but the impact stunned Dulci, and jarred down her arm. She fell, her feet losing their purchase in the glass.

She heard Jack bellow her name, she braced herself for the attacker's assault, but it never came. Faced with Jack, knife in hand, he opted to vault on to the table, making a wild scramble for the window before Jack could pull him back.

Dulci cautiously crawled to her knees, seeing the concern on Jack's face, and beyond him footmen in various states of dress materialising in the doorway. She understood the indecision that flickered across Jack's features. 'Go, Jack! Go after him! I'm fine,' she cried, flinging an arm towards the window. Jack leapt to the table, but he was already too late. The rope jerked away through the window, the attacker having enough wit to destroy the escape route upon reaching the ground.

'The back stairs!' Dulci scrabbled to her feet, running and sliding inelegantly towards the door, Jack behind her.

He seized her in the hall to halt her flight. 'I'll go. Stay here and see to getting our culprit tied up before he wakes.' Jack roughly shoved past her, running shirtless into the night, gesturing to two footmen to follow.

Dulci drew a deep breath, some of the excitement leaving her in the wake of Jack's departure.

Jack was right, of course. There was no benefit to both of them haring off into the night. They would come back to find the other intruder gone and the journal with him.

Dulci quickly organised the servants. There were actions to take and decisions to make. Some of them were sent to round up cords from the kitchen. Others were set to watch the captive until he was secure.

Her butler, Roundhouse, asked permission to call the watch. She debated the decision before deciding against it. She also wished to maintain some level of anonymity. She didn't want this break-in announced to the world. Going for the watch would only raise a host of questions. That couldn't be what Jack wanted.

The housekeeper wanted to clean up the room, but Dulci thought it would be better to wait for Jack, for the daylight, and a chance to search for clues. Instead, Dulci set the woman to work making tea and laying out an early breakfast. After a whirlwind of early morning activity, there was nothing to do but wait for Jack's return.

Dulci was dressed and coiffed, looking every inch the respectable young woman by the time

Jack came back some time after the clock chimed nine, dressed in someone's ill-fitting shirt with too-short sleeves. It seemed more than hours had passed since the break-in.

She'd never been treated to the sight of a dishevelled, unkempt, sleepless Jack called out in the middle of the night to run the streets of London. The man standing before her in the entry bore little resemblance to the couth, impeccably tailored man who'd squired her to the Mayfield ball only last night. Jack's blonde hair hung in his face, causing him to repeatedly push it out of his eyes. His trousers were ripped at the knees, his chest, where it peeked through the unbuttoned shirt, bore signs of soot and dirt.

She searched his tired face, adorned with dark circles and the blonde stubble of morning beard. He shook his head wordlessly. The intruder had got away.

'Do you want to bathe first or eat?' Dulci solicited.

'Eat, if you can stand me. I'll start with coffee if you have it.' Jack's voice was hoarse with weariness.

'I have breakfast and coffee laid out in the family dining room. I'll send someone to your lodgings for fresh clothes.' She peered closely at Jack. He seemed to sway where he stood. 'Are you all right?'

Jack managed a wry half-smile. 'There's nothing wrong with me coffee can't cure.'

Coffee, a bath and clean clothes did indeed work wonders on Jack. Dulci wondered at his reserves of stamina hours later as he briefed a small team of men, Gladstone included, in the ruins of her collection room, leading them through the burglary.

'There can be no question that the intruders had a specific destination *and* goal in mind.' Jack flashed a sharp look at Gladstone. Dulci recalled Jack's scepticism the prior evening over Gladstone's reluctance to officially name Calisto Ortiz as the prime suspect in Vasquez's murder.

'This room is set at the back of the house and is two storeys from the ground. The intruders came here instead of choosing rooms on the lower level, which would have been accessible with much more ease and without the risk of waking the occupants. It is unlikely someone sleeping on the third floor would have heard a disturbance on the lower level.'

Dulci noted how carefully Jack worded his hypothesis, delicately skirting away from any word that would imply 'we'. Unless called to it, Jack was doing his best to steer attention away from his presence in a bedchamber in an unmarried woman's home.

The three other men nodded their heads, following Jack's explanations. Dulci marvelled at how easily or perhaps willingly the men were led. It was a curious trait of the English to simply ignore what did not please them. If anyone deduced Jack had already been on the premises, no one mentioned it out loud. True to English custom, if it wasn't said, then it didn't happen.

'Did the intruder escape with the map?' one of them asked.

'No, the map is safe.' Jack's answer was direct and short.

'Do we have any idea who sent these men?' asked another.

'*I* have ideas.' Jack shot Gladstone a cool look. 'We have the second intruder in custody. He's been sent to a safe house where he awaits interrogation later this afternoon. I am confident we'll have the answers we seek by evening.'

Dulci hid a shudder. An interrogation sounded

exceedingly brutal. She wanted to protest that such extremes weren't necessary, but of course they were. To not extract the needed information from the captured intruder was the height of folly. Was Jack going to do the interrogation? He'd said 'we', implying he and one other. She'd never thought Jack capable of cold-blooded violence. His appearance seemed so immaculate and, well, *clean*, nothing out of place, nothing disturbed by any unruly conduct as if he moved in a world apart from the rest of them. But then, Calisto Ortiz had not looked like a murderer any more than Jack looked like an interrogator. So this was what he did for the king. This was his work.

'Gentlemen, if you'll follow me into the drawing room, there is one more matter we must discuss,' Jack led them down the hall towards the large room at the front. Dulci trailed in their wake, giving instructions to waiting servants that tea should be brought to the drawing room and perhaps something a bit stronger.

'The other item is Lady Dulcinea's need for protection,' Jack began once everyone was settled with tea and sandwiches. He strode meaningfully in front of the long windows, looking out to the busy street beyond the Stockport House gates, all eyes in the room riveted on him.

There was no doubt that Jack was in charge. The unprepossessing Gladstone had faded in to the upholstery of his chair without meaning to. A tremulous thrill darted unbidden through Dulci. There was something undeniably appealing about a man in command, even if that man was Jack and had much to answer for; she'd almost forgot for a moment, but his next words stirred her temper.

'We must operate on the premise that our culprit will try again in the wake of this initial failure to recover the map. That puts Lady Dulcinea at risk. That risk increases if our culprit treats her with the same assumption as he treated Señor Vasquez—that Vasquez not only possessed the map, but knew its purpose.'

She might as well be just anyone Jack was responsible for guarding for all the impassive objectivity he was showing, not the woman he'd lain naked with discovering the dratted map. She wondered what these men might say if they knew precisely the circumstances under which the good Viscount Wainsbridge came across the map.

'The house and Lady Dulcinea must be under

surveillance at all times until this situation is resolved.' Jack nodded to one of the men. 'Morrison, I will leave it to you to work out a schedule. I will station myself here as well as much as I am able. We have our jobs, gentlemen. Let's work swiftly and competently; the empire and our monarch depend on us.'

'To say nothing of Lady Dulcinea,' Gladstone said, rising from his chair with a smile that relieved some of her irritability.

'Gladstone, we must be away,' Jack snapped, striding towards them. 'The interrogation, man. They're waiting for us.'

'Might I have a word before you go?' Dulci asked.

'I am afraid not, Lady Dulcinea.' Jack smiled indulgently, coldly. There was nothing of her clever, teasing lover in that smile. 'You can give your daily schedule to Morrison. I'll return later. I will contact your brother unless you prefer to do it yourself. He should be informed.'

The limit of Dulci's tolerance had been reached. Reached and exceeded. She would not stand here and be treated like a hapless female a moment longer. 'Do not mistake me for a school-room miss. I appreciate your concern, but I am fully capable of looking after myself. It was me, after all, who knocked out our captive with a candlestick last night.'

'Yes, indeed, Lady Dulcinea,' Jack said through a thin smile. 'I can hardly forget it.'

Jack doubted he'd ever be able to shake the image of her dashing across the room, her pink-silk dressing gown billowing behind her, her hair loose, oblivious to the amazingly sensual image she created, streaks of moonlight turning the thin nightgown she wore beneath the robe gossamer. If it was truly only lust he'd have only noticed the fine fullness of her breasts in that moment. But his thoughts had been obsessed over her safety— how could he protect her when she insisted on putting herself in the centre of the action?

Jack sank back against the carriage seat, not caring that he shared the space with Gladstone. Jack could not recall being this tired in quite some time. Dulci was going to be the death of him. Had she no idea how many times she'd pushed him to the brink of fear last night? The very idea that she'd thought herself capable of taking on a man who outweighed her by at least two stone was enough to stun him, her success at doing so not withstanding.

The remembrance of the man's retaliation was nearly enough to finish him off. The only thing more frightening than Dulci's 'moonlight charge of the candlestick' against an intruder was seeing the other intruder leap for Dulci, having no scruples about attacking a woman.

Jack, who'd faced down worse than two mediocre burglars, had been scared, not of the act itself; he knew how to handle combat of all nature. He'd been scared because Dulci was at the heart of the risk. He was not used to such an emotion being attached to his work.

What *drove* that fear for Dulci was frightening in itself. He'd worked with partners before and never been frightened for them in such situations. This was not fear invoked by simple lust for another. While he wouldn't name it, he would admit that he felt something stronger than lust for Dulci.

He would not bother himself with the effort of naming that feeling right now. To do so would be imprudent and hasty until he was absolutely sure what that feeling was. Some might rashly name it love, but Jack was unwilling to do so on short acquaintance, both with the sentiment and the woman to whom he might attach the emotion.

Indeed, he wasn't even sure 'love' was the right word or feeling. Just because a man sneezed didn't mean he was catching cold. Then again, a part of his conscience nagged, this might be it, this might be love. If so, it was a deuced rotten time to work that out and he would put off admitting it to himself as long as he could. There was a lot left to work out before his conscience could say 'I told you so'.

In any case, if or when he ever decided to use the term, he would exercise the utmost caution. Love meant promises and he was a man who promised nothing.

All his philosophising could not change the reality of his emotions, which had simmered under the merest veneer of control since he'd seen the intruder lunge for Dulci.

Jack's gut had tightened with rage at the sight and remained clenched with raw, barely leashed anger. That man was going to pay. Jack had followed him into the night, exhausting every lead, every potential, fuelled by his anger. All to no avail. The crafty burglar had gone to ground; his head start out of the window had been enough to elude Jack in London's dark alleys. Jack had returned to Stockport House exhausted and empty handed.

He wouldn't be empty handed much longer. He had every confidence the interrogation would confirm all he suspected. Then he could get back to Dulci. She'd played her part beautifully today in a lovely demure dress of pale blue and lace. No one could have looked at her today and accused her of spending two intimate nights with him. He laughed silently at his mental joke. Dulci did everything beautifully. She couldn't help it. And it had paid off. Her image of quiet innocence and his objective politeness had carried the day. No one had questioned his presence in her home at the unseemly hour of four in the morning.

But Dulci was *angry* and Jack knew he had a reckoning coming. Monarchs and maps aside, Dulci felt betrayed. He knew what she thought; he could have told her sooner when they first discovered the map and he hadn't. He'd wanted to be sure. But he'd waited too long and now she suspected his motives in their brief affair. Well, there would have to be time for sorting that out after… Jack heaved a sigh, fighting the urge to close his eyes. This was an old pattern too in his life. Everything was put off until after. The only problem was that 'after' kept getting pushed further down the line. It was something of a revelation to realise that he wanted 'after' to be 'now' where Dulci was concerned.

'Well done today, Wainsbridge,' Gladstone huffed across from him. Jack did not mistake his opening as a compliment, but merely arched his eyebrow.

'You've managed to avoid scandal.' There it was, Gladstone's real reason for conversation.

'I beg your pardon?' Jack said coolly, pretending to be confounded by Gladstone's reference. If the man was going to bring up certain omissions, he would have to be blatant.

Gladstone's eyes narrowed. 'You were in Lady Dulcinea's house, sleeping in her guest room, I hope, although that hope seems misplaced.'

'Indeed I was.' Jack sat up ramrod straight. 'Lady Dulcinea was in need of immediate protection after you and I met at the Mayfield ball. When I returned to the ballroom, she was in the company of Calisto Ortiz. I escorted her straight home, but I could not leave her. Seeing that she is an old family friend, I saw no harm in staying at a home in which I've been welcomed for several years. It would have been her brother's wish if he'd known she was at risk.'

'You cleverly disguised that today.'

'For Lady Dulcinea's benefit,' Jack said staunchly, rather enjoying putting Gladstone's lurid imaginings to rest. 'Sometimes honourable intentions get lost in social translation. I had no wish for an inaccurate telling to circulate in society.'

'Where I come from, Wainsbridge, when a virtuous woman's honour is compromised, a gentleman does the right thing and marries her, especially if he is party to the compromising in the first place. He knows what needs to be done without society's prompt.' Gladstone took the high ground. 'Then there is no need for a network of lies and half-truths.'

Jack smiled politely. 'Neither I nor Lady Dulcinea have any intention of marrying, each other or otherwise, as I am sure you are well aware.'

Gladstone glowered the rest of the way, but at least, Jack mused, he was silent.

Chapter Ten

More bungling! Calisto Ortiz could hardly concentrate on Adalberto Vargas's words during the afternoon meeting at their leased headquarters, someone's currently unused town house. Vargas was laying out the agenda of their opening discussions with the British. After two weeks of parties and a 'getting to know you' phase, the time to settle down to business had finally come. Much of the business slated for discussion was *de rigeur*, such as the status of the Spanish missionaries along the Orinoco.

In fact, many of these yearly reports were usually handled by the Venezuelan government and the Governor of British Guiana, Sir Carmichael-Smythe. There was seldom a need to bother London with the mundane mechanics of colonial relations. This year, with boundaries in question, it had been deemed more expedient to go straight to London rather than relying on correspondence by steamer.

Such a strategy suited Ortiz perfectly. He'd rather pass off his map of boundaries, drawn by a biased surveyor, among people thousands of miles away who'd never set foot in South America than among people who actually lived there and were somewhat more familiar with the terrain. It would be easier to argue the former boundaries had been flawed, that the river ran at a different angle than the results previously reported.

It was all wishful thinking as of yet, seeing that he didn't have his map to hand. The map was proof that British Guiana had overstepped its physical boundaries. Without it, Vargas could only make polite overtures about 'looking into the situation'. That would take time, years even, given the distance and the expense and organisation of mounting an official expedition. The Ortiz family didn't have years. They wanted to mine the gold *now*, but as long as the territory remained in British hands, all the gold would belong to the British, too, no matter who mined it.

Vargas didn't know about the map. If he did, Vargas would object strenuously. The man was a traditionalist to his core. Calisto had planned on introducing the map on the eve of negotiations, presenting it humbly as a patriotic gift to Vargas. 'Here's a map my family commissioned once of the region,' he'd say simply, adding, 'I do believe it will help your negotiation since it clearly lays out the grounds in contention.' In one short sentence, the map would become valid proof that the territory belonged to Venezuela. Vargas would not doubt the map or even consider that the map might have been the result of money changing hands. He might even get some type of useful commendation for it.

All this could still come to pass if he could get to the map. But now, the risk was greater. Wainsbridge was sure to alert those involved that the map was a fraud and the insinuation that the map was not legitimate would cause Vargas to worry. The intruder Wainsbridge had caught in Lady Dulcinea's home had surely sung like a nightingale under the pressures of the Foreign Office. By now, Wainsbridge knew everything he'd once suspected. But a few well-placed words could mitigate Wainsbridge's claims. That wasn't what worried him.

What worried Ortiz most was that Wainsbridge had turned out to be rather more than he appeared. Calisto's instincts had been correct there.

He idly tapped a finger on the brown folder beneath his hand. The dossier had come before lunch. The viscount actively worked in a quiet but prominent capacity for the king himself. He was also something of an expert on the South American region, having been there with Schomburgk a few years back. Wainsbridge potentially knew too much about the region. He would know what was skewed on the map. He might even guess why. For those faults, Wainsbridge would have to die. Vasquez had died for much less.

Calisto Ortiz smiled with satisfaction. At the other end of the table, Vargas nodded at him, and Ortiz realised Vargas, pompous old windbag that he was, thought Ortiz was smiling at him. There'd been too much bungling already. Ortiz would handle Wainsbridge's demise. He wouldn't personally kill the man with his own hands, of course. After all, why do it himself when there were others who'd be glad to do it for him?

* * *

Jack stepped down from the carriage in front of Stockport House, tired and world weary. Dulci had lit the lamps. She'd stayed in for the evening. She'd waited for him. The thought was both comforting and unsettling.

Late spring twilight had descended and the night was mild, a perfect evening for courtship if one didn't have any other pressing matters to consider. Jack always did. It was the trademark of his life now. He took a moment to pause and drink it in. It was quiet here. Stockport House was set back from the street, away from the road noise. One could see the street, but one didn't have to hear it. Crickets chirped in the hedges, reminding Jack of home, the small manor house in the north country where he'd grown up. He closed his eyes. He could smell the roses and honeysuckle planted along the drive and his heart ached for simpler days and simpler pleasures.

It wasn't fair to paint those days as a halcyon past. Those days hadn't been perfect either but this, whatever it was he'd become now, hadn't turned out the way he'd hoped. He hardly knew the man he'd become any more, this man who carried a knife in his boot and interrogated mercilessly. Jack opened his eyes. Enough of that maudlin sentiment. If wishes were horses...

Jack laughed roughly. If wishes were horses, Dulci would be riding pillion behind him, her arms wrapped about his waist, her cheek pressed to his back, her hair streaming in the wind as they charged into the unknown. That was all he'd ever really wanted—someone to share his adventures.

To discover that Dulci was that someone was both hopeful and hopeless. How could he drag Dulci into the wilds he explored? An explorer's life was necessarily devoid of the luxuries she enjoyed without thought. And there were dangers too: disease, hostile peoples, poisonous insects, to name a few. While she might be game for such an adventure, would she be game for what it would do to her life? Unless he married her. That might be the one useful thing to come out of his title—he could make her a viscountess at least. Brandon would have to agree first and Jack couldn't see that happening. Brandon would want more for his sister than a wandering viscount, even if the wandering viscount was his best friend.

Those factors alone were enormous obstacles

to his simple wish. They didn't begin to even encompass Dulci's needs or his. How could she love a man she didn't know? He barely knew himself or even if he was capable of love. Certainly he was capable of falling into love. But sustaining it?

Jack climbed the steps and was met by Roundhouse at the door. Roundhouse informed him Dulci was in the garden, Morrison and Tredwick were in the library playing chess, alert to any suspicious behaviour. Two other men were in the garden with Dulci in case anyone attempted to penetrate the house from the garden gate on the alley side.

How much more did Dulci hate him for making her home a prison, a fortress? Stockport House had always been her refuge, the place where she could fence and collect without casting aspersions on her gender. But he'd had no choice. He could not leave the home unguarded. It had been a convenient stroke of luck that he'd been there last night. The consequences of Dulci having discovered the intruders alone did not bear thinking about.

Jack stepped out into the gardens and breathed the fresh night air. He spied Dulci immediately.

She sat at a small table, engaged in taking notes from a book. She'd changed her gown again, this time into a simple dinner dress of pale green. Her hair was done in an elegant twist, leaving her neck exposed and delicate. One could not help but be drawn to the single strand of pearls that lay at the base of her neck, innocent and unassuming where her pulse beat beneath them. Jack felt his desire rise. Even in the midst of his exhaustion, he wanted her. He wanted to touch her, to feather kisses down her neck, to feel her body beneath his hands. He would get lost in her and he would be able to forget all else.

'Jack.' Dulci had looked up and spotted him. 'You're back. I thought we'd dine alfresco.' Her greeting was polite, perhaps a bit stiff, wary. There was little warmth to it. She might have been greeting any acquaintance. She made a gesture and servants immediately began setting out dinner trays.

Jack marvelled at the efficiency. Regardless of her greeting, she'd been planning this, waiting for him. That had to mean something. Linen was spread, wine was poured. His plate was filled. Servants disappeared. There was a hardness in Dulci's eyes when she looked at him.

'I would ask you how it went, or how your day was, but that hardly seems appropriate given the circumstances. After all, it isn't as if you're coming home from a hard day's work trying a case.'

Jack raised his glass in a toast. 'Hard work, none the less. No less difficult for its form.' Behind those blue eyes of hers, she was thinking the worst of him.

'Interrogation isn't torture, Dulci,' he said in low tones, careful not to be overheard. 'I gave him a meal and a glass of ale and sat down to talk with him while he ate. That is all.'

'You gave food to a starving man. I am sure he hadn't eaten for a while,' Dulci accused.

Jack sipped his chilled wine. 'He committed a crime, against you. He deserved worse than cold chicken and conversation with me.' He could hear the emotion edging his voice.

'Heaven forbid I should be entitled to a higher sense of justice than other citizens.'

Jack set his wine glass down forcefully, liquid slopping over the rim, his anger breaking loose. 'Did you want me to announce how the map was discovered? Did you want me to say we found it dressed in blankets in between bouts of lovemaking? I had to be objective today. I could not let any of them suspect for a moment that I'd run through London half-naked for you, that I'd been scared beyond belief when the intruder went for you and you fell before I could get there.' Jack paused. 'What do you think would happen, Dulci, if anyone guessed at what we've been doing?'

For once, Dulci had the good grace to look penitent. 'I would not trap you, Jack. I would expect nothing. I would shoulder my part of the blame.'

Jack snorted. 'That would be all of the blame. It's always the woman's fault.'

Dulci chose to ignore him and turned the conversation in an entirely different direction. 'My honour aside, what did you learn today?'

'The man was sent by Ortiz. Everything is as we thought. Gladstone had to eat a small slice of humble pie.'

'Well, then, that's it,' Dulci said with a satisfied half-smile. 'The proper officials know the map is a fake. Even if Ortiz recovered it by some miraculous means, he can hardly introduce it into the talks now that everyone knows. It's over.'

How nice it must be to live in Dulci's black-and-white world. She expected blunt straightforwardness from everyone around her and gave it in return. It was hard for her to conceive of the spaces between where black and white weren't so obvious. Jack's world, however, was a bit greyer. He did not think it was over.

'We must be alert in case Ortiz tries something else.'

Dulci's gaze sharpened. 'Ortiz is not to be arrested?'

'We can't. He has diplomatic immunity. The Venezuelan government can choose to try him upon his return, but we can do nothing.'

'So he's on the loose, able to extract revenge.'

'Possibly. Your safety depends on complete honesty. I will not mince words with you. Ortiz may decide that, as a woman, you should be spared his wrath, that you could not understand the significance of the map.' Jack flashed her a wry smile. 'For once, Dulci, your gender might be the saving of you.'

'You think Ortiz will target you instead.' Dulci divined instantly the hidden message in his words. A flicker of worry flamed in her blue eyes. Jack took it as a good sign. She might be angry, but she hadn't given up on him entirely.

'Yes,' Jack said simply. 'I am sure by now that

he has a dossier compiled on me and he knows my background. He's too astute to not take the standard measures. He will know I've been to South America and that should worry him greatly. That I've turned up in the midst of this negotiation will confirm his suspicions. He knows, no matter what you knew or didn't, that *I* knew. I knew what he was after and why he was after it.'

'Then you've come to say goodbye.' Dulci looked away, making a great show of fussing with her napkin beside her plate.

Jack nodded. 'Among other things that need saying.' He gestured to the men walking the garden, motioning they could retire inside. 'Walk with me, Dulci.' He didn't want to explain what was in his heart at the same table where they'd talked of murder and conspiracies.

Dulci took his arm, but she dreaded what he was going to say. In a way, what was to come was far worse than hearing the sordid details of Calisto Ortiz's gory schemes to retrieve a map. 'The hydrangeas bloomed this week.' Dulci pointed to a large pot of blue-and-pink flowers set on the pathway. 'They were late this year. Brandon would have had a fit.'

Beside her, Jack laughed softly. 'Brandon loves to order nature around. Taming the wild suits him.'

'I threatened to let the garden go its own way this year since he wasn't coming to town.' Dulci reached out to touch a petal on the climbing roses. It was nice to talk with Jack this way, without a ballroom of people staring, without innuendo and the double meanings that wrapped most of their conversations. Yet, such a simple discussion seemed surreal. Dulci tilted her head in Jack's direction. 'How is it possible after all that has happened that we can stand here speaking about flowers and Brandon? It's almost too ordinary. My world has been turned upside down and yet it still looks the same, still acts the same. I changed my gown for dinner, I gave orders to the servants, I worked on my notes. Calamity has struck. Shouldn't *everything* be different?'

She studied Jack shrewdly. 'Do you ever get used to it? I am suddenly struck with the realisation that this is what life is like for you on any given day. How do you waltz into ballrooms and make witty conversation every night as if you've nothing more to worry about?' Why hadn't she seen it before, the duality of his life since receiving his title and what it must mean for him? It was more than the secrecy.

'You adapt,' was all Jack said. 'This will pass and your life will return to normal.' He was watching her in that way of his, the heat in his eyes being stoked to life. But there were things that needed to be dealt with before she could fan those coals.

'And your life, Jack?' They moved on down the path to sit on a bench by a statue of a water nymph surrounded by greenery and ferns, water spouting from the jug she carried into a pool of pebbles.

'My life will go on much as it has.'

'You're awfully miserly with your conversation tonight,' Dulci scolded. 'You said there were things that needed saying and yet we haven't said anything at all in that regard.'

'You're the one who wanted to talk about hydrangeas,' Jack reminded her. But she sensed a challenge beneath the scold.

'Maybe that's what we're supposed to talk about,' Dulci answered softly. Jack was leaving, never mind that he'd still be in London. He was leaving her. He would go back to his quarters and he would keep his distance in order to ensure her safety. Then he'd be off on another project for the king. What good could come from talking about other things, confusing things? Maybe she'd be better off remembering this moment with him: a peaceful moment where they'd walked and talked together without artifice instead of clouding it with ambiguous promises.

'You and I are a lot alike, Dulci. We've never been good at doing what we're supposed to. I know what you're thinking, what you're debating in that active mind of yours.' He shook his head. 'Only a coward would let us leave here with nothing more than a discussion of hydrangeas and roses to remember.'

'Jack, you don't need to explain anything. I've got it worked out. I had all day to think.' Dulci tried to stall, tried to protect herself. Jack's eyes were growing darker with desire and, Lord help her, in spite of all her misgivings, her need was rising too, the need to be in this man's arms, to let his strength surround her, to empower her, to forget the danger for a little while.

'I cannot leave knowing that you think what occurred between us was all work, some kind of subterfuge I employed to get to the map.' Jack's voice was at her ear, his mouth nipping gently at her lobe, his hand pushing back her hair. His lips were at her neck now and Dulci arched against him instinctively, wanting to be nearer. It was awkward being side by side, she couldn't get close enough.

'Tell me you know better, Dulci.' Jack breathed heavy and hoarse, dragging her on to his lap, helping her to straddle his thighs. 'Tell me you know our love-making is not an act of artifice. Tell me you know it's honest.'

The desire in his darkened eyes was arresting and potent, the window to his soul open, offering a glimpse into the depths of his character, a swirling mix of the complex and the desperate. Dulci could not deny him; indeed, her need of him was greater because of it.

'Yes, Jack. It's honest,' Dulci whispered, her arms around his neck, her breasts pressed against his chest, her mouth covering his, glorying in the taste of supper's sweet wine. Jack groaned his pleasure, letting her take the kiss where she willed, giving his mouth over to her while he worked pleasure of his own beneath her skirts, hands moving up her thighs, at their apex thumbs gently brushing damp curls, drawing back her secret lips to the tight bud hidden within, one thumb gently skimming until Dulci cried out, begging for a firmer stroke, begging for completion.

But Jack would not relent. 'Let me worship you, Dulci,' he begged, his own arousal powerful and obvious beneath her buttocks. Dulci slipped a hand between them, answering his erotic strokes with delicious strokes of her own, finding the head of his shaft beneath his trousers.

'You're an enchantress, Dulci.' Jack was hoarse, rocking hard against her, needing both his hands to steady himself on the bench. She reached for the fall of his trousers, releasing his hot member, glorying in the fulfilling power of arousing this man to such heights his very control was in question. Tonight *she'd* take *him*, riding him astride in the newly risen moonlight.

Dulci moved to push him back on the stone bench, but Jack had other ideas. 'No, tonight I want to cover you.' His voice was ragged, beyond desire. Dulci thought she heard a new desperation in it. There was wildness in his eyes as he rolled her beneath him, careful of the stone's hardness on her back.

He joined her intimately and immediately, their foreplay having served its purpose, both of them wet and ready when Jack plunged into her. There was no need to be delicate. Dulci didn't want gentle tonight. On that bench, with only nature as a witness, she wanted a release to the madness that raged inside them both. She wanted a release for the anger and despair, perhaps even a release for the impotence that had roiled inside of her all day. Most of all, she wanted Jack without doubt, without the world intruding. In these moments, with her legs wrapped about him, embracing him tightly, she could protect him from the demons in his soul, from the desperation he'd let her glimpse tonight, desperation she hadn't known was there. The knowledge of such things increased her ecstasy. Paradise was within reach, peace was within reach.

She raised her hips, feeling his own hips grind against hers, the tempo of Jack's rhythm speeding towards completion, the pressure growing in his body, his muscled arms trembling as they held his weight, and knew his crisis would soon be upon him. Her own release neared, so very close she thought she'd scream from the wanting of it. Then they were there together, Jack's climax thundering deep inside her, pulsing in waves, releasing the most intimate of tides at the shore of her womb. This was completion.

They lay still, letting their breathing return to normal, their excited hearts regain their usual pace. Dulci relished the feel of Jack's head at her shoulder, his hand lying quiet on her stomach. Something intangible marked tonight. Their love-making had taken on a different cast, driven by something she couldn't name yet.

After a while, Jack rose and adjusted his clothing. He reached down to help her up and straighten her skirts. The desperation she thought she'd viewed in his eyes was effectively driven back. His eyes, his face, held a look of firm resolve as if something had been decided and there was no going back.

His teasing smile was on his lips. But his voice was soft, a near-whisper full of sincerity. 'This will definitely be more memorable than a conversation about hydrangeas and roses.'

At the intimate sound of his voice, something warm blossomed in the feminine core of her. She felt complete, wrapped in the shared memory of their passion conjured up by his voice. She was well and thoroughly seduced. But it was more than seduction. What she felt for Jack in that moment was far beyond the abilities of lust to sustain. *She loved him.* The realisation nearly brought her to her knees. All her defences, logic and hard cold reality, had failed to protect her. Against her better intentions, she'd fallen in love with the most unlikely of candidates for her heart: a man who would not give her his.

'You're trembling, Dulci. Don't worry, you're safe now.' Jack lifted her hand to his lips and pressed a kiss upon it, his eyes holding hers with a million unspoken messages tumbling in them. That was when Dulci understood; Jack thought he was going to die.

Chapter Eleven

It was empirically true that one never feels more alive than when faced with imminent mortality. Jack dressed in preparation for the opening negotiations, life surging through him, his senses imbued with a sharper, more vital quality. Jack worked a gold cuff into place, his eyes moving outside past the heavy curtains drawn back to let in the morning light.

The sun shone brilliantly. It was going to be a nice day in spite of the fact that nice things weren't going to happen. It was hard to believe anything bad could happen on sunny days. Hard to believe anyone could die on a sunny day. Those sorts of things ought to be reserved for rainy, gloomy days.

Jack reached for the second cuff link, remembering. He'd believed such fantasy as a child.

Growing up just outside Manchester, there were plenty of grey days and in his house there'd been plenty of bad things that happened on them. Sunshine had meant freedom. Nothing bad happened on sunny days. Sunshine meant running in the meadows and fishing in the rivers with Brandon, perfect days in an imperfect life.

Satisfied with his cuffs, Jack reached for a long strip of white linen and wound it around his neck, beginning the laborious process of tying a cravat. He'd dreamed of her last night, not surprising considering the circumstances and their rather torrid farewell.

Even now in the morning light, Dulci haunted him. He could not name why or how the endless wanting of her had started, but he craved her with the intensity of an opium addict. After the madness at Christmas he'd taken the necessary precautions. He'd tried long absences. He'd tried other women. All to no avail. His methods only seemed to increase the craving and he'd ended up right back where he'd started from.

And why not? Dulci was a rare treasure to be appreciated for far more than her fairy-tale princess beauty: the dark hair, the pale skin and cherry lips. He was drawn to her wildness, to the substance of her. Perhaps he was drawn to her because she was like him. He might not know her favourite colour, or know the name of her dress-maker or any of the mundane little facts that besotted fools who imagine themselves in love know about their beloved. But he knew her ele-mentally. He knew what drove her wildness.

She was like him in all the ways that mattered. She *knew* him. She knew his family home, an awkward cold place devoid of familial love. She knew stories about him growing up. And she still cared for him, although he was playing fast and loose with that affection.

Jack tied a firm knot at his throat with a strong jerk of his hands. She knew him and he knew her, perhaps not in the traditional way people knew each other in London society, but in a way that spoke to the core of him. He might still be at-tempting to name this depth of feeling Dulci invoked in him, but he knew with a certainty that he was willing to die to save her. If Ortiz harmed her, a light would go out of the world, and Jack knew a part of himself would go out of the world with it. As long as one of the two survived… If given the choice, Jack preferred it be Dulci.

He strapped on an arm sheath and slid a small

dagger into it. He leaned down and slid another knife into his boot. Ortiz was coming. Jack just hoped he had guessed correctly and Ortiz was coming for him. He would be ready. He had no intention of dying simply because Ortiz meant him to. Still, he'd played this game long enough to know death came in many forms: a hired thug on the street, a discreet poison in a glass. Some attempts could be thwarted with a quick blade. Other attempts could not.

Jack reached into his dresser drawer and rooted beneath a pile of cravats until he found what he wanted: travelling papers and a packet of money. He faced himself in the mirror, slipping his arms into his jacket of blue superfine.

He studied the reflection, deliberately forcing his mind to slow and focus, reviewing. He'd taken all the precautions he could. He'd left Dulci in her home, surrounded by the finest bodyguards the Foreign Office could provide. He'd armed himself for a physical attack. He had money and papers in case he had to flee, a ruby ring on his little finger and a matching stick pin in his cravat to pawn. If it came to it, he could sell the buttons on his coat one by one. He was an expert when it came to survival.

Satisfied that he'd taken all measures possible to ensure Dulci's safety and his own survival, Jack grabbed up the ornate walking stick from the stand by the door and strode confidently out into the morning to face life or death, come what may, with only one regret. He knew men who had died with more.

There were no regrets, only choices, Dulci reminded herself forcefully, struggling to concentrate on the artefacts spread out before her. She'd set up a temporary workshop in an old greenhouse at the back of the garden while she waited for new cases to arrive and the windows to be repaired. But her energy was divided between the items spread before her and the items on her mind—the shocking revelations of the night before.

Jack was worried, so worried he'd attempted to draw Ortiz's fire and divert attention from her. She was not sure how she felt about that. She was used to fighting her own battles, but never had she faced a battle like this. This was not a battle over social acceptance, but about life and death. She was out of her depth when it came to secret assassins and hidden maps.

She'd spent a restless night and a restless morning trying to put the image of Jack out of her mind without success. The guards placed around the house had told her the negotiations started today.

Jack would be there by now, seated at the long table with other men, Calisto Ortiz across from him just a few feet away, close enough to strike with a dagger if Ortiz didn't mind the publicity. Why should he if he had immunity and the argument of honour on his side? Not that it was any better assuming Ortiz would refrain from a public spilling of blood. Covert activity was far worse, where even the simplest cup of tea became a weapon in an expert's hands. One sip and Jack would be gone, taken from her, sacrificed for her, just when she'd discovered she loved him.

She loved Jack. The realisation was so fresh, so new, she hardly knew what to make of it. But she did know where to start and that was with the question: Did she dare give in to it? She wasn't exactly sure she had a choice. Could you control whom you loved? But assuming she did have a choice, Dulci wasn't sure she could afford to love Jack. In the end, it might cost more of herself than she was willing to give. She would not tolerate living on the periphery of his world, even if that was the only way she could have him.

There were terrible consequences to loving Jack, she was beginning to realise with a new level of clarity. He might die. She might have to give him up and not act on her affections for the sake of saving her own soul. Either way, she'd be left alone with her love—alone and apart from Jack.

Dulci's pen slipped, smearing ink on the carefully written card. At this rate she wouldn't get any work done. Dulci flopped down into an old wicker chair that had been left or forgot when the greenhouse had been abandoned. A little cloud of dust puffed up from the faded cushions and she sneezed. Damn. She allowed herself the luxury of swearing. Would nothing go right today? Even the simple act of sitting down irritated her.

It was all Jack's fault. She'd never asked him to protect her, never asked him to stand between her and Calisto Ortiz. He did not owe her anything. But he'd stood her champion none the less and it had complicated things immensely. The thought she didn't want to think surfaced, unable to be contained by denial and anger— why had Jack done it? Had he done it out of fraternal affection for Brandon? Because Brandon would want him to protect her in his absence? Or maybe this wasn't about Brandon at all, but because there was something more between the two of them? Was it possible that he might reciprocate the intensity of feeling she carried towards him?

Dulci picked at a loose seam on the pillow. She wondered if it had ever been just sex for her, no matter what logical justifications she applied. That day in the artefact room, she'd trusted Jack with her body and he'd not let her down. Even now, he was protecting her body with his distance, his bodyguards, his attempt to direct Ortiz away from her. Jack had never pretended to offer more than a few nights of unconditional pleasure.

Yet if she knew one thing about men, it was that they protected what they loved. Was it possible that, against the odds, Jack had fallen in love with her? Had he slipped into it just as she had? If so, what did they do now? Anything? Nothing? Was it possible to be in love and do nothing? Someone would have to be brave enough to make the first move, declare their feelings and weather whatever storm came.

'Lady Dulcinea!' One of the bodyguards burst

into the greenhouse, the door banging behind him. 'There's news from the negotiations.' Ah, even love would have to give way in the wake of the empire's needs. Jack wasn't even here and she was being interrupted, her thoughts called away from their feminine daydreams to Jack's world.

The man was breathless and the look on his face was not one of excitement. 'What has happened?' Dulci's anxiety rose.

'Viscount Wainsbridge has been accused of framing Señor Ortiz in regard to presenting a forged map of boundaries.'

'It's not true,' Dulci said in consternation. The incredible claim was wildly untrue; a bigger lie she could not imagine, especially when the exact opposite was true. 'Who accuses him of such a thing?' She was on her feet, pacing. She had to do something, take some action. Jack would need her.

'Señor Ortiz himself.'

Ah, like the witch trials of old where only the afflicted was able to bear testimony against the accused. A cold thought indeed.

Calisto Ortiz was inordinately pleased with himself. This plan had hatched itself flawlessly. The negotiations had opened and the British had asked he be excused from the negotiations. They had concerns about his 'objectivity', that he was associated with the murder of an importer who'd carried cargo from Venezuela and had been in possession of a certain map. That map had fallen into the hands of a British citizen and been the source of an attempted burglary of the citizen's home. Since the map was a forgery, it appeared Señor Ortiz had a hidden agenda to swindle land from the British government. It would be best to excuse him due to a conflict of interest.

It had been nicely said, but Vargas had clearly understood the message. The old diplomat had sputtered, voicing embarrassed protests to save face. Then he'd jumped in, adding to Vargas's protests. He'd merely said, 'I've been set up by Viscount Wainsbridge, who is in possession of the map and who has a personal grudge against me over a woman. It seems to me that if I were trying to pass off a map I would have the map in my possession. Yet it is Wainsbridge who "found" the map, not in my quarters, I might add. In fact, not once has the map been in my possession since arriving on English soil.'

His claims were audacious, but the bigger the lie, the more easily believed. He didn't have to have anyone believe him. He needed only to cast enough doubt to cloud the discussion. He watched Gladstone spear Wainsbridge with a look of disgust. Ah, good, a potential ally then. Wainsbridge showed no emotion, managing to look cool, as if people levelled charges of this magnitude against him daily. For all Ortiz knew, maybe they did.

Señor Vargas turned to Ortiz. 'You swear this is the truth?'

Vargas was so damned honourable he couldn't conceive of dishonour in anyone. Ortiz stifled a smile and manufactured a look of chagrin. He laid his next layer of argument, the layer meant to distract and confuse. 'I swear this is the truth. I would encourage you, *señor*, to ask yourself why would Britain want to put a forgery into play that shows them losing land? It is to start a war.' There was a general outcry at the table. Ortiz raised a hand for silence.

'I posit Britain wants to use the false map as a chance to whip up public support for a war in which Britain is fighting to take back what Venezuela has "cheated" them out of. It would be no difficult feat for Britain, an empire with an enormous army at its disposal, to defeat

Venezuela and in the end grab *more* land. These talks are merely a prelude to war. We've been called here to be straw men. These talks mean nothing. Britain is using them for a larger, more sinister purpose and Viscount Wainsbridge is at the heart of it.'

So this was how it was going to happen. Not with a knife in the alley or poison in the tea, at least not yet. Jack watched Ortiz spin his case with steely eyes. There would be discrediting first, the maligning of a reputation, the casting of doubt until people might believe with enough certainty that he'd commit suicide over the shame of it. Of course, it wouldn't truly be a suicide. That would be when Ortiz would arrange a violent end and his body would float up from the Thames a few days later. People would whisper knowingly behind their fans that he'd had no choice really, disgraced as he was, and what could be expected when one came from such lowly antecedents, a squire's son after all?

The difficulty came in making his case. He could not say Britain had advance warning that a map might exist without exposing the intelligence network that had brought the news. He could not say Ortiz had gone to the warehouse without exposing that he'd followed Ortiz and spied on him. There was only one piece of evidence he could legitimately draw on.

Jack steepled his hands. 'Your claims are outrageous. There is no interest in starting a war with Venezuela. Your scenario is intriguing, but it does not account for the testimony we have from the one burglar who says he was paid, by you, Señor Ortiz, to retrieve a map from Lady Dulcinea's residence.'

Ortiz shook his head sadly. 'That was poor judgement on my part. I was so distraught over the news of such a map and Señor Vasquez's death. I had just heard and I was desperate to preserve my reputation. I acted hastily and foolishly. I thought if I could get the map, I could destroy it and none of this nastiness would materialise.'

'How did you know the map would be at Lady Dulcinea's?' The question seemed to flummox Ortiz for a moment before his eyes narrowed and his mouth quirked into a smirk.

'Perhaps I should ask you the same? How did you happen to be there?'

'You've been suspected from the start,' Jack growled, his anger overriding his sang-froid.

'Lying in wait for me? No doubt it's because you knew I'd come, that I'd have no choice in order to save my reputation.' Ortiz rose from his seat, his hands braced on the table. 'You've had me framed from the start, since the first night you tried to make a fool of me at the ball, all because Lady Dulcinea was taken with me, and not you.'

Gladstone coughed furiously at the far end of the table.

'I prefer to have Lady Dulcinea, who is nothing but an innocent bystander in this, left out of the discussion.' Jack rose to meet Ortiz across the table, all his instincts firing: protect, protect, protect. Protect Dulci. Protect the crown.

Gladstone rose and cleared his throat. 'Gentleman, there must be a suitable resolution to this misunderstanding. Let us take a brief recess to sort this out. Wainsbridge, a word, please?'

Jack shut the door of a small blue salon behind him. The place was quiet and private, a chance to talk. 'The man is talking nonsense,' Jack declared the moment they were alone.

'Is he? How do we prove that?' Gladstone shook his head and paced the floor. 'Can we produce the map?'

'Yes, I can get it,' Jack said evasively. If Gladstone did not leap to his defence, then Gladstone could not be trusted. The man should have done more for him back there besides cough in disbelief. 'What good will that do? It will only prove I am in possession of a map that contains boundaries unlike the ones on the Humboldt map.'

'Hmm. That would only make you look guiltier, I suppose.' Gladstone stopped to fiddle with the top on a crystal decanter. 'Wainsbridge, did you plant the map? It would have been ingenious. You hear the king and I mention the potential for the map's existence and then you decide to make that potential reality.'

Jack whirled on Gladstone incredulously. 'You heard the king, he said he needed me to stop a war, not start one.'

Gladstone shrugged. 'There's more glory in war than in peace, Jack, and you're a man who hungers for adventure.'

'I did not plant the map. Everything happened as our intelligence said—the map was hidden in Vasquez's cargo. It was a stroke of luck that Dulci happened to have it. Otherwise, the cargo would have disappeared into London.'

Gladstone nodded, cringing a bit at his easy use of Dulci's first name. 'You understand I had to ask.'

Jack met his gaze evenly. 'I understand that you're willing to sacrifice me for the sake of these negotiations.' He saw what Gladstone wanted. Gladstone wanted him to gracefully bow out of the negotiations, but that wouldn't stop the rumours circulating as to why he'd left. Such a gesture wouldn't stop Ortiz's tongue from wagging. Worst of all, if he bowed out, then Ortiz would be entirely vindicated while he would be all but ruined, the banner of scandal firmly affixed above his head for the rest of his life: the man who tried to start a war with a lie.

'I won't do it, Gladstone.' He had worked too hard to lose it all like this. It was one thing to want to give it up. It was another to be stripped of it in shame. What would Dulci think of him? He could not stand to lose her so soon after realising what she meant to him. But he'd rather give her up to protect her from his scandal than drag her down with him.

Gladstone moved towards the door, his hand hovering over the knob. 'There are a lot of ways to serve your country, Wainsbridge. Consider this yours.'

'No,' Jack said defiantly. 'I will go to the king.

I will prove the map is a fraud, drawn up at the behest of Calisto Ortiz.'

Gladstone gave a hoarse laugh. 'How will you do that? You'd have to go all the way to Guiana. You'd have to find the map-maker and wring a confession from him. You'd have to sail down the river and prove its course runs counter to the drawing.'

'Then that is what I'll do,' Jack said with grim determination. Hercules had his twelve labours, Jack had his.

Chapter Twelve

A more regal king would have sided with Gladstone and, with a show of great reluctance, washed his hands of Jack Hanley, the first Viscount Wainsbridge, a man of no account when compared to the generations of service provided by Gladstone's family. There was no one, no great family or genealogical history to offend by doing so. But William IV was of a more plebian mind. He defined his rule by his support of reform, by lessening the gap between the entitlements of gentlemen and the entitlements of the common man. As such, he felt it unnecessary to sacrifice Jack for the good of the order.

William fixed his gaze on the two men sitting before him shortly after midnight. 'This is unbecoming of you, Gladstone. I am disappointed you have not championed Wainsbridge publicly. The Venezuelans must not suspect we can be so easily divided and conquered. If they think we will break ranks over this, they may think we are easily manipulated on other issues as well.'

'I had to be sure of Wainsbridge's actions, your Majesty.' Gladstone went red in the face.

William offered him a look of disbelief. 'An Englishman does not need to doubt another Englishman. What was there to be sure of? We do not make a practice of disgracing viscounts. By disgracing Wainsbridge, you disgrace me and my good judgement.'

Jack disliked having to involve the king, but when faced with utter ruination, he needed an advocate. Left to Gladstone's mercy, he'd have ended up under house arrest and no recourse. It was a petty victory to see Gladstone red as a rooster, but a victory none the less and Jack would take it.

'Your Majesty, I appreciate your support,' Jack began humbly. 'However, there is still the issue of the map. It is not an accurate representation of landownership on the border. Until a definite, first-hand study of the border can be made, my greater fear is that this map is only the first. We make ourselves weak if we haven't the proof to defend ourselves. Venezuela will come again. There will be others like Ortiz, even if we scotch this particular effort. Humboldt's map is only a suggestion. He did not explore the Essequibo region.'

William looked thoughtful, a hand caressing his soft double chin in contemplation. 'I see your point. Undefended borders have historically been problems for all empires. What do you suggest, Wainsbridge?'

Jack leaned forwards in his excitement, careful with his words. 'I suggest we map the area immediately.'

'And who should do the mapping? Do you have anyone in mind?' A glimmer of a smile played on William's lips as if he understood the direction of Jack's thoughts.

'Robert Schomburgk, with whom I worked on the Anegada exploration, is already over there, but I would willingly offer myself to work in tandem with him, although I would gladly do it alone if he is too busy. This must be done in a timely fashion.'

'Brilliant!' William slapped his leg jovially. 'I like how you think, Wainsbridge. You're a man of action.' He turned sharp eyes on Gladstone.

'This is the perfect solution, the perfect proof. Do you see it, Gladstone?' William winked at Jack. 'Killing two birds with one stone, eh?'

Jack nodded, elation and relief filling him simultaneously after the stress of the afternoon. The map would serve two purposes. First, it would define the currently ambiguous borders of ownership between Venezuela and British Guiana, preventing future contentions. Second, it would absolve him of Ortiz's flimsy claim that he wanted to start a war. No one would create one map and then deliberately draw up another, contradictory one.

He would create an honest map that showed no need to quibble over territory because Britain already possessed it rightfully. Now, the burden of initiating hostilities would fall to the Venezuelans. *They* would be the invaders, not the British. If there was a war, Britain would not start it. And he would be clear in the process, his reputation intact. He would not be the man who betrayed Britain by giving away land. In the process, if he happened to find the man who'd been paid to draw up Ortiz's faulty map, so be it. That would be all to the better. If the man could be found, and testimony could be obtained, it would be further exoneration for him.

'How soon can you leave, Jack?' William asked.

'How soon would you like?'

'There's a ship departing at dawn. You could be in Guiana by the end of July. We could have a map in hand by the new year.' William mused out loud, 'Perhaps even a letter of some merit in the post by late autumn.'

Jack knew William was thinking of timing. Negotiations had just opened today. They would last three months at least—three months of ponderous discussion over contracts and words, polite, diplomatic haggling over titles and positions to be doled out. In all likelihood, discussions would last longer, some of the issues lingering to be dealt with during the Michaelmas session of Parliament. If so, the border discussion could be effectively tabled and then brought back as soon as he sent news.

He could see William's hidden agenda too. If he moved fast enough, there'd be a chance to discredit Ortiz before the delegation left England. Jack smiled. 'Dawn will be fine, your Majesty.'

Jack wasted no time departing. There were only five hours to make preparations. He would not worry about supplies for the expedition. It would be better to purchase supplies once he reached British Guiana and Robert would be able to help with that. The king would send a packet of papers to the ship, including a writ of purchase and an introduction. They would be waiting for him. All he needed was a quick stop at his rooms to gather his personal tools, pen a few necessary notes. Most of all, he had to see Dulci regardless of the time of night.

He needed to say goodbye.

Again.

He wouldn't disappear with nothing more than a note, although he knew leaving would probably destroy any hope of exploring the possibilities between them. He would be gone a year at least. She could not be expected to wait for a man who wasn't sure what it was he could offer her.

By the time Jack approached his rooms on Jermyn Street, he knew he was being followed. Jack slowed his steps and whirled on the shadow, taking him by surprise. Jack grabbed him by the arm, surprised himself to find the shadow was nothing more than a skinny street boy. But that didn't weaken Jack's grip. Small boys were not weaponless or any less harmless for their size. He'd been a small boy once too. 'You've been trailing me since St James's.'

'I don't mean anythin' by it, guv'nor.' The boy twisted and turned in Jack's iron hand. 'I'm to give you this note.'

Jack took the note and flipped it open one handed, not wanting to let go of the boy. He scanned it, his blood chilling. 'Get on with you, then, you've done your job.' He let the boy go. He knew all he needed. There was nothing the boy could tell him. He was just steps away from his door, from his compass and his mapping kit, but there was no time, not even the few minutes it would take to grab them. It might already be too late. There was no time to think, no time to do anything but run.

Dulci awoke with a start, a sixth sense pricking her into wakefulness. Her room was dark, still and yet it felt disturbed, altered in some small way. A cool breeze fanned her face. Dulci turned towards the window. The window was open, her curtains blowing lightly in the breeze. Worry and fear came to her. Dulci scrambled upright. That window had been closed. She specifically remembered shutting it when she'd gone to bed. Then she saw it, in the shadows, the figure of a man. Dulci opened her mouth to scream, but the figure was faster, closer than he'd appeared. He was on her in a moment, a hand clapped over her mouth, his voice at her ear, his scent in her nostrils.

His scent.

Almond.

Jack.

'Shh, Dulci, it's me. Don't scream. Just listen.' His whispered voice was firm. 'I need you to get up and dress quickly, simply. You are in danger and there isn't time to explain.'

The tone of his voice brooked no argument, brooked no exception. The fierceness in his eyes, the perspiration of his body, told her far more about the supposed danger than his words. The danger was real. Immaculate Jack was dripping with sweat as if he'd run across London in the dark. She had to trust there'd be time for explanations later.

Dulci nodded her complicity and went to her wardrobe, swiftly pulling out a carriage dress and jacket. She dressed quickly, one eye on Jack, who was moving about her room with a satchel he'd grabbed from the dressing room. He was pulling out drawers on her vanity, throwing items in the bag.

'The journal's on my bedside table,' Dulci whispered loudly, forcing her feet into serviceable half-boots. Jack had been running. She might be running too. She tried to focus only on the immediate, not on the nebulous danger that awaited her out there.

'My gun's downstairs in the study.'

Jack shook his head. 'There's no time. Can you climb?' He motioned to the window. She saw the outline of a ladder and nodded, swallowing her trepidation. Climbing down in a skirt from three storeys up was tricky business, much harder than climbing up.

'Good girl. Let's go.' Jack squeezed her hand in reassurance. 'Let me go down first.' He tossed the satchel to the ground, swung a long leg over the window sill and disappeared.

Dulci took a deep breath and glanced once more about her room. Jack had not been neat in his haste. Drawers lay on the floor, objects strewn on the carpet. Did she imagine it or was there a sound downstairs at the front door? What kind of danger was it that knocked on the door? It would take Roundhouse a few minutes to be roused and answer the summons if there truly was one. But she had to move fast.

Dulci made her descent without mishap, years of climbing trees as a child with Jack and Brandon paying off. Jack steadied her at the bottom, his hand at her waist, comforting and alluring in spite of the peril.

'Now what?' Dulci quirked a saucy smile in Jack's direction.

'Now we run, out the garden gate, into the alley and down to the docks. If we can find a hackney, we'll take it.'

'Jack, I thought I heard someone downstairs at the door.'

Jack nodded. 'Then we'll have to run fast.'

'Not the world's most sophisticated plan,' Dulci managed to remark, choking back the fear that came with the reality that Jack had only been ahead of the danger by a handful of minutes.

'No, but it will work.'

Inside the house, loud voices could be heard.

Dulci was seized with concern. 'The servants! Will they be harmed?' Involuntarily she stepped towards the house.

'There's nothing you can do, Dulci.' Jack

grabbed her hand and they ran, across the dewy garden, out the gate into the night. The idea of danger stalking them was never far from her mind, but even the danger, whatever it was, could not obliterate the excitement of running. Her hair flew loose, her cloak billowed behind her like a Gothic heroine and exhilaration filled her. She was running, with Jack, through alleys and back streets, running so fast cut-purses didn't bother them, running so fast nothing could touch them. At some point her exhilaration overwhelmed her and Dulci laughed out loud as they raced through the dark city, revelling in the thrill, the adventure, and, yes, even the danger.

Somewhere between Mayfair and the docks, Jack hailed a hackney waiting for a late-night fare, a gentleman stumbling home from his clubs. He bundled her inside and they lay on the seats, gasping for breath and laughing.

They caught their breaths and with them, sobriety. Dulci remembered all the things about this escapade that weren't laughable. 'Tell me, Jack, where are we going?' For surely they were going somewhere. Their destination sealed it.

'Do you remember when you said you'd wager I could walk out your door and be on a ship in twenty minutes with only the clothes on my back?'

'Yes.' Dulci suddenly became wary, cautious.

'Well, we're about to find out if you're right.'

Chapter Thirteen

'*Where* are we going?' Dulci asked again, her trepidation growing in the absence of a direct answer. For all her love of adventure, Jack knew this news met with a burgeoning sense of panic on her part and rightly so. She'd been pulled from bed and forced to flee her home.

'We are going to British Guiana to save your neck and to save my reputation.' His plan had been instantaneous and the best he could do under short notice.

Dulci sank back against the seat, letting the shock of the news settle over her in waves. Jack watched her closely. Maybe the past few days had been too much. He supposed even Dulci must have limits.

'Don't worry, Jack, I won't go to pieces on you,' she said with her best ballroom *élan*.

Jack smiled broadly in relief. 'I never thought you would, m'dear.'

'In that case, don't you think you'd better tell me all about the danger? I've run through the night with you and beyond my misplaced affections for you, I still don't know why.' Dulci's blue eyes sparked deliciously in the dim confines of the hackney. Trust his Dulci to maintain her sense of humour and wit in the face of crisis. Jack decided then and there that describing imminent peril to a woman one has just rescued was a deuced awkward time to be aroused. But Jack could do nothing about it. He was unmistakably aroused.

He'd like nothing better than to throw her across the carriage seat and take her before they reached the docks, but they weren't out of trouble yet. They were merely in a hiatus and so his desire would have to be put on hold as well until they were safely ensconced on board his Majesty's ship and out to sea. Then he'd have weeks stretching before him with nothing else to do.

Jack reached inside his coat and pulled the note. He passed it to Dulci. 'This is what brought me rushing to your side.'

Dulci scanned it; the note was brief and overt in its purpose. 'Ortiz, I assume? He thought to abduct me in order to gain a confession from you.' She folded the note and handed it back to him.

'It would have been a very private form of blackmail.' The unspoken details of Ortiz's intentions created lurid images best left unexplored in Jack's mind: Dulci taken unawares by rough invaders in her home, spirited away to some secret location and held there until he capitulated to Ortiz's request for a confession to the heinous activities Ortiz had charged him with. What choice would he have? He could not go to anyone for help without jeopardising Dulci's reputation, whether or not anything sinister occurred.

He could only guess what Ortiz might deign to put Dulci through; the man clearly coveted her. Jack had seen the desire rise in the man's eyes the first night, before any of these contretemps had begun. The man clearly detested him. Lust for Dulci and dislike of him was a powerful combination, which might motivate all nature of sins.

And, of course, if Ortiz held Dulci, it would be an effective tool for keeping Jack in England. If Ortiz knew Dulci was worth ransoming, he would also know Jack could never leave her behind.

Yet was taking Dulci with him any better? It saved her from the terrors of abduction, but it might also have only put off the inevitable: Dulci teetered on the brink of social disaster. The Incomparable was about to fall, something petty-minded débutantes and jealous matrons with daughters to marry off had secretly wished for years. If not tonight, then later, when it was learned she had accompanied a man unchaperoned, not even with a maid, to British Guiana. A lone, unmarried woman on a ship manned by males, into a brutal, savage land, was not something society could overlook and he would be the instrument of her downfall.

After years of wild living and questionable escapades she'd managed to carry off with discreet aplomb, her fall would be by his hand. She would hate him when she realised what he had done. Still, he reasoned it was better to have a bridge to cross later than a bridge already burned.

Jack peered out of the small window. The environs hailed their approach to the dock district. He tensed, wondering if they should get out and walk the rest of the distance to the ship. Two lone figures in the dark could slip and slide among the shadows, hardly noticeable. But they'd also be prey for other lone figures that could also slip among the shadows. He hadn't come this far today to end up skewered in the stews. If no one had picked up their hackney yet, they'd be better off to stay with it.

'You're smiling.' Dulci's eyes narrowed in suspicion.

'I'm thinking about how I've lived much longer than I expected today.'

'That's not funny, Jack. Why do you suppose Ortiz hates you so much?'

'I am all that stands between him and success. As long as I am a legitimate player in this game, he cannot have what he wants. I know the territory he wants to claim. He had not counted on that. He'd expected everyone in London to have only a two-dimensional understanding from mediocre maps, that we'd all be easy to trick. It's why the negotiations are happening here and not with the governor—too many experts there. Secondly, I caught him at his trick. We found his map before he could introduce it, so his hand was forced.'

'But his story is stupid,' Dulci said frankly. 'By blaming you for trying to frame him with a bad map, he has taken away his chance to claim the land he wants. He's admitted the boundaries are false, merely put there to induce a war.'

Jack smiled. 'Well, he has ruined his chances in that regard. All he can do now is cover his tracks. He's desperate to keep me in the country because if I go, I might find the proof that he deliberately paid someone for a faulty map and then there will be no place for him and his tattered honour to hide. I do imagine Ortiz will have many enemies if the full extent of his shenanigans comes out.'

'So now he's a desperate man.'

'Very much so.'

Dulci mused out loud, 'That will make him more dangerous, more unpredictable.'

'That's been my experience when it comes to desperate men.' Jack was grim. The next step was gaining the ship without mishap. Ortiz had eyes and ears everywhere. If he knew Jack was leaving and knew that the ruse to snatch Dulci had failed, the man might make a last stand at the wharves. So far, they'd encountered no one, but why chase them through London if Ortiz knew their final destination?

He could not reconnoitre in the hackney. It was time to get out and walk and plan. Jack banged on the side of the carriage. 'We'll get out here.'

The stench of the docks was overpowering. The smell of fish, fresh or otherwise, mingled with other unsavoury odours created when the scents of sea and land combine. Beside him, Dulci tried unsuccessfully to look unaffected. He laughed and handed her his handkerchief. 'Apparently the docks you visit don't stink.'

Dulci tossed him a nasty look, but she didn't cringe. He gave her credit for that, but by God she'd stick out like a virgin in a whorehouse just by nature; her proud carriage, the haughty cock of her head, marked her as a lady of the highest reaches. He would need to address that immediately. Fine clothes, both his and hers, could be covered with cloaks. Manners could be masked. It was time to get to work.

'Come on, Dulci, we're going shopping.' The look on her face was priceless. There was something to be said for keeping Dulci Wycroft off balance.

'Here?' For all her bravado, she couldn't keep her eyes from wandering to the nearby building fronts, none of which looked like a suitable place for the purchase of haberdashery.

Jack reached for her hand. 'I've always imagined you'd be a fine actress if given the chance, m'dear.'

Jack steered them towards a ramshackle building full of light and noise in spite of the hour nearing three in the morning. Men spilled from the building, rough men, with gin on their breaths and bawdy women on their arms. Jack didn't want to go in. He was looking for a hanger-on, a gin whore on a side street near the establishment. He found one huddled in the alley. 'Perfect,' he muttered under his breath to no one in particular. But Dulci heard him.

'Depends on one's perception.'

'Stay here.' Jack left Dulci at the mouth of the alley. He'd have to work quickly to ensure no one stumbled across Dulci alone.

'Good evening.' Jack approached the doxy, dazzling her with a smile while trying to overlook the fetid odour of her and the stink of drink.

She was all immediate attention, able to recognise Jack as a fine gentleman even in a drunken stupor. She swayed her hips, a hand moving to undo the string of her blouse and show off the jiggling cleavage further. 'What can I do you for, guv'nor? You're a handsome one, aren't you? Perhaps I could do you for free?'

'You are kindness itself, good woman. I am only looking for a cloak. Might I buy yours?' Jack rolled a gleaming coin across his knuckles.

She eyed it enviously, already calculating the cloak's worth against the amount of gin she could purchase with such a coin. 'You can have the cloak. Are you sure there's nothing else you want?'

'The cloak reeks!' Dulci held the offending garment away from herself.

'Put it on. We've got another stop to make. This is nothing. We're just getting started.' Jack gave her an infuriating wink. The damnable man was enjoying this!

'You might not enjoy this so much when you hear what I have to say.' Dulci reluctantly shrugged into the cloak, understanding the necessity for it. 'A group of men in official-looking uniforms passed by. They weren't British. It sounded like they may have been speaking Spanish. They can't stop the ship from sailing, can they, Jack? They wouldn't have any authority over a British ship departing from a British port.'

Jack shook his head. 'No, they can't stop the ship. You're right, they have no jurisdiction over it.'

'But they could stop *us*,' Dulci replied quietly. She saw immediately what Jack had omitted from his answer. If there was a warrant to detain Jack over a diplomatic concern, Ortiz could certainly raise a big enough fuss to have him removed from the ship; legalities of such an action could be sorted out later if enough paper and permits were waved in a chaotic situation.

'They could stop *me*. They couldn't stop you. There's no reason to stop you, you're a free citizen able to come and go as you please.' Jack gripped her shoulders. 'This is no time for heroics, Dulci. Promise me you will get on that ship and stay on it no matter what.'

Dulci wanted to protest, but the truth was that she'd put Jack in more danger if she didn't get on the ship. It wasn't her nature to leave someone behind, but she would not risk another unnecessarily if she could do something to prevent it. 'I hope it doesn't come to that,' she said solemnly.

'It won't, I have a plan.' Jack's levity returned. 'We're going inside that brothel over there. Stay close to me and don't take that cloak off. We're going in through the kitchen entrance at the back but still, we've got enough chances to take tonight without adding another one.'

Ten minutes later, Jack thrust a bundle of clothes at her. 'Put these on. You can use the bathing screen over there. Be quick.'

'At least these don't smell like gin.' Dulci shot Jack a displeased look.

She could do this, she told herself. She was brave. She could fence, she could take her carriage alone to warehouses on the docks, she'd participated in countless feats of daring, she could certainly do this.

Dulci slid the cheap satiny gown over her head, her hands shaking as she did up the ribbon lacing in front. This was about real danger, this was not like her other dares. Nothing more than easily replaced guineas were at stake then. The dress fit well enough for its purpose although the bodice was tight and far too revealing, her breasts pushed up high to show all but their tips.

Dulci folded her clothes and stepped around the screen, determined to make light of the gown, but she didn't get a single joke past her lips. The sight of Jack transformed was enough to render her speechless.

A common sailor stood before her in ragged trousers and blowsy shirt that must have been white years ago. A patch covered one green eye, soot from the hearth shadowed his jaw and darkened his winter-wheat hair. She would not have recognised him if it hadn't been for the careless smile he gave her. She took a step towards him and wrinkled her nose. 'You smell terrible.'

'Ready for a night on the town with ole Jackie, me luv?' Jack replied, stuffing their clothes into a bag. He laid some coins on the kitchen table and thanked the cook who'd sent him upstairs for the garments.

'I liked you better when you were a gentleman,' the cook groused when Jack bent to give her a playful kiss.

'Me too,' Jack answered heartily, sweeping Dulci out into the street and closing the door behind him.

'Pink becomes you, Dulci. You look right fetching in that gown. Perhaps you can make it the latest rage.' Jack leaned on her, causing both of them to stumble like drunks.

'Don't tease me, Jack,' Dulci hissed. 'Anyone looking at me can practically see every inch of my "bountiful charms". And I'm cold.'

'All the better to see you, m'dear,' Jack drawled, pointedly fixing his gaze on the imprint of erect nipples beneath the cheap cloth.

Dulci swatted at him. 'I am in no mood for your sordid jokes.' She made to draw the gin-soaked cloak closer about her.

'Don't you dare, Dulci,' Jack cautioned. 'Your bountiful charms are going to be our salvation. If everyone's looking at them, they won't be thinking about us.'

'It's not funny, Jack.'

Jack winked with his one 'good eye'. 'Of course it is, there's something funny in everything.'

But neither of them was laughing when they approached the ship. With an hour to go before it sailed, the docks around the boat were bustling with activity. Men strode up and down the gangplank with last-minute supplies. Early morning vendors were preparing for a new day of business. Fishermen were beginning to come in from night fishing with the day's catch. Fishwives and doxies roamed among the men. Drunkards and whores stumbled home to sleep off excesses. Amid the bustle, Ortiz's men stood at attention, questioning those who went past. To Dulci's eye, going unnoticed looked daunting and nigh on impossible.

'I don't think anyone slips by them,' Dulci whispered to Jack.

'You're right about that. But we aren't going to slip, we're going to be noticed.' Jack wore a smug smile. If she hadn't seen the concern in his eyes earlier, she would have sworn Jack was having fun, all dressed up in smelly clothes and only a step ahead of disaster. There was no trace of his doubts now.

'What are we going to do?'

'We're just going to walk right up the gang-plank.'

Dulci frowned. 'Run. Walk. You come up with great plans.'

'They work,' Jack said simply, gathering her to him. 'Now, kiss me once for courage.'

He was still kissing her, sloppy and wide-mouthed, when they emerged into the street, tripping over one another, staggering over the hem of her gown, Jack's hands wandering lewdly over her breasts, a hand occasionally dipping to squeeze her buttocks. It was quite the sinful display and Dulci knew she looked well used by the time they made the base of the gangplank. A sailor bumped into them on the gangway and swore at Jack for drunken laziness. A few others shouted up ribald comments. Jack shouted back replies in a sailor's cant Dulci didn't pretend to understand. She played her part feverishly, return-ing Jack's kisses with wanton abandon, hanging on him with a whore's desperation, which wasn't too far from her own desperation, truth be told. Her heart hammered beneath her gown. At every step, she expected them to be stopped. Surely the guards would not let them pass unquestioned, but each step took them further from notice and closer to the safety of the ship.

Down the wharf, there was a commotion, a clatter of hooves and a frustrated cry. 'Don't look,' Jack commanded in her ear, nipping fiercely at her ear lobe. 'Ortiz has arrived. But no worries, we've made it.'

'Jack, is that you? You old dog!' A booming voice that Dulci was thankful no one on the wharves could hear greeted them at the top of the gangway.

'Andrew Merryweather, I cannot believe they've gone and made you captain!' Jack returned, pumping the outstretched hand. 'Finally, a bit of luck today.'

'I got the whole report. All is in order. There's a cabin ready for you and the king's own writ and introduction have arrived. You can rest easy for a while now.'

The captain's gaze moved in her direction and Dulci tilted her chin up haughtily, gathering her pride. What must the man think of her? Surely he'd seen that little display on the gangway.

'What do we have here, Jack? I wasn't told there'd be another, ah, guest.'

'This is Lady Dulcinea, the Earl of Stockport's sister,' Jack said meaningfully. 'She was implicated in a rather nasty abduction attempt, which has left me no choice but to bring her along. You know Stockport would never forgive me if I left his sister unprotected.'

'Brandon's sister, of course. It's been ages since I've seen him. We'll all have a lot of catching up to do.'

Dulci felt the captain look at her with new eyes, polite eyes, and she bristled. It shouldn't have mattered.

'Right now, we would like to change and I need to send a note to Brandon. He'll be worried sick if any of this reaches his ears before my news does.' Jack jerked his head to indicate Calisto Ortiz on the dockside. 'Perhaps we can cast off as soon as possible. We don't want him trying to board the ship.'

'We'll be off within the half-hour. I will start immediately,' Andrew promised, his humour high. 'What a voyage this will be with you on board, Jack.'

The cabin was a little larger than expected,

but still small—space was always at a premium on board any ship. But there was a wide bed, a table to function as a desk and a sea trunk bolted to the floor. Best of all, there was a little round window.

There would be arrangements to make in regards to that bed, Dulci thought, eyeing the cabin. If Jack thought he had *carte blanche* to it and her in it, he'd best think again. There were issues that had to be hammered out between them. But that was for later. Right now, all she wanted to do was put her own clothes on.

Dulci could feel the ship start to move beneath her feet as she finished dressing. Jack had already washed his face and hair and returned to his regular self. He'd given her a few minutes alone to complete her *toilette* in the cabin and now he was back, urging her to hurry, to come on deck as the ship slipped its moorings.

'The sun is coming up, Dulci,' he urged, grabbing her hand, nearly pulling her up the stairs to the deck.

They found a place at the railing, out of the way of scurrying crew members. Fresh air blew across their faces, the sky pinkened over head. Jack was behind her, his arms about her waist, pulling her against him. For the moment, that was all she needed.

'I can't believe we made it.' Dulci sighed.

'I can. It's been quite a night, hasn't it?' Jack was nipping at her ear again.'

'You're insatiable,' she scolded, but she didn't mind. Jack was safe. She was safe.

The boat slid down the Thames. It would be a while before they reached open sea, but they were underway. There was no going back.

Impulsively, Dulci raised her arm and waved to the shore.

'Who are you waving at?' Jack asked.

'Calisto Ortiz.' Dulci turned in Jack's arms. 'Just in case he's watching.'

Jack laughed. 'Well, in that case, let's make it good.' He swept her into a kiss, and Dulci gave herself over to it. Soon the enormity of what she'd done, of what Jack had done, would sink in. She might even be appalled. But that was for later.

Chapter Fourteen

Two weeks later

More sensual surroundings Jack could not have better designed: the turquoise of the ocean sparkled beneath the sun, the breeze warm and gentle in his face as he stood on deck, Dulci a few feet ahead of him, unaware of his presence.

He wanted to drink in the sight of her as she was right now in the moment—barefooted, her black hair loose down her back, the bright cotton of the Spanish skirt they'd purchased when they'd put into port fluttering playfully at her ankles. She wore a loose white peasant's blouse, also courtesy of the local market they'd frequented, showing off her curves quite nicely. Absolutely a vision of loveliness. In the days they'd been at sea, she'd won the hearts of a sceptical crew easily and Jack yearned for her with a never-ending intensity. But he'd played the gentleman and strung up a hammock in their shared cabin, unwilling to take advantage of the situation although it was becoming tortuous to do so. This next task he had to perform would be tortuous as well. There were five weeks at sea before them and they had to talk.

He moved forwards, his boots sounding on the wood planks of the deck. Dulci turned at the sound, a content smile on her lips. 'Isn't it beautiful out here, Jack?'

'It can be,' he answered, taking up a place at the rail with her. 'It's not so beautiful in the midst of a storm, although I know that's hard to believe on such a glorious day.' There was a hub of land fast approaching and Jack pointed to it. 'That's a nice deserted island; it has a sheltered bay. Andrew plans to put in there and take a day of relaxation. The beaches are sandy, the water is warm. We should reach it by this afternoon.' Dulci's face lit up at the prospect of some adventure.

'We should talk before then, Dulci. Perhaps we should have talked days ago,' Jack began.

Dulci didn't flinch. She kept her gaze fixed on the horizon and the approaching island. 'I think we're doing fine, Jack. The cabin is working out. You needn't worry overmuch about my modesty.'

'I don't want to talk about the cabin, Dulci. I want to talk about us, about you, really.' Jack tried again. 'Maybe I should begin with an apology. I've put you in a horrible position. I've ruined you quite thoroughly with this gambit of mine. Incomparables can't run off to sea with gentlemen even if they are viscounts.'

Dulci gave a slow nod of her head. 'I am well aware of that, Jack. But what's done is done and there's no going back. We didn't have much of a choice.' She gave a delicate shrug of her shoulders. 'I was tired of being an Incomparable anyway.'

Jack gave a snort of disbelief. 'You? Tired of ruling London? I don't believe it, Dulci.'

Dulci turned at his challenge and leaned back against the railing. 'Believe it, Jack. I've been tired of it for some time. Frankly, I'm surprised I lasted this long, but maybe I was afraid to let it go when it really came down to it. Being an Incomparable is difficult work: all the gowns, always looking fresh, and all those silly young men.' Dulci rolled her eyes. 'All those puppies needing their egos stroked and a woman to laugh at their jokes. It was fun at first, a great game. But then my friends I came out with began to marry and have their own families and I was more and more alone every year.'

'The races? The dares?' Jack prodded, fascinated by this look into Dulci's thoughts. 'Am I to believe they were all products of your boredom?'

'I like a challenge.' Dulci's eyes held a teasing glint. 'Maybe that's why I put up with you.'

'I *am* a good kisser,' Jack replied. He was already thinking about what he'd like to do once they reached the island. He'd stopped here once before with Andrew and knew of a private cove where he and Dulci could get up to all kinds of sinful decadence.

'That's all I expect, Jack. Good kisses.' Dulci was all seriousness now, returning to the topic at hand. 'I've been thinking these past weeks about my future. If British Guiana is promising, maybe I'll stay. I don't think London will ever be the same, at least not for me. But whatever I decide, it will be my decision. You don't have to be responsible for me, Jack. You don't owe me anything. You saved me in London and I won't repay you for that by trapping you into something you don't want.'

The island neared and Jack felt a sense of disappointment swamp him. She didn't want anything from him? Didn't expect anything beyond the immediate adventure to hand? That should fill him with elation, but it left him with a certain emptiness he couldn't explain. Did she think he wasn't capable of offering more? Such a thought wounded his male ego. But he had five weeks to change her mind, to show her he could offer more than sin and seduction. *If he wanted.*

Ah, that was the real question. Thankfully he had five weeks to sort that out too. Was he actually in love with Dulci Wycroft? Maybe it was finally time to name the amorphous emotion that had floated through him since the night she'd downed an intruder with a candlestick. If he could name it, then maybe he could decide what he ought to do about Dulci. Regardless of the answers yet to be revealed, the five weeks started today.

The ship sailed smoothly into the sheltered bay and the island lay before them, pristine and quiet. There was the sound of the anchor chain being lowered as preparations were made to go ashore. Dulci had been strangely silent during the process, her head averted, taking in the island to the exclusion of all else, fully lost in thought. Apparently, he wasn't the only one wrestling with the unnameable something between them. But unlike him, it appeared that Dulci had arrived at some sort of conclusion for the present.

Dulci boldly moved against him, her arms twining around his neck, the familiar scent of her filling his nostrils with her nearness. She reached up to whisper in his ear, 'Take me to the island, Jack.'

His body reacted fiercely and immediately at her invitation. His voice was hoarse with desire when he answered her, gruff and impatient with his need, 'Come on, then, Dulci, they're lowering the boats.'

Sin and seduction aside, all she wanted was to be with Jack. She'd decided at the rail that morning she was done with the awkward limbo their relationship hung in. She was thoroughly ruined in rumour, she might as well be thoroughly ruined in truth. Dulci Wycroft the Incomparable had tumbled from her pinnacle. It might as well be for a good reason and Jack was the best reason she could think of. Her body craved him and the wildness he unleashed in her. This passion would not last for ever. Jack was not capable of that, had never professed to be. But she would take what she could have and be satisfied with it. Sharing close quarters with Jack had rendered her entirely aroused in a most unladylike way. The island seemed to provide a perfect antidote for what ailed her.

The island was any woman's romantic paradise. She'd not bothered with shoes when they'd climbed on a boat to row ashore and now her feet sank into the pleasant warmth of the sand as Jack led her apart from the group, saying only, 'I know a spot.'

Dulci was all too happy to let Jack take her hand and lead her around the headland of the island, the ocean waves lapping occasionally at their feet. Jack carried his shoes in his other hand, having stopped to take them off and roll up his trouser legs once they were out of sight.

They rounded a corner and out of nowhere the private cove Jack sought appeared. Dulci gasped in delight. On their left was the aquamarine ocean, placidly rushing towards the shore. On their right against the island wall set back from the beach was a waterfall splashing into a pool of clear water. Between the beach and the falls was an expanse of white sand, warm and clean and entirely theirs.

'This is the most beautiful place on earth,' Dulci breathed in awe. 'What shall we do first?' The afternoon stretched out like a blissful eternity before her.

'This,' Jack whispered, capturing her mouth in a full, passionate kiss that resonated to the core of her. His hands were on her, undressing her until her body was gloriously naked to the breeze and the sun, the decadence of what they were about to do a potent aphrodisiac that spurred her on, her hands anxious to strip him.

His arousal was unyielding against her bare skin and the moment he was freed, he took her to the sand, driving into her hard and fast until she screamed out in unmitigated pleasure, the sand warm against her back, Jack hard and deep inside her, the rhythm of the ocean adding its cadence to their love-making. Dulci doubted nothing in her life would ever compare to that single moment when Jack shattered with her and the ocean drowned the sound of their cries.

The glories of the afternoon were not done. When they could stand, they swam in the ocean, letting the warm waves lift their bodies and carry them towards shore. It was an erotic luxury to spend the day utterly naked, to let the elements touch her, to feel Jack's unabashed gaze upon her, and to look her fill of him. Jack's nude body was a wonder. He carried his nakedness effortlessly and without shame, a veritable wonder of the world. She said as much and Jack laughed, a seductive smile on his lips as he promised to show her another wonder of the forbidden world.

'This is our Eden today,' he whispered, taking her down to the sand. 'Today we eat from all the trees of the garden.'

This time the love-making was a languid perusal, as Jack worshipped her with his hands and she thought she'd weep from the beauty of it. Afterwards, he traced her footprints in the sand. 'I didn't know life could be like this. I guessed, I wondered, but I didn't know until today,' Dulci murmured. The sky above her was losing its afternoon brightness, the sun moving slowly towards the horizon. The idyll was nearly over. 'It seems as though society is cheating us of all of the things that matter with its rules and strictures.'

Jack stretched out beside her, running a hand up the length of her leg. 'Perfect days are rare gems indeed. When I was growing up, I lived for the sun because that meant Brandon and I could romp the meadows without anyone shouting for us. Those were perfect days, away from the house and all its ill humours.' He smiled briefly at Dulci, but she could see the emotions flickering behind his eyes. She knew about his dismal home life. Brandon had talked of it on occasion. But Jack had never shared anything of his youth with her before and such a disclosure touched her.

'Was it bad?' she coaxed gently.

'It wasn't bad so much as it was apathetic.' Jack took a finger and drew a gentle line down her torso to her belly. 'No one cared for anyone. It was probably a blessing to be ignored most of the time.' Jack shrugged. 'I had Brandon. His friendship made up for a lot in those days.' He paused.

Dulci could read his thoughts. She covered Jack's hand with her own where it lay warm on her belly. 'Don't feel guilty, Jack. Brandon will understand, once Nora calms him down, of course. Besides, this has to be about us, about our choices.' Dulci stood up. She brushed at the sand that clung to her legs. The waterfall caught her eye. 'Is that waterfall fresh water?'

'Yes.' A slow grin took Jack's face. 'What are you thinking?'

Dulci tossed her ocean-soaked hair and gave him a coy smile. 'I'm thinking you need a bath.'

Dulci and Jack stood beneath the falls, letting the cool fresh water sluice over their sand-caked bodies, the grit of the beach and the salt of the ocean washing away. Her body tingled with an awareness of itself, life coursing through her at the sensation. Jack helped her with her hair, freeing it from dried sand, his fingers combing through the thick tresses. 'I'll brush it for you later tonight,' he promised under the roar of the falls and Dulci could imagine how that would go with a little tremor of anticipation.

The basin of the falls was deep enough for a little swimming, the bottom of the clear pool never too far from their feet and they swam out from the waterfall when they were clean, enjoying the quiet pool in the setting sun.

Jack had his arms about her, his hands cupping her breasts in the last rays of the day. 'Have you ever made love in water before?' His voice was husky with need.

'I hope that's a rhetorical question,' Dulci teased. 'You know I haven't, Jack.'

'Then you should. It is an experience not to be

missed,' Jack murmured hotly against her neck, his member pushing at her buttocks.

'Show me.' Dulci leaned her head back against his shoulder.

'You'll have to turn around.' Jack turned her, and lifted her, her legs wrapped about him of their own volition. Her body knew what to do. She could see his eyes darkened with passion as he entered her. There was an indefinable intimate quality to their last joining, face to face, their bodies so tightly joined. Dulci clung to him as their passion crested and Jack filled her.

She could have stayed on that island for ever, Dulci thought. But all too soon the lantern signalled from the ship and it was time to head back. She dressed in her cotton blouse and skirt and Jack held out his hand to lead her back across the sand.

The sun had fallen out of the sky by the time they reached the rowboat and the sand had turned colder in its absence. As they neared the rowboat and the lanterns of the ship beyond it in the bay, Dulci's mind was made up. She'd wasted two weeks already grappling with her thoughts. She'd made up her mind. For the next five weeks, she'd be his, the future be damned.

Jack handed her into the rowboat and she leaned near his ear, whispering, 'Jack, take down your hammock.'

Chapter Fifteen

Dulci leaned on the ship's railing, eyes fixed unswervingly on the growing shoreline in front of her. After seven weeks, they were here. Georgetown, capital of British Guiana, loomed ever closer in the early morning. They would not dock for a while yet. But she could not wait. She was admittedly nervous. For seven weeks, the ship had been home. Cocooned in the isolated society of a ship at sea, she'd been able to avoid thinking about what came next.

The daily life of surviving at sea had been enough to worry over. When there had been moments of tranquillity, she and Jack had seized them in celebration of life. They had swum in warm waters when the ship had put in at an island. They had lazed together on deck in the sun, the sea calm after a two-day summer storm had kept the ship roiling. Those times had been too precious to interrupt with 'what ifs' and 'whens'. If she'd learned anything on the journey it was the very precariousness of life. By comparison, she could see now how many petty assumptions proved the foundation of her life in London, how many things she took for granted. It was embarrassing to note how trivial her life had been. In the last seven weeks, she'd climbed rigging, she'd swum in the sea, she'd worked side by side with men to save the ship. She'd done far more in seven weeks than she'd done in the previous twenty-six years.

Jack had been there to encourage her, not always with praise—in fact, very seldom with praise, more often with a dare or well-aimed quip about her capabilities. And she knew the truth. For all her independence, she'd relied on him. Not in obvious, clinging female ways, but in mental ways. She recognised he was her only link between the old world she'd left behind and the new world about to open up. Colonial living was both a blessing and a curse. A blessing because society was less established, people had the latitude to be the making of themselves through hard work. Those of modest social status who would not be received in the higher reaches of London society were important arbiters of social norms in the colonies.

But there were still expectations. A single woman travelling alone with a man was still a sinner. Everyone would think she was Jack's mistress and while it wouldn't matter as much as it mattered in London, it mattered enough to make Dulci wonder what would become of her here. On board ship, there'd been activity aplenty and the isolation of being at sea to dull the sharp reality of what she'd done. This was no small dare done under the cover of dark in Richmond. The idea that she might have left London and the life of an Incomparable behind for good carried a certain uneasy thrill.

Not all of her thoughts at the railing were focused on the enormity of what she'd done. She also thought too of what lay ahead. She was excited about the prospect of seeing Georgetown, of their quest to track down the map-maker Ortiz had bribed and to venture out into the country-side with Jack's own mission to map an accurate border for the king. Jack had mentioned they'd encounter the indigenous tribes on their journey and she was looking forward to seeing their lives, their tools up close. The mapping journey would be an enormous opportunity for her.

She'd always believed she craved adventure. Always thought she'd be rather good at the life of an adventuress. Now was her chance.

Dulci felt someone come up behind her. Jack. He took up a place at the railing next to her, dressed in his London clothes, as she thought of them now. He'd worn the loose trousers of a seaman and a few borrowed shirts of the captain's for most of the voyage. Today, he was turned out in high form. She was too for that matter in her dark-blue carriage ensemble. She'd put the outfit away after their quick stop in Spain where she'd purchased full cotton skirts at coastal market. The confines of her garments felt strange and foreign after weeks of freedom.

'It seems an age since I climbed out the window with you, Jack.'

'Would you rather I had left you to take your chances with Ortiz?'

'Do you think we're through with him, Jack?' Dulci ventured.

'I don't know. It will depend on how desperate his circumstances are. But even if he follows us, it will take him some time. It's no easy task to jump on board a ship at whim. He'll have arrangements that will need making and plenty of explanations.' Jack pointed to the nearing shore and changed the subject.

'Look, the seawall is coming into view.' Dulci's gaze followed the direction of his hand.

'The city is actually built below the level of the sea. There's a very real danger of flooding, so centuries ago when the Dutch owned the territory, they put in a system of streets with canals and sluices to protect against high-tide flooding. It's fairly ingenious.'

'Like Venice, only with better plumbing,' Dulci said offhandedly although she didn't really know. She'd never been to Venice, only read about it.

Jack didn't hold up his end of the conversation and an awkward silence descended in the gap of his lapse. In the weeks of their haphazard association, they'd tacitly agreed not to discuss the future, any future. And now, they were forced to it, forced to admit they were bound to one another. He'd brought her here. He was the only person in this half of the world she knew for the time being.

'We should discuss the particulars of our situation,' Jack began, sounding terribly officious and very much like the viscount, a persona he hadn't donned for weeks. 'We'll be staying with the governor. I have not met him personally. He didn't take over the position until two years ago. But his reputation precedes him. He is well liked.' Jack flashed her a wry grin. 'You will like him as well. He's a great supporter of freedom and has a specific issue in advancing the rights of female slaves.'

'He doesn't know we're coming,' Dulci put in. 'How could he know to expect us?' It seemed highly uncivilised to simply show up on the man's doorstep.

Jack shrugged. 'No matter, I have an introduction from the king. Carmichael-Smythe will be glad to accommodate us. It's how things are done here. Time is not the precise commodity it is in London. Here, we know within a given week what ships should arrive. But we can not tell the exact day or hour. Besides, surprise arrivals spice up a rather dull social calendar in these parts.'

'We'll be quite the surprise.'

'Yes, as to that. I've given much thought to our personal circumstances. You shall be Lady Dulcinea, the sister of my good friend the earl, a woman who is interested in the region's culture. Perhaps we could even say you are looking into the potential for investment on your brother's behalf since he is home with the birth of a new son.'

'That sounds so proper.'

'It needs to be, Dulci. You will go back to London and you will need every thread of decency you can collect to keep your reputation intact.'

It was on the tip of her tongue to ask who he'd be. While she was busy fabricating a facsimile of the blue-stocking spinster, what would he be doing? Would he be the strong, shirtless sailor she'd seen climbing the rigging in a storm to save the main mast? Would he be the shrewd diplomat who'd avoided scandal and routed Ortiz's accusations with the sharp acuity of his mind? Would he be the rakish viscount who charmed women nightly in London's ballrooms, England's most whispered-about lover? Would he be the friend she told secrets to in the dark of their little cabin? Would he be the rugged explorer who'd journeyed beside Schomburgk in Anegada?

With Jack it was hard to know. It was what made him an exciting lover. Jack's bid to establish her as a respectable woman seemed to rule out the possibility of experiencing any of that further though. His next words confirmed it.

'I'll be absent a good portion of most days and I'll be preparing for a trek into the interior for the mapping. Of course, that will take me out of Georgetown for several weeks.'

'I'll be fine, Jack. I know how to amuse myself and I'll have work of my own.' It was all true. Dulci had no intentions of letting this once-in-a-lifetime experience go to waste and if Jack was going into the interior without her, he'd find he was sorely mistaken. Still, she felt a small wave of abandonment sweep her. Jack had discharged his duty, acted as nobly as the situation allowed and now he was ready to move on to the other action items on his list.

Jack wouldn't want her to cling, to beg him not to desert her. Of course he wasn't deserting her. He'd seen to all of her needs; she had a fine place to stay, there would be decent clothes and there would be funds at her disposal. Dulci knew too that he'd taken pains to secure her own social success in Georgetown. The governor and his wife would not let a house guest languish in isolation. Dulci stiffened her spine and stood a little straighter. She'd show Jack she didn't need to cling to him in the least bit. Georgetown or London, she'd show him she could be an Incomparable anywhere.

An hour later as their carriage rolled towards Water Street, Dulci wondered if she'd been precipitous. From the ship, Georgetown had looked placid, organised, far more civilised than it was after one disembarked. In reality, Georgetown was a whole new world. She'd never seen so many dark-skinned persons in one place or so many scantily clothed people. Although they might have the right of it, Dulci admitted privately to herself. The climate was mild and, while it wasn't scorchingly hot, the weather wasn't made for wearing her heavy carriage dress with its linen blouse, requisite jacket and stock. Yet Jack sat beside her in equally warm clothing without giving off a sign of discomfort.

The streets were dirt. Nothing was paved, but the Parliament building offered a sense of 'civilisation' with its classical pillars, which Jack informed her had been built in 1833 and was a relatively new addition to the town. Past the building, they veered west on to Water Street, passing what proved to be a bustling market centre. Dulci distracted her mind from the heat by staring at the wide variety of goods on display and fruits she'd never seen; clothing, even jewellery, was for sale in the odd market.

'That's Stabroek market,' Jack supplied. 'You can find anything from vegetables to gold in that market. It's the commercial hub of the city. It's fascinating, but don't go alone. It's not exactly Bond Street.'

If she had a parasol to hand she would have raised it with a haughty air and effectively turned her head against Jack's ridiculous comment. One minute he was making it clear that he was leaving her to her own devices as soon as he could possibly manage it, the other he was playing the protective escort, as if he'd be around to arrange field trips to the market for her.

She didn't have a parasol. She was left only with the tool of a crisp response. 'Don't worry, Jack. I'm not a naïve innocent abroad. You needn't be concerned that I'll act irrationally.'

'It's precisely because you're not a naïve innocent that I am worried.' Jack leaned close to her ear to be heard above the din of the marketplace, making her shiver in spite of the heat. 'Those of us who are capable sometimes overestimate our abilities. Such an assumption can lead to unfortunate situations.'

'I am sure there's a compliment in there somewhere,' Dulci replied curtly, keeping her eyes straight ahead, fixed on the driver's back, giving away no sign of her annoyance. 'You will have to decide, you know. You can't have it both ways—my erstwhile protector one minute and the disappearing viscount the next, who is so eager to leave me to my own devices. When you've decided, let me know.'

Her aplomb might have been more effective if the carriage hadn't hit a bump in the road at that moment, kicking up a cloud of dust. Dulci inelegantly sucked in a breath of dusty air and choked.

Jack laughed and handed her a handkerchief. 'Maybe you're the one who needs to decide. Seems like you just might need both.'

The carriage rounded a bend in the road and laboured up a rise to a magnificent home, reminiscent of an English estate with its round drive and columned entrance. There'd been an effort to cultivate a lawn and to garden the grounds. Dulci would never admit it to Jack on principle, but the home looked like an oasis full of the comforts she'd so recently took for granted. There might even be a full tub for bathing. That would be absolutely heaven.

Jack helped her down and she self-consciously reached a hand to her hair in a last effort at a *toilette*. 'You look fine.'

There he went again, changing on her. The sharp tones of their little quarrel in the carriage had given way to the low-toned reassurance of a trusted friend.

Dulci looked up at the house and favoured Jack with a smile. 'You can say I'm right any time you'd like.'

'Right about what? It's hard to tell, Dulci, you like to be right about so many things. A man needs a bigger clue.'

Dulci elbowed Jack playfully in the ribs. 'About walking out of my house and going halfway around the world with nothing but the clothes on our backs. We made it.'

Jack grinned, his eyes sparkling with his special brand of mischief. 'I'm sure there's a compliment in there somewhere, Lady Dulcinea.'

Dulci winked. 'There is.'

The sea stretched grey and endless from the deck of the ship, so far from land there weren't even any seagulls to break the sound of the waves. Wind filled the sails, but nothing could move Calisto Ortiz's boat fast enough for him. By his calculations, Wainsbridge would be in British Guiana by now and he was still two weeks out if all luck held.

There'd been no choice but to follow Wainsbridge. Vargas had raked him over the proverbial coals after news had come regarding Wainsbridge's departure and with the king's sanction to do so. Vargas had been furious about Ortiz's accusations in the first place. When Gladstone had announced Wainsbridge had left to investigate the claims first hand with the king's approval, Vargas had wanted to strangle him, because no one would set out across the ocean with the king's approval if they're wrong or guilty.

What was worse was that Ortiz suspected Wainsbridge wasn't going solely for the honour of his country at the negotiating table, or even to clear his own name. Wainsbridge was going for the purpose of ruining him. Wainsbridge would find that map-maker and then all would be irrevocably linked back to him. The only advantage he had over Wainsbridge now was that he knew where to find the map-maker. He could go straight to the man, whereas Wainsbridge would have to make enquiries. Ortiz hoped it would be enough to slow Wainsbridge down and even the distance between the two weeks that separated them.

Too much was at stake for Wainsbridge to ever see London again. If Dulcinea Wycroft had actually fled with him, all the better. No one knew where she'd disappeared to, but she was most assuredly missing from London. Ortiz was an expert at turning misfortune into opportunity. He'd hoped to use her as a lure, as blackmail to keep Wainsbridge in London, but he'd been too slow by minutes. Here, she could serve the same purpose. Wainsbridge had thought to save her, but in truth the man had flung her out of the pan and into the fire.

Ortiz stared out over the horizon as if he could make land appear all that much faster. He was coming for the man who'd wronged him and hell was coming with him.

Chapter Sixteen

Dulci proved to be absolutely charming. The Carmichael-Smythes adored her, the governor's wife making every effort to incorporate her into the female society of town. She took Dulci to tea with the rector of St Andrew's wife, she took Dulci to the embroidery circle, ladies' political and charity meetings. It certainly helped that Dulci was newly come from London and an earl's sister, but Jack knew the women would have loved her anyway. She was vivacious, friendly to all she met, and she glowed with the climate of her new circumstances.

Through the window of the second-floor library, Jack watched Dulci and Lady Carmichael-Smythe pile into the open carriage, chatting amiably as they set off to run errands for the welcoming ball to be held in a few days' time. Dulci was wearing a blue gown trimmed in simple lace, a wide straw hat with a matching ribbon, and sporting a new sprinkle of freckles across the bridge of her nose. There seemed to be no hat brim wide enough to adequately shelter Dulci's face from the tropical sun. But she didn't mind. The colour agreed with her. The ladies had showed her how to mix a lotion to protect her skin from burning and Lady Carmichael-Smythe plied her endlessly with hats. Jack thought Dulci had never looked finer.

The carriage pulled out of the drive and Dulci hazarded a glance up towards the window. She shielded her eyes against the bright sun. He fancied for a moment that she sensed his presence before she turned back to Lady Carmichael-Smythe.

Jack stared after the departing carriage. It seemed he was doing a lot of watching from afar these days. Dulci was busy, caught up in the little social whirl of Georgetown and busy with her work. The governor had eagerly introduced her to a scientist staying in town between expeditions who had knowledge of the tribes and she spent her free afternoons visiting with him in the governor's home, taking copious notes under the watchful, motherly eye of Lady Carmichael-Smythe.

The good lady's motherly eye extended to all aspects of Dulci's conduct. The diplomatic woman never expressed regret over Dulci's arrival in the presence of a single male, but the woman made sure such a lapse would not occur again on her watch. The woman, whose own son was grown and back in England, took great efforts to keep Dulci's reputation pristine. Dulci's chambers were in the opposite wing of the gubernatorial mansion by no mistake.

There was no chance of sneaking in and out of her rooms undetected. Not that he'd intended to engage in such behaviour in their host's house, but he'd never been much good at keeping honourable intentions when Dulci was around. Breaking those rules seemed more and more unlikely and Jack found that he was inexplicably jealous as time wore on.

Jealous of Dulci and the transition she'd made into this new place. If the transition had been difficult, she gave no outer signs of it. Looking at her, one would never imagine a few months ago she'd aspired to settings far grander than the ones she now found herself in, or that she'd worn gowns far more exquisite than the ones she wore now with the same personal elegance. In short, she looked as if she belonged. Worse, she *acted* as if she belonged. In honesty, Jack had to admit she more than acted, she *did* belong and that was the source of his jealousy.

She didn't need him.

He'd rather thought she would. She was halfway across the world. She knew no one. Anyone else, man or woman, would have been grateful for his mentorship. But Dulci had not. From the moment Lady Carmichael-Smythe had whisked her upstairs for a hot bath and a look through her wardrobe for suitable gowns, Dulci had not needed him. It begged the question if she ever had. He conveniently chose to ignore that he'd planned to put distance between them on purpose for her protection. But it wasn't working.

He'd wanted Dulci to need him, wanted her to recognise him as someone more than her erstwhile lover, someone more than a foil for her wit and eccentricities, a partner in occasional wildness. But Dulci defied all logic.

He should be thankful. He had work to do, evidenced by the papers piled on his desk. Luck was with him. Schomburgk was in town, preparing for a botanical expedition. He'd had a letter from the man today, wanting to renew their acquaintance. Jack knew all he had to do was ask and Schomburgk would gladly take him on and assist in the mapping portion of his mission. It was all working out just as he'd outlined to Dulci their last morning on board ship.

Jack sifted through the items on his desk. Along with the note from Schomburgk there were replies to his enquiries about the map-maker who might have drawn up Ortiz's map. Soon it would be time to go and meet people, to make the mapping journey, time to leave Dulci. No matter what she thought or imagined, the interior was no place for a woman, or for some men. The swarms of midges, the humid climate, the mosquitoes, made it intolerable for all but the most intrepid. Dulci would hardly miss him when he went and perhaps, thanks to all the diversions she'd acquired, she wouldn't protest his going without her.

Jack knew he should be thankful. Dulci wasn't clinging to him, impeding him from achieving his goals, slowing him down. She was well adjusted and off on her own sort of adventures. What was wrong with him that he wished she wasn't? He might privately confess to himself that he'd fallen in love. But he could not declare those sentiments until the mission was complete and he knew

Dulci was safe. Right now, association with him risked putting her in danger if Ortiz followed them.

Oh, he didn't want to change Dulci into a simpering pattern card of English womanhood. He liked Dulci exactly as she was. It was her very character that drew him to her. But he'd like to know, just once, where he stood with her. Of course, that raised a whole host of other concerns that he didn't want to examine too closely. The foremost being, why did he care about where he stood with Dulci? Followed by, what would happen if she didn't hold him in any great regard? Could he stand the truth if the truth was she enjoyed him as a lover and nothing more? In the past he would have found the unchanging nature of such an association reassuring.

Or, his conscience prompted, did he want a different answer? Was the old answer no longer reassuring? What if she felt something more? What would happen if she said she was in love with him?

Was that the answer he wanted? It shook Jack to his core. He stared blankly at the papers in front of him. That *was* the answer he wanted. He could not doubt he was in love with her, or continue perhaps to ignore that reality, pushing it to the back of his mind. One only wanted someone to love them, if he loved them in return. Jack had to be careful here. Unrequited love was for fools and he preferred to learn from their mistakes instead of making his own, especially in a world where he'd had to prove himself to those who felt only those with titles were worth any regard.

There were those like Gladstone who'd never truly accept him. There were others who accepted him only on the grounds that he was a novelty to include in their menagerie. Jack hadn't really cared about their opinions. They meant little enough. But he did care about Dulci's opinion, which seemed to remain unaltered, although there were times when he wondered if her regard was all it seemed, that perhaps he'd underestimated her feelings. A woman could not love as she did and emerge emotionally un-changed. Jack knew women and he knew Dulci.

It was on these assumptions he would bet this next roll of the dice. It was clear she was not going to declare her feelings. If he wanted to know where he stood with her, he would have to ask her. The ball in his honour would take place in a few days prior to his intended departure with Schomburgk. Perhaps it would provide the perfect setting for such a disclosure. If the disclosure was positive, he could leave her in Georgetown with plans to make. If the disclosure was negative, he'd leave her with time and distance, a chance for both of them to manage their embarrassment over the awkwardness that would remain. It would enable them to pick up with a thread of normalcy when he returned.

Jack fiddled with a quill, laughing at himself planning his strategy like a general amassing an army for a frontal attack. Of all the frightening things he'd faced in his life, love topped the list.

'These ribbons will look delightful with your dress for the ball.' Lady Carmichael-Smythe held up a length of yellow ribbon the shade of spring daffodils. 'Another thing we can cross off our list,' she said happily, putting the ribbons in Dulci's already full shopping basket. 'There's nothing like bright ribbons to turn a man's head.' She shot Dulci a sly look as they moved on to another market stall. 'Not that the viscount needs to have his head turned, my dear. It's already full-pivot in your direction.'

'He is merely attentive.' Dulci wrinkled her nose at the meat stand they passed. She would never get over the odd variety of goods sold next to each other in this marketplace. Jewellery sold next to fish, cloth sold next to vegetables. Anything and everything was on display here. No wonder people often called it the bizarre bazaar.

'Of course he is, you are his responsibility,' she pressed. 'I think you're very brave to come all this way for the sake of your studies and your brother's business interests.' She peered at Dulci from under the brim of her hat. 'It's easier to be brave when there's a handsome face at stake, don't you think?'

Dulci took a studied interest in a bolt of fabric at the next booth, hoping to avoid any direct discussion of Jack. 'The viscount has been my escort across the sea. Beyond that, we have no claim upon each other outside of his friendship with my brother.' Dulci hoped to end any further enquiry.

Nothing was going as she hoped with Jack. Her plan to show him how successful she could be here hadn't reaped the desired results. The more she dazzled, the more he withdrew. He wasn't supposed to withdraw. He was supposed to *pursue*. Any other man in her court would have run himself ragged behind her. But Jack was not entranced with her and she doubted daffodil-coloured ribbons would change that. Jack had his work and his king and he'd never made any pretences to offering her more than his body on occasion. She was a practical woman by nature, and she knew the merits of something being better than nothing.

'The blue would look pretty with your eyes.' Lady Carmichael-Smythe held up a bolt of cloth. 'This would make into a nice afternoon gown. Perhaps a lovely dress and a little encouragement would change things with the viscount. I cannot believe he is indifferent to you. Long journeys have a way of changing one's perceptions. What was once taken for granted often becomes quite dear in such circumstances.' Her eyes sparked with romantic mischief.

'It may be that I do not wish things to change between myself and the viscount.' Dulci teased, the older woman's good humour infectious in spite of her denials.

'He is the most handsome man to step foot in the colony for ages...' Lady Carmichael-Smythe laughed '...excepting my dear James, that is. Everyone will line up to dance with him at the ball.'

Dulci turned deadly sombre for a moment, schooling her features in the most serious expression she could master, ready to have a little fun with her hostess. She leaned forwards confidentially and whispered in Lady Carmichael-Smythe's ear, 'It's a good thing Wainsbridge is so handsome. His looks make up for his lack of skill on the dance floor. His dancing is deplorable.'

Lady Carmichael-Smythe looked genuinely horrified by her revelation. 'Oh dear, I never would have expected...' she stuttered. 'It will be such a disappointment...'

Dulci's frown dissolved. 'Do not worry, he dances divinely.' She laughed. 'But the look on your face was worth guineas.'

Lady Carmichael-Smythe laughed, sharing in the joke. 'You're terrible to tease me. A hostess must take these things seriously. We can't have our guest of honour made a laughingstock.' Her eyes twinkled and she linked her arm through Dulci's as they made their way out of the market. 'You know what they say, dear. You can tell a man's prowess in the bedroom from the way he dances.'

I know, Dulci thought. Too bad there wasn't a similarly simple indicator of his heart. Instead,

Dulci smiled back and said, 'And your James? He's a good dancer?'

The woman grinned broadly. 'Oh, yes, the best.'

The carriage ride home was filled with chatter about the ball, most of it originating with Lady Carmichael-Smythe. Dulci made the right noises at the right times, but the entirety of her thoughts were elsewhere. She did understand that Jack had an ambitious agenda and time was of the essence. The faster he could accomplish his goals and get himself or the information back to England, the better it would be. Still, she had not anticipated being so thoroughly cast off, so obviously shut out.

Jack would leave in the mornings for meetings. He would spend the heat of the afternoon in the study beneath the punkah fan writing letter after letter and making list after list.

She had lists, too, but hers were of balls. His lists were for the inevitable expedition he would take to make William's map; an expedition that would exclude her if she didn't do something about it soon. For all her social outings and her work with her artefacts, she was lonely and not just any company would do. She was lonely for

Jack. They'd gone from the intimacy of daily proximity on board ship to virtual separation in the governor's mansion. She craved a touch, a kiss, a stolen moment in an alcove.

The carriage turned into the drive and a servant met them on the steps, whispering a hurried message to Lady Carmichael-Smythe. 'For dinner tonight?' she breathed in excitement. 'Tell Cook we'll manage something.'

'What is it?'

An excited hand fluttered to Lady Carmichael-Smythe's breast. 'We're to have a guest for dinner, my dear. Robert Schomburgk is to dine with us tonight.'

Dulci met the announcement with part-dismay and part-anticipation. In her ruminations on the way home, she'd half-thought of trying to get Jack alone. A supper guest would preclude any efforts in that regard. Surely sneaking off for a tryst in the alcove was considered bad form even in the colonies. But to talk with a man who'd seen so much of the southern Americas was an incredible opportunity. This would mean much for her research.

Dulci dressed carefully for dinner from her selection of borrowed and altered gowns Lady

Carmichael-Smythe had so generously provided. She settled on a gown of sea-foam green with a tight bodice and a plunging neckline delicately accompanied by a white lace fichu that gave the illusion of modesty, just in case opportunities for something other than research arose. One always had to go prepared.

Chapter Seventeen

Robert Schomburgk's moderate good looks were greatly enhanced by his excitement for his subject, Dulci decided over the soup course. Dinner was proving to be eminently enjoyable. Originally, she'd begrudged the presence of a dinner guest as a barrier to Jack. But Schomburgk was an entertaining addition to the table. Together, he and Jack regaled them all with tales of their Anegada expedition.

'Jack and I were as brown as natives and smelled worse than hogs when we got back after spending a month smeared with that paste.'

Jack raised his glass across the table from Schomburgk. 'Thanks to the paste we survived. Without it, we would have been eaten alive.'

'To the paste, disgusting as it was.' Schomburgk

joined him in making a great show of drinking their toast.

Schomburgk turned to her. 'All joking aside, Lady Dulcinea, Jack saved my life on more than one occasion. It's one thing to tell stories in hindsight, full of high spirits. It's another to remember the moments of true desperation. I came down with a fever. I thought I was done for. I've never felt so weak, so helpless. I couldn't move a single muscle in my body to save myself. I was delirious and out of my mind. But Jack carried me to safety and nursed me through the fever at great risk to himself. Those are the less glorious moments of an explorer's life.'

Jack. Schomburgk had used Jack's given name all night. They must be fast friends indeed, no casual acquaintance. Dulci could name two people in England who called him Jack. Dulci sipped her wine, a rich excellent red from France, and studied the two gentlemen: Schomburgk lean and slender to the point of emaciation from his travails in foreign lands, his skin tanned to a leathery consistency; Jack the epitome of the perfectly groomed gentleman, his golden hair shining beneath the chandelier.

It was hard to picture Jack muddy, covered in the

paste they described and stinking, carrying Schomburgk through the forest to safety. And yet the image was not surprising. He'd come for her against Ortiz, come to her rescue when it could have jeopardised his chance to sail and clear his name from the slander Ortiz heaped on it. He'd stood by her brother, Brandon, when he was in need of a stalwart friend even unto the point of challenging the law. Schomburgk's story illuminated for her something that she had heretofore overlooked: Jack took great risks where his friends were concerned, where his love was concerned.

Jack caught her staring, a small secret smile quirking his lips. He reached for his wine glass. He nodded his head in her direction in the most minute of gestures as if to say he knew precisely what she was thinking and it was about him.

Arrogant man! But two could play this seductive, clandestine game. Dulci averted her gaze in feigned innocence, her hand alternately plucking and smoothing the white lace fichu at her bodice in a self-conscious gesture of modest reticence.

She felt Jack's eyes on her from across the table, but it was Schomburgk beside her who held her attention. 'I understand you've met the

Arawak people during your travels. I'm writing an article about them in hopes of seeing it published with the Royal Geographic Society.'

Schomburgk's eyes lit up at her show of genuine interest. 'I'm fascinated by their lifestyle and I am worried about that lifestyle as well. I fear that European colonisation will pose a grave threat to their future. Their culture is so different that adopting new ways of living will prove to be too foreign.'

When Dulci showed continued interest, he went on. 'The most immediate threat comes in the form of land ownership. Each tribe is ruled by a *cacique* and he is advised by *nitayanos*, his nobles. These elders are the ones who hold the knowledge about the tribe's boundaries and are the memory of the tribe. They're the ones who know if any agreements have been made with other tribes, they negotiate new treaties and are the memory keepers of tribal law.'

Schomburgk shook his head. 'Nothing is written down. All law, all rules, survive simply by memory. The concept of a written contract or a map is so entirely outside the scope of the Arawak imagining that it makes understanding their significance impossible.'

Dulci nodded, the ramifications of how an oral tradition would interact with European traditions that relied heavily on written word clear. 'They will be lost.'

'I very much fear it,' Schomburgk averred.

'Robert is a great advocate for the rights of indigenous people. His efforts are to be commended,' Governor Carmichael-Smythe voiced from the head of the table, his friendly affection for their guest obvious. Like Robert Schomburgk, Governor Carmichael-Smythe was also lauded by many for his efforts in the fair treatment and emancipation of the slaves in his colonies.

Dulci was about to comment on the Arawak when a stockinged foot slipped up her skirt, nuzzling her ankle bone with delicious, tickling strokes. It was terribly difficult to concentrate and she had to cede the conversation to others. She shot Jack a scolding look under cover of servants serving up the fish course.

Jack answered with an innocent look of his own as if to say he hadn't a clue what he'd done to distress her while his foot moved up her leg. 'Ah, Atlantic salmon,' Jack exclaimed benignly over the course. 'Robert, when you come to

England, we must go fishing together. There's a river I know that serves up the best trout.' Jack shot a glance at Dulci. 'Tickling trout is an enjoyable pastime, and a delicious one too. Do you enjoy tickling, Lady Dulcinea?' He was all conversational innocence while his foot made naughty overtures beneath her skirts.

'On occasion,' Dulci answered, her eyes meeting Jack's evenly, a little smile playing on her lips. She kicked off her slipper under the table and went on the offensive, nudging Jack's foot away while she ran her toes the length of his calf.

'Perhaps you prefer to be the tickler,' Jack remarked.

Lady Carmichael-Smythe coughed delicately and sipped her wine, looking from Jack to Dulci.

Jack changed the subject. 'I've heard you mean to go back out and do some mapping.'

'I do mean to, very shortly. Within the week, actually. As you know, I am a devout student of Alexander Humboldt who mapped a large portion of this region around the Orinoco River. But it has come to my attention that Humboldt did not map the Essequibo river basin or the Corentyne.' He nodded in Jack's direction. 'Those are the boundaries you're concerned about and rightly so. Until they are determined, there's all kinds of mischief that can be wrought regarding the peoples and resources of that region.' He turned to Dulci by way of explanation. 'Guiana has outlawed slavery recently, but Venezuela and Brazil have not. Peoples living in Guyanese territory have no fear of slavery, but slavers crossing into our territory thinking they're still in their own lands have taken free peoples as slaves. Then it becomes a border discussion when determining whose laws apply.'

The conversation turned political after that, focusing on the governor's latest work in that regard. Lady Carmichael-Smythe eventually rose, signalling it was time to leave the gentlemen to their brandy and cigars.

The men didn't leave them for long. They were soon joined in the blue drawing room by the three men and the tea cart. Jack came to stand beside her, wicked intent gleaming from his eyes. 'Did I toe the line sufficiently during dinner?' he said *sotto voce* for her ears alone.

'You certainly toed something. You're a naughty boy, Jack,' Dulci replied, sipping her tea and trying to ignore the sensual breath against her ear.

'Bad boys often make good men,' Jack

answered easily. 'Perhaps you would accompany me out to the verandah and I can show you just how good.'

After all their flirtations, Jack could still make her cheeks burn. 'I think I could use some fresh air.' Dulci set down the delicate tea cup, feeling the heat from her cheeks.

'There, that's better.' Jack shut the French-paned door behind them. 'Now, as for you, Lady Dulcinea, you might be cooler if you wore fewer clothes.' His eyes sparked with their green mischief and he reached for the fichu. 'Starting with this. Now it's my turn to tease.' Jack drew the scrap of cloth by one end, trailing the lace lightly over one sea-foam silk-clad breast. Dulci shivered in involuntary delight, her nipple hardening beneath her gown at the tantalising contact.

'So you do like being tickled,' Jack whispered huskily, one hand about her waist, drawing her close. 'How are you, Dulci? I've missed you.' He stole a kiss, long and lingering.

'They'll be sure to see,' Dulci protested before he could launch another.

'Only if they're looking.' Jack chuckled. 'My sweet hypocrite, you don't mind breaking the rules, you just mind getting caught.' Jack winked.

'I don't think any of them are bad mannered enough to look. We're safe.'

He might be safe, but she certainly wasn't. Dulci knew she'd be far safer inside next to the tea cart. Instead she was out on the verandah with a wolf in sheep's clothing; Jack dressed up as a gentleman was every woman's fairy tale and he worked on her like a tonic, his eyes, his body promising all nature of happy ever afters.

'You're incorrigible, Jack. You've hauled me out here to kiss me. Should I be flattered or do you think I'll come at your beck and call?' This was his chance. Dulci had been proposed to enough to know how to provide any willing gentleman the perfect opening for his declaration. If Jack was looking for a way to profess his changing feelings, this was it.

A considering glance swept Jack's face, shadowing his hot eyes. For a moment she thought she had him. The back of his knuckles gently stroked her cheek.

'I have no answer for you. Your question is unanswerable. If I say you should be flattered, you will fly at me and call me arrogant to my core. If I say I think you're at my call, you'll think I find you fast. I do not think you're fast, Dulci.'

Hardly the declaration she was looking for. Dulci twined her arms about his neck and pressed her body flat against his. 'I think you are.'

'You think I'm fast?' Jack arched a blond eyebrow in a mock display of wounded pride.

'Absolutely.' Dulci moved her hand between them to discreetly stroke his length, finding his desire stirring, hardening beneath her hand. 'I heard the most intriguing speculation today,' she whispered provocatively. 'I heard that dancing ability is a fair judge of a man's skill at bedsport.'

Jack's hand lingered on her breast, his hand making a small caressing motion over her nipple. 'Just speculation? In true scientific method, perhaps we should test this hypothesis. Why don't you save me a dance tomorrow night and we'll find out?'

A figure moved behind them in the doorway. 'Ah, Lady Carmichael-Smythe believes we've been out here long enough, guardian of your virtue as she is,' Jack said ruefully and Dulci stepped away, taking her fichu from Jack and tucking it into her low bodice.

'I liked the dress better without it,' Jack groused. 'Go on in, I'll be along in a minute.'

Jack leaned on the railing, taking in the spectacular view that reached all the way to the harbour as if he were really seeing it. All his thoughts, all his senses, were focused on Dulci and his failure this evening.

He had not told Dulci what he'd meant to tell her: he was leaving with Robert the day after the ball. Robert had all his supplies ready and was willing to wait two days for Jack to join the expedition. Jack knew he could not be luckier. Schomburgk was heading out in the very direction he himself needed to go to complete the king's commission. Robert's presence would validate the expedition on an entirely higher plane. With Robert's reputation as an explorer and scholar behind the results of the mapping, no one could doubt the integrity of his findings. There would be no grounds on which to argue that it was merely his crooked map against Ortiz's.

But Dulci would be angry. Furious.

There was no question of her going. Jack hoped the stories he and Robert shared over supper would work to subtly dissuade her from wanting to go. Her desire for such an adventure no doubt sprang from a fanciful notion of what that adventure entailed.

He understood that initial untried image of exploring. He'd had a similar image, too, when he'd first set out: meeting the natives, sitting cross-legged with chieftains and engaging in parley, trading goods, eating strange foods and seeing spectacular places.

The reality was far from that. There were insects and all sorts of dangers on the ground where one sat cross-legged with chieftains and the food, while living up to the 'strange' expectations, always tasted far worse than anything conjured up in prior imaginings. But one ate it to survive. One smeared mud and animal grease on oneself as well to survive. A man got to a point where nothing else mattered. A man learned he was capable of anything to survive. He didn't want that for Dulci. If she'd seen him when they'd emerged into civilisation after Anegada, she wouldn't have recognised him: gaunt, sun-burned, ragged remnants of trousers hanging off his hips, a dirty beard covering his jaw. No, he didn't want that for his beautiful Dulci. Georgetown was as far as she was going.

He'd wanted to tell her tonight. He didn't want to wait until the ball. He had other plans for the ball that didn't include making Dulci angry.

But his well-laid plans had gone astray the moment she'd sat down at the dinner table looking delectable in her borrowed finery, her dark hair piled high on her head, showing off her lovely neck and the slope of her bosom, artfully covered by that damn fichu. The whole presence of the fichu introduced the idea that the bodice was too low to begin with and Jack had spent most of the meal trying to follow the conversation while visualising Dulci's gown without the offending modesty piece.

If women knew what men really thought about fichus, they might dispose of the flimsy pieces altogether. Jack was strongly of the opinion that fichus didn't preserve decency as much as they promoted indecency in male thought patterns. Then again, maybe women knew and they did it on purpose. Dulci had known precisely what she was doing at the dinner table with her hand skimming her chest, fluttering so modestly at her neckline.

It had succeeded, to say nothing of her deft footwork beneath the table. He was so aroused by the time she left the men to brandy and cigars, Jack had forgone the cigar and swallowed Carmichael-Smythe's fine brandy in one fell gulp. It was no surprise the verandah had turned into a lovers' interlude instead.

Now, everything hinged on tomorrow night. There'd be no chance to tell her tomorrow morning. In the morning, he was off to pound the first nail in Ortiz's political coffin. That was the other news he'd meant to share. He'd located the map-maker. In the morning, he'd pay the man a visit and gain his confession by whatever means necessary.

The door behind him opened again and Robert Schomburgk stepped out, taking up a silent post beside Jack. 'You didn't tell her, did you?'

'No.'

Robert had the good grace to leave the easy rejoinder alone. 'It's a beautiful night.' Robert breathed in a healthy lungful of air.

'I hadn't noticed.'

He was indifferent to the sweet smell of hyacinth and the special warmth of a tropical night, to the flickering lantern lights bobbing on ships in the distance and the stars glistening overhead in the night sky.

Even if he wasn't indifferent, he still could not have pierced the darkness and seen the rowboat lowered from the big ship anchored at the mouth of the harbour and rowed by a tall, dark-cloaked man towards the Demerara river on the west side of town.

Calisto Ortiz had arrived.

Chapter Eighteen

Morning sun shone warm through the windows of the breakfast room. Dulci helped herself to the dishes on the sideboard containing English specialties and the lovely pyramid of fresh fruits unique to this part of the world and so readily available. This was fast becoming her favourite time of day. She rose early here to ride before the sun became too hot. Afterwards, she was still the only person abroad in the house and had the luxury of eating in quiet, alone with her thoughts.

She had not realised how much she enjoyed the private time. In London, the town house usually teemed with various Wycrofts. This Season had been something of an exception in that regard. Her four sisters and Brandon were all otherwise occupied. Dulci plucked a kiwi from the colourful pyramid. Jack had posted a letter from her when they docked in Spain. Surely it would have reached Brandon by now and he would know she was well and that she was with Jack. She'd wanted to dispel the initial panic he would no doubt have felt in the wake of Jack's hurried note from the ship when they departed.

A servant stepped forwards to pour tea for her as she settled at the empty table. What would he say about his sister carrying on with his best friend? It wasn't that Brandon would mind them falling in love and having a traditional courtship. Jack was as good as a brother already to Brandon. The sticking point was whether or not Brandon would insist on the relationship being honourable in society's eyes. He would insist on marriage.

She and Jack had to be free to make their own terms with one another. She did not want Jack coerced and she certainly didn't want herself coerced.

Dulci buttered her toast and bit into it with relish, savouring the simple pleasure of toast with butter melting across the surface. It would be the only simple thing today. She'd known in advance the day would be complicated, full of last-minute preparations for the ball. Any day of such an event was bound to be so. Lady Carmichael-Smythe wanted her to help oversee all the particulars. There would be flowers and food, decorations and details. But then there would be tonight. There would be dancing and Jack. She would be at her charming best in order to hold his attention. Tonight he could not bury himself in business and pretend to ignore her. Tonight she would make sure he gave pursuit. A glimmer of a smile hovered on her lips. Footsteps sounded on the hardwood floor outside the room. Dulci quickly schooled her features, concentrating hard on her eggs.

'Good morning, Dulci.' Jack sounded surprised, his step faltering. 'I'd not expected to see anyone up so early given the long day ahead. I thought everyone would be sleeping a little later to marshal their strength for the big night.' Jack helped himself to some eggs and sausage and settled across from her at the table.

'I went riding. I like to ride in the morning. It's better for seeing the birds. There's such a marvellous variety here. The colours are extraordinary.' Jack was being awfully convivial, almost too friendly.

'Why are you up so early?' She was starting to

suspect he'd hoped to be alone. Alone or undetected? 'Are you skulking about?'

'I have some early business to see to,' Jack answered vaguely. Now he was being evasive and trying to sound friendly about it.

She would indulge him and redirect the conversation. He was definitely up to something he didn't want her to know about. If he didn't want her to know, then he'd definitely not tell her if she asked him outright. It did no good to keep probing.

'Lady Carmichael-Smythe is excited about the turnout for the ball. You'll be able to meet a lot of people tonight. Maybe one of them will know about the map-maker who helped Ortiz,' Dulci said.

Jack nodded and added a few desultory comments to the conversation. He excused himself after a few minutes, clearly eager to be off.

Dulci let him go, giving him a three-minute head start. She raced upstairs to her room and rummaged through her dresser drawer, beneath lacy undergarments until her hand met with the cold steel of a small pistol. She smiled to herself and slipped it into her skirt pocket. It had not been difficult to find a weapon at the market. The bizarre bazaar had lived up to its reputation. Right next to a fabric merchant, there'd been a small arms dealer happy to assist her. It had been one of the first things she'd purchased.

Careful not to be seen, Dulci peered out her window from behind a frothy curtain. Her room commanded a view of the drive and she was able to spot Jack trotting down the lane and turning on to the road, away from town.

That was her cue. Dulci raced down the stairs to the stable. The groom offered to bring her usual mare and Dulci saddled the horse in short order. 'Where did Viscount Wainsbridge say he was going?' She ignored the strange looks the groom gave her. She'd only brought the horse back an hour ago.

The groom shook his head. 'He didn't say.'

Definitely not a pleasure ride, then. Dulci's instincts were on high alert. How dare Jack ride off without telling her? It was almost certain he'd uncovered something about their mission. When she caught up with him, she was going to be very angry. She was tired of being nothing more than an accessory. Jack was acting as if this was his mission alone. He'd conveniently forgot her artefacts had been destroyed, her house had been burgled, her very person had been the target of a failed kidnapping effort. She had not endured the hardships of the voyage, forsaken her home and risked her reputation to be treated like a fragile bauble.

Dulci set out after Jack, picking up his cloud of dust moving down the dry dirt road. She kept a careful distance, not wanting to give herself away with the noise of an approaching horse or by sight.

The ride was not a long one. Whoever Jack was seeking, they lived only a little way out of town. Jack turned down a narrow lane choked with weeds and dismounted in front of a dilapidated shack with a sagging porch. Dulci was surprised the building didn't collapse at the merest flick of a finger. She kept her distance, watching the steps take Jack's weight with some amazement. At the door, Jack bent swiftly to his boot and loosened something there. She could not see what precisely, but she had her guesses. Dulci's hand closed reassuringly over the little gun in her pocket. In her experience, there was only one thing gentlemen kept in their boots and that was knives. Jack expected trouble.

No one came to the door and Jack stepped aggressively inside, drawing the knife from his boot, confirming her suspicions. From her distance, it was hard to see the exact dynamics of the situation, but it appeared no one was home. At least now it was safe to dismount. She hastily picketed her horse at the entrance to the lane. She didn't dare risk riding into the dirt space in front of the shack. This wasn't a place that saw many visitors and Jack's horse would surely whinny and give away her arrival.

Dulci crept forwards, keeping her form below window level, although she doubted the broken panes afforded much view of any newcomers.

There was a yell and Jack swore loudly. There was a loud crash from inside. Jack was in trouble. Dulci's heart raced. She gave up any pretence of subtlety. She pulled out her gun and ran up the steps with a roar of her own, hoping to take any attackers by surprise.

But the surprise was all hers. Jack was alone in the shambles of the room. Broken furniture lay on the floor along with smashed crockery.

They spoke at once.

'You're not hurt?'

'What are you doing here?'

Jack strode towards her, forceful hands on her shoulders, anger emanating from his body in waves. He roughly propelled her towards the door.

But it was too late. A slow wafting unpleasant smell caught her nostrils, her eyes fell on an awkwardly positioned object—no, not an object. A body.

Dulci screamed her shock, her horror growing as she connected the smell to the body lying under the debris of broken furniture. She pummelled at Jack's chest with her fists irrationally in her horror, fighting his attempts to bundle her out of the shack.

'Dulci, breathe, darling,' Jack counselled once they gained the yard. 'It's all right.' Of course it wasn't.

'I thought you were in danger. I heard you shout.' Dulci gulped in great breaths of air.

Jack's anger was fading as the shock of the encounter wore off. 'What are you doing here, Dulci? This is no place for you, it's too dangerous as you can very well see.'

Dulci felt her balance returning. 'You were being so secretive at breakfast. I knew something was up. You could have needed me.'

Jack's jaw clenched. 'I was trying to keep you safe. I would have asked you to come if it was appropriate.'

Dulci's earlier anger rose in the wake of her

passing shock. 'I don't need to be kept safe, Jack. I want to be part of this. It was my house that was broken into, my artefacts that were destroyed. You are not the only one Ortiz has put in jeopardy. I cannot be swept aside and ignored, although God knows you've tried.'

Jack's face clouded. 'Do you know who that man was?'

Dulci shook her head.

'The map-maker.' Jack took her none too gently by the elbow and led her to his horse. 'This is the man who did the map for Ortiz. He's dead, just recently. Probably murdered in the night. I was just a few hours too late.'

Dulci didn't have to be told what that meant. 'Ortiz is here,' she whispered, looking about their surroundings as if the man would pop out of the bushes.

Jack nodded. 'He's here and he'll be looking for us.'

'We won't be hard to find.' In a city the size of Georgetown, anyone would be memorable and people like she and Jack stood out like diamonds among coals. 'What should we do?'

'We go back to the governor's house and dance.'

'There you go with your simple plans again. Run. Walk. Dance.'

'We'll hide in plain sight. There's nothing Ortiz can do while we're at the governor's. He's on British soil here. No one will be very sympathetic to his claims. When he's here, he hunts alone. He must be very covert. He hasn't the prestige of his position.'

'He's desperate, Jack,' Dulci put in as they walked the lane towards her horse picketed on the road.

'Necessarily so, my dear. What man sails halfway around the world and sets aside his comforts on a whim?'

Dulci shot him a sidelong glance. 'You do.'

'As I said, a desperate man.' Jack boosted her up into the saddle, squeezed her leg and checked her stirrup. 'Stay close to me on the way back in case Ortiz is in the area.'

It was the first time, fleeting though it was, that she'd truly sensed Jack's concern over the task facing him. All through the weeks on board ship, the few weeks here in Guiana, he'd seemed so confident, so much on the offensive. It had never occurred to her that Jack was worried about completing his mission. Jack always seemed confident, always seemed in charge.

Silence surrounded them as they walked their horses towards the Carmichaels'. Only the occasional bird call interrupted the stillness of the morning. 'Are you leaving soon, Jack?' Dulci ventured. 'I think you must be. If Ortiz is here, you cannot wait to finish the map.'

Beside her, Jack drew a deep breath. 'I meant to tell you last night. Robert and I leave tomorrow. He's already delayed his departure a week to accommodate me.' One more thing he'd been doing without consulting her. Dulci's heart sank. She'd hoped, even believed, she'd meant more to him than this. She'd wanted to be his partner in this.

'I want to go with you.' It was a fruitless request, Jack's answer a foregone conclusion.

'Absolutely not. The dangers of the forest, the rivers, are enough even without Ortiz thrown into the equation, Dulci. Now that he's here, what's to stop him from following me into the jungle? At least by following me, he can't be following you at the same time.'

'I can take care of myself.'

'In London. Among a court of gentlemen. Yes, you do very well. There's none better under those circumstances. These circumstances are vastly different.'

Dulci opened her mouth to protest. But Jack silenced her with an imperious wave of his hand. 'The discussion is over, Dulci.' She'd been dismissed like a petulant child.

By him.

The man she thought she loved.

Dulci was still in an unmitigated temper by the time evening approached. Her disappointment, her anger at Jack, had simmered all day. To be honest, she was angry with herself, too. She'd hoped for more from Jack. Perhaps not marriage, or the things women traditionally expected from men. But she'd thought he respected her, admired her, even loved her. Now she saw that she was merely tolerated for her novelty. In some regards she was no different than the other women Jack had affairs with.

The realisation hurt. The shoe was definitely on the other foot. She was not used to being the jilted suitor in this scenario. Is this what her suitors had felt when she'd refused them? Now more than ever, she had to stiffen her spine. Jack had made his position clear. It would do no good to break down now.

Lady Carmichael-Smythe's maid came to help

her dress and do her hair. Dulci let her string a length of pearls through her coiffure. She let the maid slide the lovely lavender gown over her head and slip her feet into matching slippers with tiny bows.

She would go to the ball and she'd go looking and acting like a queen, graciously bestowing her favours on her court. She would dance, and she would laugh and she would spare Jack the knowledge that her heart was breaking.

He would do it tonight. He would put his cards on the proverbial table and say the words, 'I love you.' He wanted her to know before he left. Beyond that, he could promise nothing.

Jack stood at the base of the sweeping stairs of Carmichael House with Robert, admiring the bunting draping the banister, nodding to the women who traipsed up and down the stairs to the retiring room to check hems before the dancing started. In his mind, he knew how childish his mental bet was. It was like the silly 'if this, then that' arguments he had with himself growing up. If the clouds passed the church steeple before the church bells stopped ringing, then his father wouldn't be angry over his late return for dinner. If he did well at school, then his father would love him. Foolish arguments all.

'She quite steals my breath.' Robert nudged him gently in the ribs with an elbow, calling his attention to the top of the stairs.

Dulci stood there, staring down, catching his eye with a dazzling smile. She might have been in the finest ballroom in London. He'd seen her countless times and yet her beauty did not cease to astonish him. What man could not look at her and not love her? For all his self-proclaimed rules and self-imposed absences, he could not tell his heart not to love her, futile though it was.

Her lavender skirts swayed delicately as she descended, showing delightful peeps of the cunning slippers beneath. She looked fresh, innocent and yet not without intelligence—in short, the way a virtuous woman looked. Such a woman was not for him, although he could not stop his heart from loving her. Dulci belonged in London and he had to ensure her safety. The further away she was from him, the safer she'd be. His life was dirty, full of secrets he could not tell. Gladstone was right. There were some things a man could not earn, some things a man was born with or without. Perhaps nobility was one of those things after all. He could no more be noble, no matter how many titles William hurled at his head, than Gladstone could be common.

They'd had plans for tonight, but Dulci's pique with him at the shack and the developments of the morning had probably effectively ruined them, much to his regret. He would have liked one more glorious night with her, something to remember her by, for she surely would not want to see him again after he told her what he'd decided. This time, their goodbye would not be temporary. He did not anticipate there'd be a reunion after she had a few months to cool her temper. This time, goodbye would be permanent.

Lady Carmichael-Smythe bustled forwards, taking Dulci's hands at the bottom stair. 'There you are, Lady Dulcinea. The musicians are just starting. You're in time to lead out the opening dance with Viscount Wainsbridge.'

Jack summoned his usual ballroom smile and bowed in Dulci's direction as her eyes met his. Beneath his polished sophistication, she would never know his heart was breaking. In the meanwhile, he would have a few last things to remember her by, starting with this dance.

Chapter Nineteen

'We're always dancing, Jack. Have you noticed?' Dulci was all brilliant smiles, but her tone was brittle, almost wearied as they led off the ball. Perhaps Jack had finally worn her out. He'd certainly led her a merry chase in all ways. Or perhaps she'd finally given up. It was hard to think of it as being the latter. She was no quitter and yet there seemed to be no other solution. At some point one had to give up a fruitless hunt or resign oneself to mediocrity and half-measures. She wasn't sure she could live with half-measures where Jack was concerned. She wanted his heart and his body, all of him.

'Will you do something for me, Dulci?' Jack swung them through the first turn, his grip tight at her waist, his efforts careful to keep her at the proper distance.

'I can't commit to anything until I know what it is first,' Dulci said stubbornly.

Jack's face looked serious, his eyes narrowing. 'Governor Carmichael-Smythe has informed me that Andrew's boat is ready to sail back to England. There's a place for you on that boat. It leaves in a couple of days. You have time to pack and say your goodbyes.'

She played the flirt, trying to hide her extreme dismay with a saucy toss of her head and a lilting little laugh as if this were the silliest of suggestions, a grand joke. 'Jack, we've barely just arrived. This is our *welcome* ball, for heaven's sake. It's been barely two weeks. It took longer to get here.' This request of his was more final than she'd expected. It was worse than being left behind to wait for his return from the expedition. At least then she'd still be here. Now, he was sending her away. If she left, who knew when she'd see him again.

'Thank you for the offer, but I'll choose to stay a while. There's still some work I need to do for my articles. There will be other boats when the time comes.' She was cautious to avoid saying she wanted to wait for him. A thousand tragedies could befall him in the jungles. She wanted to be close. What if he needed her?

Jack's gaze hardened at her refusal. 'I need you to get on that ship,' he said bluntly.

She was still the flirt. 'That's not exactly how a girl wants to be needed, Jack.'

'With Ortiz here, Georgetown has become too dangerous for you. I cannot guess with certainty what Ortiz will do next. Brandon will kill me if any harm comes to you.'

Dulci's heart sank another notch. Push and flirt as she might, she could not wring a single word of personal affection from Jack. He wanted her on the boat for Brandon's sake and her own safety. Even if he'd said he needed her on the boat for his own peace of mind, because he cared for her too much to place her in jeopardy, she might have considered it.

Why had she thought he would be any different tonight? Not once had he uttered love words, words of affection to her. His level of concern was based on respect and responsibility, which, however noble, was comparatively empty.

'All things considered, Jack, I think I will stay,' Dulci said coolly. The music stopped and Dulci curtsied. 'Thank you for the dance.'

She meant to hurry off to the next dance partner, but Jack's eyes glittered dangerously. He did not like being rebuffed.

'What do you think of Lady Carmichael-Smythe's hypothesis now?' he asked casually with his usual lazy sensuality.

'I think it will remain a hypothesis.' She had to escape. If he touched her one more time, the slightest of caresses would destroy her. She would give in. She knew herself well enough to know she was on the brink of giving him what he wanted, of getting on that ship simply because he needed it regardless of his reasons for wanting it. Dulci turned sharply on her heel and began walking to the sidelines, to safety.

One…two…three… She was going to make it. She made it five steps before Jack's hand closed about her arm, his voice harsh in her ear. 'Come with me, now.'

How like Jack to wait until she was convinced he wasn't coming after her, that she was finally free of his spell.

There was no verandah this time, no garden stroll, no dark library. He marched her straight to her rooms down an unpeopled hallway and locked the door behind them.

'I am sure it's bad form here as well to deprive a hostess of her honoured guests all at once,' Dulci began, but underneath her light tone she was scared. She'd never seen Jack this angry before. She didn't worry that he would hurt her. He was a far too controlled man for such mindless violence. But she did worry he would question her and he was an expert interrogator. All he'd done was feed the burglar dinner, offer conversation and he had the confession he needed to prove Ortiz guilty of masterminding the break in. He wouldn't need nearly that much skill to have her babbling all sorts of craziness. Then he really would be done with her. He wouldn't want a clinging woman who begged him for the crumbs of his attention.

With a savage jerk, Jack pulled off his carefully tied cravat.

'What are you doing?' Dulci was all wariness.

Jack shot her a sharp look, his eyes stalking her, assessing her, his voice like danger wrapped in silk. 'My dear, I am redefining the nature of our relationship.'

Why did he bother to plan anything when it came to Dulci? This wasn't going according to any blueprint he'd mentally laid out when he'd decided to declare his feelings. He'd wanted a serene setting: champagne, stars overhead, a quiet walk in the garden. Instead, he had Dulci locked in her room, spitting-cat mad over his request she take the boat home, Dulci flirting and flippant, arguing against a sensible notion, all out of stubborn pride.

There wasn't time to coax her into a better disposition. He was leaving on the morrow for an indefinite period of time. He had to know she would be safe. He had to know if there was a reason to return to England when his work here was done. She was in no mood to listen and he was in no mood to be patient.

An explosive combination if ever there was one.

'Redefine?' Dulci gave him that cold, arched-eyebrow look of hers. She sat in an overstuffed chair by the window, arranging her skirts and managing to look like a queen on her throne.

'Yes, redefine, dammit,' Jack growled.

'That presumes there was something defined to start with.' Her haughty tone suggested she didn't care one iota. Tonight, he could not believe that. Tonight, he could not be put off by her practised wiles, used on others to enforce their distance. He would not be treated as an indifferent suitor.

Jack shrugged out of his evening coat, aware that Dulci eyed him with great speculation, hungry speculation in spite of her cool comments to the contrary.

'We can no longer be lovers, Dulci.'

She merely looked at him, a tolerant queen allowing her subject the luxury of speaking freely in her presence, but something flickered in her eyes. 'And why is that, Jack?'

He advanced towards her chair, gratified to see her eyes widen at his approach. She was not as immune as she wanted to appear. He trapped her, an arm on each side of the chair. 'I want more than sex from you, Dulci.' The terms were blunt and honest. There was no more time for mis-interpretations and cross-purposes. He did not want a war of wits with her. If they were to fight, he wanted to fight without the stealth of double meanings. If she wanted to argue, she would have to do it without artifice.

'What *do* you want, Jack?' The last bastion of her coyness teased, her tongue darted lightly over her lips, whetting them provocatively.

Jack leaned close, delicately feathering his

breath over a sensitive ear lobe. Dulci shuddered beneath him and Jack felt a lover's elation surge within him. He pressed his advantage. 'I want you, Dulci, all of you: mind, body, soul.' He pushed down the shoulders of her gown perhaps a bit roughly, freeing her breasts, then lowered his mouth to them, kissing each in turn, sucking on her nipples until they sprang sweetly erect in his mouth and Dulci moaned. Jack sat back on his haunches, pushing up her full skirts, baring her thighs, his hands riding high on her legs at the warm juncture between them. He would seduce the right answer out of her if he had to. His thumbs stroked her curls, warm and damp, her cleft already wet with want. His thumb parted her soft, secret lips and teased the taut nubbin within.

From his intimate crouch, he watched Dulci with a lover's delight. Her head was thrown back, her hair starting to fall in provocative fullness from its pins, her breasts naked and raised, her gown crushed about her, her mind absorbed with the heat of passion for the moment instead of hot argument.

Jack bent his head, placed his mouth where his thumb had been and blew gently. Dulci cried out, the half-pant, half-gasping sob of a woman thoroughly caught up in her fulfilment. She arched against him. He held her possessively, his hands bracketing her hips, bracing her, as his mouth took her in the most intimate of fashions in the most intimate of places. This was his woman, complete and ready for him, not abashed by his boldness, but joining him in it, not afraid of her own pleasure. Before the night was through he would prove the rightness of his possession to her. He would brook no refusal and she would give him none.

Dulci rocked against him, her hands clenching his hair, driving him to give her greater pleasure. His arousal was heavy and full, yearning for its own completion. He freed himself, sliding Dulci to the floor. Overstuffed or not, the chair would not hold them both, not as wild as they both were. He rose over her, covering her with his length, surrounding her with his strength. Her body answered, her passion surging as she took all of him, her body revelling in the power of him as it slid into hers, commanding the rhythm of their joining, leading them to utter completion. Dulci bucked hard beneath them, shattering in her pleasure and he shuddered deep within her, filling her.

He had no desire to move from the floor, only to lay there with her, basking in the afterglow of their spent passions. They were calmer now, their passion not being the only emotion quenched by a bout of lovemaking. For the moment she was tamed. Now was the time to tell her what his body had shown her.

Jack traced a light finger from the pulse in the base of her neck, in the valley between her breasts. 'Dulci, I love you.'

Dulci's eyes fluttered open. Surprise and shock were mirrored there in the moments before she became guarded, once more the Incomparable who'd spent most of her adult life rejecting proposals, protecting herself from those who would claim her as a prize. 'What does that mean, Jack?' She was all business, not exactly the tone he'd expected from a woman who had just been so thoroughly pleasured.

'It means I want us to be together, no more wondering if each time is the last.'

Dulci hoisted herself up on one elbow, looking like a well-tumbled woman, her hair falling gloriously to one side. Jack felt the intensity of her veiled gaze as she studied him for a long moment, contemplating, weighing. When she spoke, her tone carried a mordant edge. 'Why, Jack, is this a marriage proposal?'

So Dulci wanted to duel albeit without their rapiers. Jack schooled his own features into a devil-may-care expression that gave away no sign of his disappointment. He'd never told a woman he loved her before and Dulci had all but thrown the words back in his face. Who knew, the night was young, she still might.

'If it was, would you accept?'

'Answer my question first,' Dulci countered. 'Are you proposing marriage?'

He'd meant only to declare his feelings tonight. There was too much ahead of them yet to think of marriage. Perhaps he would contemplate marriage after the mission was complete and he knew he had something to offer her besides a viscount with a ruined reputation if the mission failed. Jack hesitated only fractionally, but Dulci's insights were too keen. She noted the reluctance almost immediately and seized on it.

'So it's not a marriage proposal, but perhaps a proposal of a different kind. Eh, Jack?'

Jack leapt to his feet, adjusting his trousers. 'No, damn it. I am not asking you to be my mistress. Do you think I have no honour when it comes to you?' The very thought was appalling and he was

angry with her for even thinking such an arrangement spoke to the quality of their relationship.

'But you're not asking me to be your wife.'

Jack's temper flared. 'Not tonight. How can I
think of marriage with all the dangers that lie
ahead? I cannot responsibly make a proposal
until my name is cleared.'

Dulci gained her feet, her voice in deadly
earnest. 'Don't bother. I wouldn't accept.'

'I deserve better from you, Dulci, than hot
words. I said I loved you. In my mind, that's
worth more than any marriage proposal.' Love
meant promises, surely she knew that? Saw what
he was offering her?

'Love is not enough when it's offered from a
man who has all but ignored me since our arrival,
who hasn't allowed me to be a partner in this
venture although I have risked everything and
followed him halfway around the world, who
makes his work for the king the single most important priority in his life to the exclusion of all
else. I dare say if the king knocked on the door
right now, you'd be gone without a backward
glance. No woman wants to exist on the sidelines
of her husband's life.'

'You know it doesn't work that way in my case.

It's too dangerous.' Jack drew a ragged, frustrated breath. She was asking for too much, far more than he could give. How could he function in a world where Dulci was at constant risk?

Dulci gave a slight nod of her head. 'I will not be marginalised, Jack.'

He had been dismissed. It was over. All that remained was to say goodbye, but Dulci had one last thing to say.

'Do you really think saying "I love you" would change anything? For that matter, that marriage would change anything? Neither will stop you from running at the king's command into secret missions you can't share or leaving for months on end.'

'This man *does* love you, Dulci,' Jack said firmly.

'Then let me in, Jack,' Dulci fired back.

Jack gave her a short, sardonic bow. A smart man knew when it was time to move on. He would return to the ball and make his excuses. He had a departure to make in the morning.

At the door his hand stalled on the knob. 'If you ever cared an ounce for me, Dulci, you'll get on that ship.' He shut the door behind him and stepped out into the hall, feeling as if part of his soul had been left behind with a woman who had all he could give and still found it to be not enough. He wondered if he really blamed her. If positions were reversed, he'd not settle for what he'd offered her either. But all the same, she had to understand he could offer nothing more.

Dulci collapsed on to the bed, fighting sobs. If she started crying now, she'd never stop. He was gone, really gone this time. How had they moved from spectacular love-making to farewell in the span of an hour? She was trembling, shaking from the emotion of it.

How dare he put her in the position of having to decide what would become of them? How dare he say he love her and expect the words to be enough? How dare he give her exactly what she'd secretly craved but never voiced—he'd said he loved her?

Truth was, she believed him. A man like Jack would far rather bare his body than his feelings. To tell her he loved her must have cost him dearly, no matter how much he meant it. To go to those depths meant two things: Jack was worried beyond obsession about Ortiz. And he must have wanted her on that boat pretty badly to use love as a negotiating tool.

Well, she wasn't about to desert Jack in his

time of need. If he was worried about Ortiz, then he needed her beside him. A woman didn't abandon the man she loved.

That was her truth. She did love Jack; loved him too much to let him pretend that marriage and words would give them the answers they were looking for. She did want to be with Jack, but not like this with so much unresolved between them. Despite her harsh rejection earlier, she wanted to marry Jack in the sense that she wanted no other man but him, wanted to share his life fully with him—*that* was marriage, not some empty ceremony and piece of paper filed on the parish records. She wanted a life with Jack, not a disaster. Jack was not ready to share a life with her. Until Jack could accept that she meant to be his partner, that she would not be left behind mentally or physically, she could not commit to a future with him.

Dulci drew a deep steadying breath—best to begin as she meant to go on. She had to show Jack the acceptance she wanted and she had to do it with actions. She could not tell him she wanted to be accepted. She had to show him and she knew how. Dulci smiled in the darkness. What was that word he'd used earlier? Ah, 'redefining'. That was exactly what she intended to do.

* * *

Morning saw a type of constrained chaos reigning at the governor's mansion. Schomburgk was outside with his retainers for the expedition, waiting for Jack and the governor to send them off. Partygoers had not departed the ball, which had run until four in the morning, in hopes of seeing the adventurers off. They milled on the drive and on the wide front porch.

Dressed in khakis, with her hair tucked up under a concealing hat, Dulci sat astride a big horse at the rear of the group, trying to draw as little attention to herself as possible. She was impatiently waiting with the rest. At last they were off with the governor's prayer and his blessing. Jack rode at the head of the column next to Robert. She was careful to stay clear of Jack, keeping herself with the other retainers and trying to say as little as possible.

Dulci waited until they reached the first river to reveal herself to Jack. The group began the process of loading goods into the many boats that would be far more useful to them than horses on this venture. She saw Jack say something to Robert and slip off into the privacy of the trees.

She waited until he was decent before she stepped out into his path, pulling off her hat and letting her hair fall while Jack started back in what she hoped was surprise.

'Hello, Jack.'

Confusion and shock dominated his features. She watched them settle, transmuted into something more formidable as the consequences of her appearance in the jungle became obvious.

'What the bloody hell are you doing here?' This was not the tone of a man who'd been presented with a pleasant surprise. She'd best tread carefully here before she found herself marched back to Georgetown. Jack was not a man who tolerated defiance, even when it was for his own good.

While she'd hoped for a more friendly reception, she'd expected this. Dulci stood her ground in the wake of his anger. 'I am redefining the nature of our relationship.'

'And what might that be? Your terms seemed fairly well defined last night.'

She was not put off by Jack's insouciant manner. 'I am here to prove I don't have to be left behind, that I can be your partner in all ways, in bed and out.' She stepped towards him, closing the distance, and stopping his mouth with a kiss as fierce as her arguments.

Chapter Twenty

Jack was furious. Aroused, but furious. Sisyphus had an easy task compared to him, Jack thought once he got over the extraordinary shock of Dulci here of all places, kissing him senseless. He'd rolled his proverbial stone uphill only to see it roll back down. He'd seen to her safety, secured her passage on a ship back to the sanctuary of London and her brother's protection. Ortiz could not touch her there. But here she was, professing nonsense about redefining the nature of their re-lationship. Didn't she understand there was nothing to redefine? That it couldn't be any other way? To be any other way was to bring his night-mares to life. Worse, it gave those nightmares a face and it was hers. Yet, he couldn't deny the jubilation that warred with his anger. She'd come! In spite of all her arguments last night, she'd come.

'So, Dulci, you've decided to become an adventurer,' Jack drawled once she broke her kiss.

Dulci fixed him with a speculative stare, like a gambler assessing the table. 'I've decided to become something more than an adventurer, although I dare say there are numerous similarities. I love you, Jack, but the one thing I must have is a place in your life. I will prove it to you. Put aside your anger and let me have a chance.'

'Do you know why I am angry?' When he'd accepted his commissions with the king, he'd also accepted living with an amorphous fear, that the people he loved might be endangered simply by association. Up until now, the fear had not been claimed, no one had captured his affections long enough to be put at risk. Dulci had changed all that; she demanded his partnership and, by doing so, made his fear real. Dulci would be the one imperilled.

'You're angry because I broke your rules and you can't stand being challenged.'

'My rules are there for good reason,' Jack ground out; his emotions were out of sorts. He needed time to think, to reconcile the elation at her being here and the fear. She started to reply. Jack shook his head. 'We have to get back to camp or else Robert will worry. And, Dulci, say nothing. I have to work out what to do.' For once, Dulci complied, walking stoically beside him back to camp while he sifted through his thoughts.

Some men might leap for joy at the prospect of having the woman they loved follow them in to the wilds, and in truth, part of Jack thrilled to the prospect of showing Dulci the jungle. She would love it and they would be beyond the boundaries of rules, far from society's and the governor's wife's watchful eyes. But there was no small amount of guilt overlaying those decadent fantasies. Entwined with the elation was anger. Jack wanted to throttle her. The moment she'd said 'hello, Jack' his two worlds had collided, his efforts in keeping them separate all for naught.

He was torn between what he should do and what he wanted to do. He should send her back to Georgetown with a couple of the younger assistants. It would help restore balance to his two separate worlds. But beyond that, it would do little good. Andrew's ship sailed on the dawn tide. Dulci would not make that sailing. She would be no more than a sitting duck in Georgetown for Ortiz if she went back and he would be miles away up some unknown river branch, unable to rescue her should the worst happen.

On the other hand, keeping Dulci with him would keep her safe and under his direct protection. Jack shot a sideways glance at the long-legged beauty beside him. His decision was made. It looked like he'd get to do what he wanted; to keep the intrepid Dulci Wycroft by his side and have this incredible adventure with her, guilt aside. Maybe just this once it would be better for his two worlds to mix.

Of course, he still worried about her ability to cope with the perils of such an expedition. No matter how much she protested to the contrary, she wasn't prepared for the rigours of travel in the Guiana interior. Still, if he had to choose—and apparently he did, Dulci having botched his former plans—he would rather take those chances than leave her to her own devices against an angry Calisto Ortiz.

The decision made, Jack felt some of his anger evaporate. He allowed himself to celebrate the turn of events privately. At least for the duration of the expedition, Dulci was his, even if he couldn't have her for ever.

'How long are you going to stay mad, Jack?' Dulci asked, the boat launch coming into sight.

Jack allowed for the luxury of a smile. 'There's no use crying over spilt milk, is there?' He reached for her hand and squeezed it. 'I was angry because you put your safety at risk, not because you were here.' He hoped that made sense to her. It did. Dulci smiled and the last of the tension between them evaporated.

The loading of supplies was nearly complete on the keel boat-styled watercraft that would take them down the river. Departure was imminent. Jack drew a deep breath. More than one type of journey was being embarked on from the shores of the river. For him, the bigger journey might be the mental one he was embarking on with Dulci. She wanted to be his partner. So he would try.

With careful words he hoped she'd appreciate, Jack said, 'We'll send the horses back with the horse handler. From this point, the insects, the swamps and the rivers make horses literal beasts of burden. We'll travel by boat.' Jack paused and tossed Dulci a questioning look. It was her last chance to turn back. 'If you want to go back,

Dulci, you can. The handler is reliable and you can trust him to get you home to the Carmichael-Smythes.'

Dulci shook her head. 'My place is with you, you'll see.' She gave him a saucy grin that warmed him. 'You're not the only one who can master both ballrooms and nature.'

'I thought you'd say that.' Jack sprang up on to the deck of one of the keel boats and bent down to offer her a hand. 'But you do understand that I had to ask.'

'After today, Jack, there's no going back.' Dulci swung up beside him. Ahead of them, Robert's boat pushed off into the river and the men at the poles gave shouts of celebration as they got underway.

In spite of the excitement of setting off down the river, she captured all his attention, his body stirring at the brave sight of her, seductive and lovely in her tight-fitting trousers and long boots, her wide hat with mosquito netting hanging down her back.

Jack closed his eyes briefly, wanting to capture this moment for the entirety of his life, wanting to see the two of them, he and Dulci, the way they might look to someone standing on the shore;

two proud people standing defiantly at the front of the boat, setting off into the unknown, the breeze off the river ruffling their hair back from their faces, their love of a challenge, their love for each other etched into their expressions—a man with the woman he loved and the woman who loved him.

He gave himself over to the fantasy.

These were the best days of his life. Jack could not imagine being happier. The three boats made their way down the treacherous riverways without mishap, the current but sketchy maps proving accurate as they poled the river branches towards the Essequibo.

In the cool of the morning, he would take Dulci on shore with him and Robert for scouting. Robert would collect botanical samples, and he would set up his borrowed surveying equipment for assaying the contours of the land. He would climb hills and look ahead down the river for miles, seeing the turns and twists it would take through the valley below. Dulci did as she pleased, sometimes assisting Robert and drawing the colourful birds that lived high in the trees. Sometimes she would come with him, helping

328   *A Thoroughly Compromised Lady*

with the equipment, learning how to use the compass and many occasions contributing her own insights and knowledge about the terrain.

They kept a look out for any signs of the Arawak or other tribes, but so far, to Dulci's disappointment, had seen none. Jack thought privately they were better off for it. The Arawak had unique and brutal tribal customs.

When it became too hot, too humid for exploring on land, they rejoined the boats that had slowly made their way down river. Usually it was easy to find a nice place to pull out, where there were safe pools of water for swimming beneath waterfalls without fear of the ever-present river piranhas and water snakes. The team would spend the afternoons swimming beneath the gorgeous cataracts, mending equipment, and writing copious notes regarding their findings. All in all, Jack found these days idyllic in spite of the constant danger that surrounded them from insects, snakes and any number of creatures.

Dulci was adapting well, easily lending herself to the tasks of the boat camp and picking up on the rituals of the more seasoned explorers. She checked her boots for scorpions and other insects before pulling them on. She brushed her luxurious hair out every night and then braided it tightly to keep it clean. She found ways to be modest yet not fussy about conditions that offered the barest of privacies. The men adored Jack's woman. Much like she had aboard Andrew's ship, Dulci fitted seamlessly into a man's world while still maintaining her wonderful brand of femininity.

The days ended when the sun set, no one willing to waste more lantern oil than needed. In the dark, one of the assistants would pull out his fiddle and play while the others chatted on their floating homes, settling for the night, stars filling the sky until it seemed there were more pricks of diamond light than there was dark canopy to hold them.

In the privacy of the dark, Dulci would snuggle close to him, remarking that the stars never shone so brilliantly in London. And when he was certain there was no one to see, he would make exquisite love to her and she to him.

Afterwards, he would lie beside Dulci on the deck of the boat, surrounded by protective netting, the stars bright overhead and think that this was what it meant to be alive. This was what it meant to love…*and to be loved*.

That was perhaps the most profound discovery

Jack had made yet on the exploration. He'd known for some time that he loved Dulci, loved her so much in fact that he was willing to bow to the social convention of marriage. He'd thought he knew what love meant; that he must marry her, protect her, shelter her from the hard truths and experiences that ruled his life.

To do so meant leaving her behind so that she couldn't see his life or be sullied by it. It meant she'd be living with half a man, that he could not be himself with her. He had not considered the other portion of the equation: being loved, especially being loved by Dulci, a woman who wanted the whole of him and would not settle for less.

With each day that passed, Jack grappled with an additional reality. Dulci not only wanted to be his partner, but she was also capable of it. Such competence presented Jack with an awkward dilemma—even with her capabilities, did he dare risk her? It was one thing out here in the jungle with few people around and his twenty-four-hour presence. Other missions would be different. On the other hand, if he did not risk her, it meant losing her entirely.

He did not know which risk was more unpalatable. He had underestimated what being loved meant and the realisation rocked him to the core as he held her beside him in the dark. Because she loved him, she wanted to be his partner in all things. She didn't want to be left behind. She didn't care about the dirt and imperfect realities that sustained his viscountcy. She cared only that she was with him. She wanted to protect him as much as he wanted to protect her.

She shouldn't have had to prove herself to him, but she had time and time again. First on board ship, although he'd been too blind to see it. She'd proven her ability to adapt to colonial life in Georgetown. Not once had she complained that life was not to London standards. She'd proven herself again on this trek. Not only could Dulci endure, she could thrive. She was actually enjoying this, hardships and all.

If ever there was a woman to match him, it was she. In the dark of the night, Jack could see with acute accuracy the rightness of Dulci in his life. As long as he'd believed a wife had to be tucked away in the safety of London, she'd been right to refuse his offer of marriage. Such a marriage would have been an unhappy farce. Each day that passed proved that was no longer the case, if he would just take the chance. If he could accede to that reality, untold happiness awaited him and in that happiness, London seemed very far away. Calisto Ortiz seemed very far away.

Calisto Ortiz slammed the articulated levels of his telescope into the base. They were headed towards the Essequibo, perhaps a day ahead of him. Their progress was not built on speed, whereas his was. He had no interest in stopping to appreciate the flora and fauna, or the wildlife. He had no interest in swimming beneath the waterfalls and their thundering roar. His was not a botanical expedition. His goal was singlefold: stop Wainsbridge from bringing back a map of the Essequibo River Valley and any news of what the Essequibo River might hold. There was gold in the river basin, gold discovered by him and his uncle. Well, not technically by the two of them, but by men who'd been hired by them.

Ortiz had no intention of turning that wealth over to any government. He meant for it to be private wealth for the vast Ortiz family coffers. But he couldn't begin to petition the Venezuelan government for a tract of land the government didn't possess.

The importer, Vasquez, had died for this, the map-maker who'd made the dummy map was rotting in his cabin for this. They were martyrs to a cause, really, people who might know too much and accidentally expose his secrets. They would not have died in vain. Ortiz would silence Wainsbridge and all would be well.

Although he wouldn't have agreed at the time, Ortiz was now thinking things had worked out quite well. It would be far easier to kill Wainsbridge in the wilds of Guiana than it would have been in London. In England, there would have been too many questions, too many coincidences. He was certain Wainsbridge's friend, Lady Dulcinea's brother, the Earl of Stockport, would have mounted a brutal inquiry until the truth had been ferreted out. It would have been messy and Vargas would have seen him ruined over it. The stuffy old man couldn't stand the breath of scandal even if it was for the good of the country.

Out here, there were so many ways to die and no one would know the difference between murder or the dire consequences of travelling in a difficult land. Likely, no one would even think of murder. The expedition would simply not come back. Whole expeditions had failed to come back before. The trick would be in ensuring there were no survivors. That's what he had the Arawak priest for.

Calisto Ortiz made his way down the hillside to the motley band he'd assembled for his work. There were his trusted Venezuelan henchmen, one of whom spoke the Arawak language and understood many of their customs. There were the Arawak themselves, among them one of the tribal priests.

Ortiz called the translator and the priest to his side. 'Tell him that we are only a day behind the land stealers.'

He waited for the translation. The Arawak priest made a long response. The translator nodded and turned to Ortiz.

'He says that is good. We will catch the people who would steal the land and they will pay the penalty. All of them.'

Ortiz suppressed a delighted shudder. Among the Arawak, the penalty for violating boundaries, for taking land, was far fiercer than even the penalty for murder. Wainsbridge and his party would suffer greatly for crossing Calisto Ortiz. 'But not the woman,' Ortiz replied. 'Tell him the woman is mine, she is not to be punished. She is not there of her own volition. The land stealer, the blond-haired one, took her out of her own home, stole her away.' Dulcinea Wycroft would find ways to be very thankful he'd spared her. Very thankful indeed.

The priest scowled and the translator said, 'He says of course the woman will be spared. These are issues between men, this is a man's punishment.'

Ortiz nodded. 'Very good. We'll travel fast today, close in on them tomorrow and spring the trap the next day when they are only a day out from the main river.' Ortiz looked to the sky, what he could see of it through the thick forest canopy. Viscount Wainsbridge did not know it, but he had only two days left to live. His uncle would be pleased at last, perhaps pleased enough to allow him to marry an Englishwoman.

Dulci wiped the sweat from her brow, taking a rest from her labours through the forested bank of the shore-line. She was certain this was an entirely different sun than the one they had in England. This sun was hot and penetrating, not like the weak bit of light that made few appearances in her part of the world.

Jack called out yards ahead that he'd found a spot to put down his tripod. She smiled and waved, trudging forwards. Jack was indefatigable. She'd seen so many faces of Jack, but she'd not yet seen this side of him, the side that could tramp through the waist-high foliage of the river bank, study the contours of the land with such precision he could return to his camp table and turn his findings into maps of detailed precision.

Dulci watched the play of his shoulders beneath his shirt as he adjusted the tripod to a preferable height. It was just the two of them today. The boats were some way ahead, just specks on the water. Robert and the boats would wait for them up around the next bend in preparation for turning into the Essequibo tomorrow. Today was Jack's last day of surveying before they began the final leg of the journey, perhaps the most important part of the trip, the part where they'd establish the British border of Guiana.

Then they would head back to Georgetown, civilization and decisions. Adventuring was hard work. Jack had been right, it required a certain fortitude. The simplest of pleasures seemed like the most sinful of luxuries. She'd give a fortune for a hot bath and a clean cotton dress, for being able to slip on her shoes without worrying sudden death waited inside. All that aside, she wouldn't have missed this for the world.

Every fibre of her body sang with vitality the moment she awoke each day. There was no such thing here as boring. Every day was exciting and she saw it all with Jack beside her. She had not told Jack yet, but she was not convinced she wanted to go back to England. She wanted to stay in Georgetown. She'd prefer Jack to stay, too, but she could not dictate his future. She could only love him for what he was. Surely the king needed an emissary with Jack's skills here, someone who wasn't attached to the government already, but someone who could act in a respectable but unofficial capacity. Perhaps Jack could be convinced.

The prospect of such a future filled her with a sudden burst of happiness that couldn't be contained. She flung her arms wide and turned her face to the sky to bask in her joy. Life was so amazingly good, so much more extraordinary than she'd known. If she didn't do another thing, she could die happy.

Dulci blamed herself for what happened next. If she had been paying attention, not lost in thoughts of future plans, she might have called out a warning in time.

A whistle of wind shot past her, so close she felt the little puff on her cheek. Just feet in front of her, Jack crumpled without notice. 'Jack!'

She fell to her knees beside him, horrified that one moment he'd been all flexing muscles as he worked with his equipment, all fluid motion, and now he lay in a boneless heap on the ground. She saw the cause immediately, high on his neck where there was brief bit of exposed skin between his hat and the collar of his white shirt—the tiny hunting dart of the Arawak. She recognised it right away from her own drawings and research.

That meant she wasn't alone. Adrenalin raced through Dulci. There was so much to do. She stood up, searching for signs of the hunter, looking for a stick she could make a flag with to signal Robert on the boats.

Jack needed help. She had no way of knowing if the dart was poisoned for instant death or if it was only dipped in the stunning potion hunters used to bring down small game. Jack still breathed. If he made it the next ten minutes, she would know.

Dulci reached for a long stick. A hand shot out of the brush, wrapping around her wrist. Dulci screamed, the forest devouring the sound. A stocky man of modest height and black bristly hair emerged from the brush, dragging her forwards, away from Jack. All around her the forest came alive. The man was not alone. Men surrounded Jack, lifting his body.

'No, leave him,' Dulci gabbled, trying to move towards him. 'You've hit him by mistake. He's hurt.' Her captor would not release her and no one understood the words she spoke. Panic threatened to swamp her. Jack was unconscious, Robert was far ahead, unaware. The Arawak would disappear with them into the forest and Robert would be hard pressed to track them. She was alone. There was only her. She forced herself to calm down, to remember the Arawak words, few as they were, that she had learned from the scholar in Georgetown.

'I am peaceful,' she said in their words. The man holding her looked at her strangely, then jerked his head to indicate a spot behind him.

Dulci watched in fascinated terror as Calisto Ortiz stepped into view. 'Please, you must help me.'

'Of course, *mi querida*, I will help you.' He

nodded to where the men had tied Jack's limp form to a long pole as if he were a wild boar. 'It is him I cannot help. He is a land thief and shall be prosecuted accordingly.'

'You cannot do this.' Dulci felt the panic rise again. She had her gun in the pocket of her trousers. It had always been a comfort to her, she'd always felt invincible when she carried it. But now she saw the impotent truth of it. Her little gun wouldn't save her now. But maybe her wits would.

Chapter Twenty-One

Dulci stumbled through the undergrowth of the forest beside Calisto Ortiz. The Arawak leader had wanted to bind her hands, but Ortiz had laughed off the need, saying she was already as good as bound as long as they held the land stealer. Then his mouth had curved into a wicked smile and he'd bent close to her ear. 'Remember the little favours you owe me, *mi querida*. I am sure we can find a way for you to show your gratitude. Who knows what other degradations I can save you from with the proper motivation?'

Dulci struggled to curb her tongue. She wanted nothing more than to lash out with a cutting comment, but that would gain her nothing. Already, he suspected Jack's worth to her. He would not believe her if she suddenly played the jilt and ignored Jack. But she was a woman, and Ortiz thought very little of women beyond their physical allure. She could use that. Ortiz was the only choice for an ally at the moment. She had to use him until it was time not to.

'How long have you been following us?' Dulci asked in a conversational tone. It would help to know how much he'd seen, how much he knew or how much he was merely guessing at.

'A while.' He gave her a hot studied look. 'Long enough to see what you and the good viscount get up to when you think no one is looking.'

So he did know the depth of her devotion to Jack. 'Why did you wait until now to take him?'

'I wanted to be well away from any sign of civilisation.' He shot a disgusted look at the Arawak. 'I can't get much further than this. These people are barbarians, but they have their uses. You needn't worry. You shall not be one of their uses as long as you are under my protection.'

There was significant unrevealed information in that comment. He was acting alone, privately, without sponsorship from his government, but hoping for their protection in the aftermath. The Essequibo River marked the boundary between Guiana and Venezuela. The other reason Ortiz did not want to seize Jack too close to Georgetown was that it made his own escape more difficult. If there was trouble with the British, he could head over the river and be out of British jurisdiction. He would be Venezuela's responsibility and with his connections, no one would look too closely to a murky happening on another country's holdings. There would be no justice for Ortiz, Dulci mused, unless she managed to mete it out herself.

Likewise, she saw the danger for herself as well. She did not want to set a foot outside British territory for fear of losing what little protection she had. If she disappeared into Venezuela, it might prove difficult to extract her. It would certainly take time. Letters would have to cross an ocean. Brandon would not hear of this until months after it had occurred. If, in that time, she became a wife to a Venezuelan national, her own citizenship might be in question. She would have no voice.

'You cannot save him,' Ortiz said. 'You can save yourself. I would look to my own hide if I were you and start thinking of all the ways you can aid your own survival.'

Dulci met his obsidian gaze evenly. 'I am not you, thank goodness.'

'Your repartee is charming, *mi querida*, although I think in the end, you will be quite glad to be me.' He spoke the last with arrogant confidence. 'Ah, here we are.' They stepped into a large glade and Dulci was amazed to see the village appear so abruptly.

Caneye, the sturdy Arawak dwellings of wood and woven cane, ringed the perimeter. People worked outside the dwellings. They stopped their tasks now and looked up at the party entering the clearing, the men with Jack strung up between them and sagging. He'd still not regained consciousness, but perhaps that was for the better.

Ahead of them at the top of the circle stood the *bohio*, the chief's house. It was bigger than the other dwellings and the little band headed there with their prize. Instinctively, Dulci followed, wanting to keep Jack in sight. She didn't want him to wake without her being there. She could only imagine the confusion and fear that would follow his waking. Not even a man of Jack's fortitude and experience could wake calmly under these circumstances without some terror.

Ortiz's hand grabbed at her arm, his voice rough. 'Stay with me if you value what freedom you have here. Women are less than nothing and you're a prisoner at best for the moment.' He dragged her with him to the chief's circle and pushed his way through the gathered throng, everyone eager to see the prisoner, everyone eager to see what excitement had arrived to break up the usual routine of the day.

Ortiz stood next to his translator. 'We...' he gestured to include his band of Spaniards and the Arawak hunters who'd accompanied them '...have returned successful. We have caught the man who has stolen on to your land and who would claim it for his tribe even though it already belongs to you.'

Dulci waited impatiently for the message to be relayed to the chief and for the chief to respond. The chief was slow to answer. He walked around the men carrying Jack, studying Jack with intent.

'He has hair of gold. Is this usual in his tribe?'

Ortiz looked disgusted. Dulci saw her own impatience mirrored in his hard look. He wanted to do business, not talk about hair colour.'

'Many of his people have hair the colour of gold,' Ortiz replied.

The chief nodded at the response. Some of the women moved forwards, eager to touch Jack's hair when it seemed he wouldn't move and the chief had shown interest. 'You say he is a land stealer. We will see what he says when he awakes. He must have a chance to vouch for himself.' The chief turned his attention to Dulci. She held still, trying not to squirm under the intense scrutiny.

'She does not have the gold hair,' the chief said in tones that conveyed his disappointment clearly enough to be understood without a translator. He looked accusingly at Ortiz. 'You said she was a rare beauty.'

Ortiz tightened the grip on her arm. 'She is a rare beauty to my people.'

'Then you may have her when we've disposed of the man she travels with,' came the reply. Ortiz's grip lessened on her arm and Dulci sensed some unknown test had been accomplished. It also became clear that the chief held all the power. He decided how goods and possessions were disbursed.

The chief was gesturing and talking again, giving instructions. The men with Jack moved away, taking him with them. Dulci sprang forwards, but Ortiz held her fast. 'Do not go to him,' he whispered harshly. 'Do not undo what has already been done. You were very lucky a few moments ago even though you don't realise it.'

'Where are they taking him?' Dulci's gaze did not waver from the men hauling Jack off.

Ortiz shrugged. 'I don't know. To one of the *caneye*, I suppose. Women will look after him. He will not be harmed until the chief has heard him speak. Imminent danger has passed for a short time. As for you, you will come with me. They have given me a *caneye* here, next to the chief's.'

'He's called a *cacique*,' Dulci grumbled.

Ortiz looked at her with disdain. 'I forgot you fancied yourself an anthropologist of sorts.' He shoved her inside the single opening of the round house.

It was dark inside. A pit for a cook fire was in the centre of the room, a hole for the smoke in the roof overhead. There were woven mats on the floor, but beyond that, the room was empty.

'What do you suppose would have happened if the *cacique*—' he emphasised the last word with a condescending sneer '—had found you beautiful? You would have become another of his wives or his concubine. You might even have hastened the viscount's death.' Ortiz stood behind her, his breath on her neck as he undid the tight braid, combing it out with his fingers. Dulci struggled not to cringe at his intimate familiarity. 'Your dark hair, which I find lovely beyond belief, *mi querida*, saved you and saved him. It is considered plain to the *cacique*, who is no friend of yours, I might add.' Ortiz lifted the heavy weight of her hair and sifted it through his hands.

'I would not cringe, *mi querida*. You must understand I am a far preferable alternative than becoming the concubine of a pagan *cacique*. He did not want you. Perhaps he would have given you to one of his council, one of his *nitayanos*. But I spoke for you, and he has given you to me.'

A leer lit his dark eyes and Dulci wondered how she could have ever found him handsome. All the same features were still there in his face— the smooth olive skin, the exotic dark eyes, the full sensual lips—but these were unattractive features now, shaded as they were by this man's unlimited avarice and complete lack of ethics.

'I could change his mind.' He whispered the threat, his arm imprisoning her against him, back to chest. She could feel the hard strength of his torso, feel his member rising with lust. His hand palmed her breast and Dulci shut her eyes. How far would he go just now? Should she fight? What would happen if she gained the opening and darted out into the village? Nothing. She could only hope to run blindly into the forest with no direction, without Jack. Ortiz was right. As long as Jack was here, she was as good as bound to a stake in the ground. She could only endure.

'I could change the *cacique*'s mind, you know. I could remind him how your blue eyes are like sapphires; how your skin beneath the shirt is whiter than anything he's ever seen. Think of that the next time you choose not to rouse to me.'

He stepped away then and Dulci moved across the room, eager to put space between them. He smirked. 'I will see about food. Later tonight, there will be hunting. The men will go out at dark for the *hutio*. There will be preparations for the viscount's trial. It will be a great celebration for them, all the excitement of a trial and subsequent punishment that will follow. The viscount will be quite the diversion.'

Dulci stayed in the *caneye* the rest of the day. Women brought her cassava cakes and fruits to eat. They were also left to guard the hut in case she tried to step outside. Whenever she peered out, women looked up from their work. Finally, one of them took pity on her and gestured for her to come and sit with them. They were weaving cotton fibres and Dulci joined them, trying to imitate their skill, trying to find the words to ask about Jack, but no one understood. The women just smiled and patted her hands.

The shadows began to lengthen, dark began to fall. Women served the men their meals, waiting until the men finished before taking their own food. Ortiz had returned to the *caneye* to be fed, saying smugly to Dulci, who'd been pressed into service to bring him food, 'Quaint custom, don't you think?'

'Take me to Jack,' Dulci demanded, serving him some of the special cassava cakes usually reserved for the *cacique*. 'Has he woken? How is he?'

'I don't think that will be necessary.' Ortiz nodded to the gathering of men and the stir of activity by the *cacique*'s *bohio*. He stood up and dusted off his trousers. 'Come with me and we will see what's to be done.'

Jack blinked in the light, trying hard not to stumble as they brought him out of the hut. His hands were still bound, making balance surprisingly difficult, but he was determined to show no outward signs of ill treatment or effects from the dart. He did not want to appear weak before the chief and he did not want Dulci worrying more than she already was. Despite his efforts, he stumbled once, the two men who flanked him jerking him back to his feet.

He hated his weakness. What he could hide from the eyes of the Arawak, he could not hide from himself. He'd taken poorly to the poison on the dart. Even now, nearly eight hours after he'd been taken, the potion left his throat dry and his stomach in uncertain turmoil. All he wanted to do was lie down and sleep. He didn't want to think, didn't want to strategise. But those were the things that demanded his priority. Dulci needed him and he needed a clear head if he was going to get her out of here.

She was here and it was his fault. Every fear he'd ever harboured in this regard had proved founded. Concern over Dulci's safety was no longer an academic exercise in argument.

He stood before the *cacique* and the council of elders, his eyes searching the ground around the chief. Where was she? Fear gripped his belly in a cold vise. Had she already been killed? Defiled and hidden away? Then, in answer to his desire, she was there, tripping into view. Jack fought the urge to call out, to expel a telling breath of relief. He didn't want the *cacique* to guess too much. He didn't want Dulci used as negotiating leverage for whatever was going on and yet the joy surging through him at the sight of her, whole and apparently unharmed, was almost impossible to hide.

Joy aside, he knew that wasn't the intention. Reassurance wasn't the reason he'd been shown Dulci. He was being reminded that she had not escaped and bringing any assistance. The sight of her was meant to remind him that they had no hope, they were utterly alone.

A man stepped forwards and seized Dulci roughly by the arm, drawing Jack's gaze.

Ortiz!

Jack's blood heated, the desire to pummel the man to an inch of his miserable existence nearly unbearable. But beneath Jack's rising fury was cold understanding. Ortiz's presence explained much of the unknown surrounding this abduction. The bastard had followed them into the jungle and aligned himself with the Arawak. Ortiz was at the heart of whatever plot was afoot. Jack briefly wondered what crime Ortiz had convinced the chieftain he'd committed. It hardly mattered. By his life or death, the only priority was seeing Dulci safely reunited with Robert and the expedition.

Jack kept his gaze riveted on Dulci, willing her with the quiet message of his eyes to save herself, to leave him if the opportunity came. Ortiz made to pull her back into the crowd and she resisted for a moment, shouting loudly over the murmurs of villagers.

'I am fine. Ortiz claims you're stealing land!' It was all she could manage before Ortiz clapped a hand over her mouth and dragged her back into the crowd, stoking Jack's anger at Ortiz's rough handling of her and his own impotence to stop it.

The *cacique* gestured for Ortiz and the translator to come forwards. Somewhere to Jack's left, he was aware of Dulci sitting on the ground with the rest of the tribe. Apparently the trial had begun. Jack fought the rising bout of nausea in his stomach and focused his attentions on what passed for Arawak justice. If they meant to portray him as an intruding Englishman, they might be surprised.

The translator, one of Ortiz's men, explained

the charges to him in English. 'You've been accused of violating the tribal boundaries of these lands with the intent of claiming them for your own tribe. This is theft, the greatest crime someone can commit against the tribe. If you are found guilty of these charges, you shall be impaled on a stick until death.' A gruesome gesture followed.

In the crowd, Dulci bit back a strangled gasp, but Jack stood stalwart, unfazed by this turn of events. He'd not expected Ortiz to waste his time on a misdemeanour. He'd also not risk a translator being too honest. Who was there to stop the man from saying whatever suited Ortiz's cause? It was time for Jack to take matters into his own hands.

'Does the *cacique* speak Spanish?' Jack asked.

'Why, yes, of course—' the translator began.

Jack interrupted, cutting the translator off entirely. He fixed his gaze on the *cacique* and stepped forwards, making it clear he'd deal with the *cacique* directly.

'Who accuses me?' Jack said, his Spanish confident and fluent; he did not grope for words.

'Señor Ortiz,' the *cacique* answered, eyeing Jack warily.

Jack shook his head. 'I am here only to make

a map, a drawing, for my *cacique* who lives far across the waters.'

The *cacique* looked puzzled. 'Why would your chief want a map of a land that isn't his?'

'Because it is beautiful and my *cacique* values beautiful things,' Jack replied with amazing calm. He could feel Dulci's eyes on him, waiting, watching, counting on him, desperate to know what was being said in a language she didn't understand. Dulci hated being left out.

The *cacique* waved his arm in an expansive gesture to encompass all the land in sight. 'I fear your chieftain may covet such a beautiful land and take it for his own.'

Someone yelled something from the people gathered about the circle, breaking Jack's rapport with the chieftain. Others picked up the cry. Noise broke out. The chief nodded and raised a hand to silence the disturbance. Jack hazarded a glance about the circle of onlookers, desperate for a sign. He needed to understand what was happening. Surely his verdict had not been determined already?

When the *cacique* turned his attention back to Jack, his voice was cold and sceptical. 'My people say you are going to steal this land. They don't trust your answers. There have been whites here before. They always bring change.'

Jack tamped down a small surge of panic. The tribe could not go down this road. The *cacique* had to believe him! With an outward calm he did not feel, Jack nodded his head towards Ortiz. 'Tell your people, the Spaniard among you sows dissent. If there's anyone among us who means to steal this land, it is he.' Jack made an awkward gesture with his bound hands towards Ortiz to be sure the chieftain might guess at his message.

The chief's eyes darted to Ortiz. 'What kind of mischief?'

'He wishes to claim this land for his country. He believes there's gold in the river basin further up. If he claims this land for his tribe, they will seek to enslave your people.'

The chief rubbed thoughtfully at his chin and looked consideringly between Jack and a livid Ortiz. 'What proof do you have?' he asked and Jack breathed a sigh of relief. He'd succeeded in sowing doubt, a good sign. But providing proof was another thing. He had none, not concrete proof anyway.

Jack shook his head. 'No more than he has

against me. You are willing to accept his word. I ask you also consider mine.'

Jack watched the *cacique* carefully. The chief *did* look uncertain, splitting his gaze between Jack and Ortiz, who had moved to protest, but found himself restrained. 'Wait, you must hear me out, it's a lie!' Ortiz struggled. But it was too late. Jack's damage was done and just in time. His stomach wouldn't last much longer. When it went, his legs would go as well.

The chief gathered his *nitayanos* about him and rose, all indecision gone now, his decision made. 'We will deliberate. Take them to the *caneyes* and keep them under guard. We will decide at sunrise.'

There was utter confusion. Ortiz and his men decided to struggle, fighting broke out, but Ortiz's group was unprepared for sudden action. In the mêlée, Dulci slipped unnoticed to Jack's side as his guards led him back to the hut. The guards looked uncertain, but Dulci spoke forcefully in broken Arawak as she gestured. 'I stay with him. I am his woman.'

They shrugged and said nothing. But their shrugs and easy capitulation were worrisome, Jack thought. Were they thinking what did it matter if the golden-hair had his woman with him for one last night? He would die in the morning and perhaps she too.

Inside the dark hut, Jack fell on to one of the woven pallets, a groan escaping his lips. 'Water, Dulci. I need water. There's some in the gourd in the corner.'

Dulci hurried as best she could in the dark. He could hear her groping. She brought the gourd and the dipper to Jack's lips, splashing water on his chest in her haste. 'Are you very sick, Jack?'

'Whatever the dart was dipped in has unsettled my stomach and it wearies me. It will wear off eventually. The water helps. I didn't think I'd be able to stand there much longer.'

Dulci felt for his hand. 'Everything will be fine, just rest, Jack.' Her touch was heaven. It felt good to feel her, to hear her voice. But he could not give in to the temptation of her presence.

'To be brutally honest, things won't be fine,' Jack corrected. 'In the morning, they'll probably kill both Ortiz and I and you'll become the *cacique*'s next wife. If I am lucky, perhaps I'll get to face Ortiz in combat instead.'

Dulci knew, of course; she'd heard the charges and the consequences read to him in English. But her grip on his hand tightened at the brutal reminder articulated so plainly, so baldly. 'Well, then I think we need a plan.' She was doing her level best to shrug off her fear. 'If we stay here, we're done for.' She stood up and started pacing. 'The first part of any plan is to assess our resources.'

'That won't take very long,' Jack said drily from the pallet. If he closed his eyes he could ease the discomfort.

'We have my gun and we have your navigation skills. I think that's all we need.' Dulci's bravado was hard won. She must know how desperate her plan was. She had one shot in that little gun.

'What do you think Robert is doing?' she asked thoughtfully. 'Is there any help from his corner?'

'He will have moored the boats at the river where he last saw us. That's the plan if anyone goes missing.'

'Perfect. Then all we have to do is meet him at the river,' Dulci said brightly. 'And the river is which direction, Jack?'

'It's south of here. I was unconscious—how long did it take to get here? An hour? More than that?'

'A little over an hour, I think.'

'Then we're four or five miles from the river,' Jack said resolutely. 'But, Dulci, even if we found enough stars to navigate by, we still have to get out of the hut and the village. There's a reason they build these *caneyes* the way they do. The cane walls are sturdy.'

'Strong enough to withstand a hurricane,' Dulci recited absently from one of her readings. 'Yes, I know. We aren't going to be able to tear the back wall apart and go out that way.'

'What do you propose?'

Dulci knelt down by the pallet. He could smell the pleasant scent of her, still lingering from their bath under a waterfall a day ago. 'I propose we walk out of here an hour before sunrise.'

'Walk out?'

'Well, my plan isn't as simple as yours usually are. I will need you to quietly overpower the guard while I dispatch the other one to fetch water or something. Then, we'll walk out when the village is quiet and no one is looking. We'll just step behind this hut and fade into the perimeter of the village and into the forest.'

She peered at Jack in the dark. 'Are you well enough to attempt it? Perhaps if we wait until dawn, you will regain your strength. A few more hours might cleanse your system.'

Jack laughed softly at her suppositions. 'I'll

be fine, Dulci.' He'd have to be. They didn't have a choice.

'Come, let me hold you, Dulci, I'm not so sick that I can't enjoy the feel of you.' And, he hoped, offer her the comfort of his body. She'd been courageous today, but that didn't mean she hadn't also been scared to death. He would give her what comfort he could, even if it was simply the length of his body pressed against hers, a reminder that she'd not been abandoned to an unknown fate. He wrapped his arm about her, feeling the rise and fall of her breathing against his chest as she settled into him.

There was peace in that rhythm for him too. He would make things right for her and then he'd take himself as far from her as possible so that she'd be safe. There was no need to speak. It was enough to feel the rise and fall of her head against his chest, but Jack wanted to talk. There were words that needed saying in case the worst happened.

'I love you, Dulci,' he began hesitantly, holding her tight. He had so much he wanted to say it was hard to know where to start. His mind was full to bursting with all he needed to tell her. He hoped he had the strength, the voice to convey it all.

'Shh, Jack, save your strength. You shouldn't talk too much now.' Dulci shifted in his arms, turning to face him. 'We can talk on the boat when you're better.'

Jack shook his head in the darkness. 'I know you're being brave, Dulci, and I love you for it. But we have to also be realists. If I die tomorrow there are things I want you to know so that you have no doubts.'

To her credit, Dulci did not protest. 'Then tell me, Jack,' she whispered.

'You are my heart, Dulci. I've been a foolish man. I've always thought of myself as unconventional, that I wasn't a traditionalist like Gladstone. It's something of an irony to come to the potential end of my life and realise at the last that I was not as unconventional as I thought when it came to you. I wanted to shelter you, I still do. But my reasons are different now. In the beginning, I was afraid of what you might think of me if you saw the sum of my life, what I did for the king, how I lived. This is hardly the life the viscounts you know in London live. But now it's different. I want to shelter you because I can't bear to lose you.'

'You won't lose me, Jack,' Dulci whispered.

'Don't make empty promises, Dulci. We both know I am going to lose you, only just for different reasons than before.'

'You're not going to die,' she insisted fervently.

'Maybe, maybe not.' Jack shrugged. 'That's not the loss I'm talking about. You came on this journey to prove to me you could be my partner. You've done that. Every day, I could see your strength and your commitment. But, Dulci, I can't let you do it. I love you too much to lose you, to know that I singlehandedly put you in danger.' He felt as if he were babbling. Perhaps he had a touch of fever after all.

Dulci tensed. He was probably lucky he couldn't see the fury sparking her eyes. 'So even by winning, I lose?' she said slowly.

A cool drop of moisture seeped through the linen of his shirt where Dulci's head lay. 'Dulci?' Jack reached a hand to her cheek. 'I didn't mean to make you cry.'

Stupid man. She'd kill him for this when they got back to the boats. Whoever thought love solved everything? In this case, love had made it worse. She'd hoped love would ease the way towards Jack's acceptance of her as a partner in life. But it seemed that love, once realised, had now become an obstacle. She could weep at the irony of it. Or, she could seize what moments she had. Dulci preferred the latter. If she could not have him for ever, she would have him for the night.

'Give me your hand, Jack.' Dulci sat up and reached for a thong that held back her hair.

'What are you doing?' Jack strained to see in the dark, struggling a little as she tied the cord around his wrist and her own.

'We're handfasting. We will have this marriage if no other,' Dulci said, a tell-tale tremble in her voice. 'I would have you as a husband who accepts me as a partner entirely for one night at least. I never thought love would drive us apart. I rather thought it would be the making of us, the one realisation that would save us.'

Dulci lay back down beside him, their hands lightly bound by the thong. 'We'll use the ancient words.'

She drew a quiet breath. 'I take you, Jack, to be the partner of my soul and the husband of my heart as long as we both shall live.'

Jack repeated them, his own voice shaky and hoarse and then it was done: short in text but long on meaning. They lay in silence, savouring the sanctity of the moment, feeling the import of their words. 'As long as we both shall live sounds ominous under these circumstances,' Jack said thoughtfully.

'There are a lot of ways to die, Jack,' Dulci whispered in the dark.

'Well, Lady Wainsbridge, I think we need a happier custom. Ah, I know just the thing.' With that he kissed her deeply and fully, competently conveying regrets that his strength would not allow him to do more.

'Dulci, there's one more thing I have to tell you.' Jack pushed back her loose hair so that his hands framed her face, his long fingers tracing the contours of her jaw and the smooth lines of brow.

'If anything happens to me, you must escape at all costs. You must go to the king and clear my name. Tell him everything you know about Ortiz. I am trusting you with this mission, Dulci. Promise me, Dulci?'

'Of course, I'll go to the king,' Dulci murmured half-heartedly. This was morbid talk, but she'd appease him.

'No, Dulci, I need your pledge.' Jack was

adamant, unfooled by her consent. 'I will take care of you, even from the grave if needed. William will listen to you. I want my name cleared. It might save you from scandal even if I'm not there. And Dulci...' He paused before going on. 'If there are any children, you must go to the king and petition for my estates. Tell William I meant for my heirs to be recognised.'

'What are you talking about?' They'd been careful. Jack had shown her how to count the days of her cycle and how to stay away from the most fertile days. On several occasions, he'd consciously withdrawn. They'd taken every precaution.

Jack covered her breast with a gentle hand. 'I would plan for all eventualities, Dulci. A man can never be too careful with what he loves.' Jack kissed her again, this time on the forehead. 'Come and sleep a little. There's a few hours yet until we make our dash.'

Chapter Twenty-Two

'Dulci, it's time.' Jack was shaking her. She made a moan of complaint and then sat bolt upright, everything flooding back to her. She wasn't in Jack's arms on the boat. They were in the Arawak village.

'Moan a bit, Jack. Pretend you're desperately ill.'

'That shouldn't be hard.'

'It's not funny, Jack.'

Jack moaned, putting on a loud performance that would have done Drury Lane proud. Once he'd moaned long enough to show real distress, Dulci went to the opening of the hut. 'Help me.' She gestured to Jack, thrashing on the pallet, doing her best to look frightened and nearly hysterical. 'Needs drink.'

One of the guards hurried off to find water. Dulci pulled at the other one. 'Come, look at him.' She frantically dragged him inside, knowing time was of the essence. Her frantic behaviour wasn't all that feigned. She knew it wouldn't be long before the water bearer was back.

'He die?' Dulci asked, urging the man to bend over Jack.

The moment he was close enough, Jack seized the man in a stranglehold. They wrestled, but Jack quickly subdued the shorter man and he slumped on to the pallet.

Jack was panting from his exertions and Dulci was worried as he rose to his feet a bit unsteady. 'Hurry,' was all she said.

Outside, they slipped unnoticed into the perimeter of the village behind the hut and then into the forest. Now it was all up to Jack.

The darkness was thick and the forest canopy blocked out the sky in places, making it impossible to navigate consistently. The only benefit was that if they couldn't see, the Arawak wouldn't be able to see them either unless they brought torches or delayed the search until sunrise. They didn't have much of a head start to count on. The water bearer would notice immediately that they had gone.

'This way,' Jack whispered, gripping her hand fiercely. 'The *cacique*'s *bohio* faced the south entrance of the village, so it would put the southerly direction to our left.'

The going was painfully slow as the forest gradually began to lighten with daybreak. With daybreak, it became less frightening too, the nocturnal sounds of animals becoming less noisome and Dulci breathed a sigh of relief once the sun was up.

They'd done well so far with their simple plan. But Jack was tiring. His tanned face was pale, his step unsteady. Dulci braced him on one side and he used a long stick for support on the other. 'Do you think Robert is looking for us?' she asked.

Jack nodded. 'I hope so. With luck, he's found my equipment. He won't have any idea which way we went, but since the village isn't too far inland, he'll quickly eliminate the alternatives.'

'And the Arawak, are they looking for us?'

'Yes, I fear so. They will have had time to assemble search parties. While they are not warriors, they are fierce hunters and trackers. There's no telling what kind of trail we've left behind in the dark.'

Dulci drew a deep breath. 'Then we'll have to hurry. How are we doing on direction?'

'That's our one piece of good news. We've headed south. We are close to the river. Can you see the change in the foliage? This is river growth. We'll see more of it as we get closer.' Jack paused. 'Dulci, listen to me. If the Arawak close in, I want you to run. I want you to leave me. Get away. You're healthy and I will slow you down. I just ask that you leave me your gun.'

'There's only one shot in it, Jack. I can't see it would do you any good.' Realisation swamped her. One shot was all he'd need. 'I won't leave you, Jack,' she said staunchly.

'This is no time for heroics, Dulci. I wouldn't even be asking it if I thought I stood any sort of chance of outrunning them.'

He was panting now to keep up the pace even with her help. 'Maybe it won't come to that,' Dulci encouraged.

'Maybe it won't.' But Jack's tone implied otherwise and his eyes kept darting around the undergrowth as if he expected to see the Arawak jump out at any moment.

Dulci was sweating profusely, perspiration staining her shirt liberally as they continued to trudge forwards. A few times they heard rustling in the tall grasses and they'd attempted to hide.

Each time was a false alarm. Jack's breathing was laboured now, sweat rolling off his face. He needed water. He was rapidly becoming dehydrated and it was obvious his stomach pained him, but still he persisted. His strength was astonishing. She would not lose him. That became her mantra as they eked out the distance to the river. She would drag him if she had to.

A ribbon of silver glinted through the trees. Dulci thought she'd cry from the joy of it. The river! At last. They'd made it. 'We're here, Jack. It will just be a bit further,' she said encouragingly.

She did drag him at that point, Jack stumbling and she stumbling with him, towards the river. 'Be careful,' Jack muttered, his speech slurring with exhaustion. 'Watsh for crawshodiles.'

'I know, I know,' Dulci responded hastily. At the shore, she shielded her eyes against the brighter sun and looked for the boats. Luck was with them! The boats were just ahead, maybe a hundred yards. Jack's direction had been unerring. But she'd never dared to hope they'd come out so close to the boats. For all she'd guessed, they'd come out at the river and then have to follow it until they ran into Robert.

The terrain by the river was harder going, the swampy ooze making it difficult to go quickly. Jack seemed to find some extra strength now that they were nearly safe. She could see figures on the boats and Dulci waved, hazarding a shout.

That was when the first dart whistled past, missing them by inches. Dulci dragged them both down. There was commotion on the boats. They were poling away! Dulci screamed again and dragged Jack forwards. They were so close! One of the crew saw them.

A cry went down the line. She could hear Robert's voice giving orders as she struggled forwards. A rope went over the edge of the boat. All she had to do was wade out into the water and grab it. The Arawak were more interested in the boats than anything that lurked below at the moment, having assumed she and Jack were already on board.

Braving the potential dangers of the river, Dulci gripped the rope and tied it around Jack so she wouldn't lose him in the current. Then she grabbed the second rope for herself and gave the signal. She closed her eyes, hardly daring to look for fear of seeing one of the darts headed her way.

At last she felt the hard wood of the deck beneath her and she collapsed flat, crawling to Jack's side, words coming out of her mouth in a babbling torrent.

After a few moments she realised everyone was standing, no one was worried about the darts any more. The attack had stopped. She looked quizzically at Robert.

He smiled. 'We're no longer on their territory. Their territory ends at the river.'

Dulci breathed a sigh of relief. 'We're safe. What about Jack? Can you help him? It's poison from a dart. His system has reacted poorly to it.'

Robert knelt beside his friend, checking his pulse and noting the shallow breathing. 'I have some herbs in my kit that will offset the poison. We'll mix him a tea.'

After Jack was made comfortable and roused enough to take the tea, Robert pulled Dulci aside.

'He'll be all right, but he's in no shape to continue the trip. I want you and a few of the assistants to take one boat back to Georgetown so he can rest. That journey alone will be enough to tax him. But it's better to turn back versus an indeterminate exploration ahead with no guarantees. If he doesn't go back, he might ruin his health entirely.'

'But the mapping,' Dulci protested, recalling Jack's plea the previous night. 'He needs this map to clear his name.'

'He'll have the map. I'll get those boundaries,' Robert promised.

That night, Jack showed marked signs of improvement, Robert's herbs having settled his stomach and his body having had an afternoon of rest. 'You rescued me, Dulci.' He reached for her hand, squeezing it where it lay in her lap.

'I owed you. You saved me in London,' Dulci said lightly, braiding her fingers through his. 'Robert and I have been talking and he thinks it's best if you and I go back to Georgetown. He will continue with the mapping…' She paused and looked up. It was good to see Jack recovering, but it meant the adventure was over, for them at least. It also meant she had to face the unpleasant truth regarding her and Jack.

'I love you too much, Jack, to risk you again. I think we should go back as well. Your health requires it.'

She waited for the protest to come. Jack's eyes were fixed on hers, his face solemn. He did not argue. 'If we go back, I can see you safely aboard a ship to London. Where I should have sent you all along.'

Dulci shook her head. 'I don't think I'll return to London. I like it here.' Then she added, 'With or without you, Jack, although I'd much prefer the former.' There, she'd said it. The battle was engaged. Last night had not been the time to fight over his crisis-induced decision to push her out of his life. But now, the crisis had passed and they needed to resolve their personal future.

Jack looked to the sky, regret tingeing his features for what might have been. 'Believe me, I want things to be different. These weeks with you here beside me, sharing this journey, have been beyond incredible. I didn't know love could be like this, how it could bring so much pleasure and hurt so much. When I saw Ortiz lay his hands on you yesterday and attempt to use you against me, all I could think was "This is my fault. She wouldn't be here if it wasn't for me." Before we came out here, I only thought I understood the risk of having you beside me. Now I know, and the cost is far more than I can bear. I know it's not what you want to hear—'

Dulci interrupted abruptly. 'What about the cost of not having me beside you? Is that so negligible as to be discounted as nothing, not worth any risk?'

'You would be alive and safe. There would be some peace in knowing you were out there in the world, somewhere.'

Dulci snorted and stood up, her anger rising with her. 'You forgot alone. And you would be too, Jack. As for me, I don't look forward to spending the rest of my days as an un-united half of a whole and I don't think you do either, whether you admit it or not. I wish I didn't love you. It would make things a lot easier.'

'You've never been one for easy,' Jack said lightly. This time his attempts to cajole her back to his side wouldn't work.

'You aren't either. Which is why this response of yours is somewhat mystifying,' Dulci said. 'I never considered you a coward, Jack.'

She'd called him a coward and simply walked away! Granted, she'd only walked to the other side of the boat, but he couldn't go after her just now. The reality of his choice began to sink in—how would it be when she was weeks away from him? There'd be no going after her then either. In truth, Jack knew if he let her get off this boat, there'd be no going after her, period. That was the most dismal prospect of all.

His life would be filled up with several 'nevers'. He'd never turn around during a surveying expedition and see her standing there, telescope in one hand looking out across the land. He'd never bathe beneath a waterfall again with her, reveling in the sheer joy of being alive together. He'd never lie down beside her at night, the stars overhead, and make perfect love that left him so completely fulfilled that his demons disappeared.

The stars came out. The boats settled for the night. Jack wished Dulci would come back to him and curl up beneath their blankets. But she didn't. She stubbornly remained as far from him as the boat allowed.

He idly rubbed at his wrist where Dulci had tied their hands together last night, the words of their ceremony drifting through his mind 'so long as we both shall live'. The phrase had not made much sense when she'd spoken it after declaring she'd rather have him as a husband for one night than never have him at all. What else had she said? 'There are a lot of ways to die.'

At the time, he'd been too focused on the prospect of a literal physical death to entertain the notion of an internal death, a waking death that left one with a body but no spirit. It occurred to him with a clarity that physically hurt that such a death was precisely what his choice had doomed them to. *Them.* Not just himself.

Dulci deserved better than that. He meant every word he'd said last night—she had earned the right to be his partner. She was capable of sharing the rigours of his life. She'd proven she did understand the life he led and she was not ashamed of it or him. She loved him unconditionally—well, that part wasn't entirely true. Dulci had her condition. She wanted a partnership of body and soul, no less. And he wanted to give that to her if…

Coward.

Dulci's challenge rang in his head. His ruminations had come full circle. When had he become so bloody cautious? In his work, he was known for bold and intrepid dealings. It was time to apply those tactics to his personal life before he lost the only thing really worth fighting for. Gladstone and her other suitors were cautious men and Dulci had rejected them for it. She wanted a man bold enough to claim her, brave enough to make her his partner and, by God, Jack was going to show her that he could be that man, that her faith in him had not been wrong, just merely misplaced until he came to his senses.

Jack pushed up from the pallet, balancing himself against the exterior wall of the small supply cabin. Whoa, he was wobbly. He stood for long moments, breathing deeply, regaining his equilibrium. The world stopped tilting. He took a few tentative steps, the wobbles disappearing. He fixed his eyes on Dulci's form and started to walk.

'Sometimes a man is stupid,' he said softly.

She startled a little at his voice and turned from the railing. 'More often in some cases than others.'

Jack cleared his throat. 'Ahem, yes, I suppose that might appear to be true.' Somehow, in the euphoria of his decision, he'd forgot Dulci might still be in a pique.

She gave one of her head tosses, her tone dispassionate. 'What have you come to say, Jack? If you've come to argue the rightness of your position one more time, I'm in no mood for it. I disagree with it entirely and I don't see that changing.'

'I agree,' Jack said simply. That was one way to end an argument and in this case, a rather effective choice.

'Agree? As in agree to disagree?' Dulci sighed

heavily. 'I'm too tired to work out your double negatives.'

'No, agree as in you're right to disagree with my earlier position. I disagree with it too. You're only across the boat and I can't stand it. I don't think I could survive sending you away, and frankly, I don't want to—send you away, that is,' Jack clarified.

Dulci's eyes narrowed as she studied him. Jack couldn't decide if that was good or bad. 'What has brought this on?' she asked, far too coolly detached for Jack's tastes.

'I took a good hard look at the reality I was creating for both of us. I'd only thought of it philosophically before. But when I started thinking about what it honestly meant to give you up, to never lie beside you, to not have you with me when I see land no Englishman has ever set foot on…' Jack shook his head. 'Well, I knew if I couldn't stand imagining it, I surely couldn't stand living it. Dulci, I was wrong when I said there would be peace in knowing you would be out there somewhere, safe. It wouldn't be peace at all. It would be hell, the worst torture I could devise for myself.'

'What exactly are you saying, Jack?' Dulci's

eyes had lost their hardness, her voice was soft and breathless in the dark.

'I'm saying I want you for my wife, my partner in all things. You already are, I told you as much last night.'

Dulci took a step towards him, closing the gap. She held out her hands to him, that coy smile of hers on her lips. 'I'm already your wife too, if I recall correctly.' She ran her thumb over his wrist.

'Yes, you're already my wife.' Jack laughed, drawing her against him. 'You and I know it, but we'll probably want to do it again in a church just to appease the legal system.'

Dulci looked up at him, serious for the moment. 'And the risks, Jack? What changed your mind about those?'

'There are always risks, just different sorts. Being without you is not a risk I am willing to take any longer. But, Dulci, being my partner, being my wife, won't stop me from wanting to protect you. A man protects what he loves.'

Dulci smiled at him warmly, her blue eyes dancing. 'So does a woman, Jack.'

Epilogue

October, roughly three months later

Jack stood at the front of the sanctuary, aware that he was the focus of the collective gaze of guests assembled in the pews of St Andrew's Kirk. Some were there out of curiosity; it wasn't every day a viscount was married in their midst. Some were there out of friendship. But whatever their motives for attending, Jack had no eyes for them. His gaze fixed on his future moving towards him down the aisle on Governor Carmichael-Smythe's arm: Dulci, a radiant vision in a gown of pale blue trimmed with pale yellow ribbons, a bouquet of creamy roses in her hands, her own gaze steady and unwavering for him alone, not the least distracted by the guests lining the pews.

Of course, there were notable absences, too,

Jack reflected. Neither he nor Dulci had family present, nor was Robert yet returned from the mapping expedition.

They had not wanted to wait.

Robert's date of return was ambiguous and there would be no more ships until spring even if Brandon and Nora were to brave the voyage. Jack could not fathom waiting six more months to make Dulci his wife.

Counting their return journey from the jungles and the time it had taken for him to make a few necessary arrangements—such as a house for them—it had already been three months since he and Dulci had committed to each other. The words they had shared in the dark on board their travelling boat would for ever be etched in his mind for their potency. No vows could ever be more compelling to Jack than their promise to protect one another, this belief that protection was not a man's duty alone.

Those words bound them together irrevocably in Jack's eyes. In the eyes of his pagan ancestors perhaps they were bound even earlier than that in Dulci's simple handfasting.

Dulci neared and Jack took her hand firmly in his own, unable to contain the smile that had lurked at the corners of his mouth any longer. Today he would marry this fine woman. They would feast at the governor's table in celebration of their nuptials and of Jack's new post. Confident that Jack's name would be officially cleared when Schomburgk returned, Governor Carmichael-Smythe had already appointed him to a position in the gubernatorial cabinet.

Then he would take her home to begin the most important journey of his life.

They were together. That was all that mattered. There'd been no sense in waiting for Schomburgk's findings or a letter from the king or Brandon's consent. Those things would come in time and would not alter their love.

Dulci turned her face up to him, her eyes shining with proof that their love lived in a kingdom of its own, ungoverned by the caprices of politics and princes. Jack bent close to her ear as the ceremony began. 'Dulci, you're my greatest adventure.'

She reached up on her tip-toes, oblivious to the onlookers to whisper in response, 'And you, Jack, are mine.'

* * * * *